**Also available from
Brenda Jackson
and HQN**

Catalina Cove

*LOVE IN CATALINA COVE
FORGET ME NOT
FINDING HOME AGAIN
FOLLOW YOUR HEART
ONE CHRISTMAS WISH*

The Protectors

*FORGED IN DESIRE
SEIZED BY SEDUCTION
LOCKED IN TEMPTATION*

The Grangers

*A BROTHER'S HONOR
A MAN'S PROMISE
A LOVER'S VOW*

For additional books by
New York Times bestselling author Brenda Jackson,
visit her website, www.brendajackson.net.

One Christmas Wish

BRENDA JACKSON

One Christmas Wish

ISBN-13: 978-1-335-52908-4

One Christmas Wish
Copyright © 2021 by Brenda Streater Jackson

The New Testament in Modern English by J.B. Phillips.
Copyright © 1958, 1960, 1972 J.B. Phillips.

This edition published by arrangement with Harlequin Books S.A.

For questions and comments about the quality of this book, please contact us
at CustomerService@Harlequin.com.

HQN
22 Adelaide St. West, 40th Floor
Toronto, Ontario M5H 4E3, Canada
www.Harlequin.com

Printed in U.S.A.

To the man who will always and forever be the love of my life, Gerald Jackson Sr. My hero. My everything.

To my sons, Gerald Jr. and Brandon. You guys are the greatest and continue to make me and your dad proud.

To my classmates of William M. Raines Class of 1971. Our fifty-year class reunion was wonderful. Thanks for reading my stories in high school and for reading my books now. You are the best!

Love knows no limit to its endurance, no end to its trust, no fading of its hope; it can outlast anything.
—*1 Corinthians* 13:7–8

One Christmas Wish

PROLOGUE

"Vaughn? Are you awake?"

Vaughn Miller rubbed sleep from his eyes, shifted in bed and adjusted his cell phone against his ear. He recognized the caller immediately. "I'm awake now, Deke. What's going on?" There had to be a reason Deke Hollister was calling him at three in the morning.

"I wanted you to know before it hit the papers that your name is being cleared."

Vaughn jerked upright in bed. "Say that again."

Deke chuckled. "You heard me, pal. I couldn't say anything before now, but the FBI uncovered a white-collar crime syndicate that stretched across several states including New York. They were able to link the group to what happened at your former employer on Wall Street. Arrests have been made and several confessions collected. One of which will exonerate you of all charges. I'm sure some type of restitution will also be in order."

Vaughn rubbed a hand down his face. No amount of restitution could make up for the two years that his freedom had been taken away from him. Not only his freedom, but also his respect and dignity.

"Thanks for everything you did, Deke. You're one of the few who believed in my innocence." The two had met years ago while in college at Yale. Whereas Vaughn had chosen a career on Wall Street, Deke had always wanted to be a crime fighter, and after a short time in the marines, he went to work for the FBI as one of their top agents investigating domestic terrorism. Last year he left the Bureau and started his own security/investigative firm in DC. He was doing quite well for himself due to his ability to solve crimes and the close connections he still had with the FBI.

"There were others who believed in your innocence as well, Vaughn. Don't forget the people of Catalina Cove welcomed you home."

Yes, they had. Thirty-five years ago, he was born in Catalina Cove, Louisiana, a small shipping town an hour's drive from New Orleans. When he'd left for college, he only returned a few times to visit his parents and sister. When they'd eventually moved away as well, there had been no reason to ever return.

When Vaughn decided to return to the cove to live four years ago, he was aware that some of the locals knew he'd served time. It honestly didn't matter since Reid Lacroix, the wealthiest man in Catalina Cove, had trusted Vaughn enough to immediately hire him as part of his executive team at Lacroix Industries. That hadn't come as a big surprise to many since, while growing up in the cove, Vaughn and Reid's son Julius had been best friends. Julius had also been Vaughn's roommate in college for four years. Sadly, Julius had been killed in a car accident close to nine years ago. He'd been like a brother to Vaughn and it was a loss that still pained him.

"I told you why they were so quick to welcome me, Deke," Vaughn said. "If Reid Lacroix likes you then the entire town loves you. Very few people go against Reid on anything." Reid was still the wealthiest man in town. Half the people living in the cove worked at the Lacroix blueberry plant. Back in the day, the Lacroix and Miller families had run in the same circles since both were part of the cove's old money elites.

The difference between Reid and some of the other wealthy people in town was that not only did Reid have a big heart, but he also genuinely cared about the welfare of Catalina Cove and the people who lived here. He paid his employees a more than fair wage, which is why very few people left until retirement. And Reid believed in giving hefty bonuses. When his companies did well, he had no problem rewarding his employees. Because of his generosity people were very loyal to him.

A part of Vaughn was glad he had decided to return. Although no comments were ever made about him serving time, he often felt there were those who hadn't been all that certain of his innocence. He hoped his name being cleared would remove all doubt.

"With both you and Sawyer there," Deke said, pulling Vaughn's focus back to the conversation, "when I get the time, I plan to visit the cove more often to get some fishing in."

"You do that. I owe you, buddy, for everything."

"You would have done the same for me, Vaughn."

Yes, he would have. A short while later, Vaughn ended the call with Deke. His friend had believed in his innocence from day one and had promised Vaughn that he would clear his name. When Vaughn was released from prison and decided to move back to Catalina Cove, Deke had paved the way by contacting the cove's new sheriff, Sawyer Grisham, who happened to be a former FBI agent and good friend of Deke's.

In addition to Reid, Sawyer and Sawyer's wife, Vashti, who'd been a classmate of Vaughn's, a number of former classmates had gone out of their way to welcome him back.

His thoughts shifted to Camila Elderberry, his girlfriend at the time he'd been arrested. The moment charges had been filed, she'd bolted, and hadn't even waited for the trial.

And then there had been Marie.

She was the person he'd come to think of as "his Marie." He'd never met her, but she had touched his life through her letters. She'd been part of the prison's Inmate Pen Pal Program, an agency that connected an inmate with someone on the outside who they exchanged letters with, whose sole purpose was keeping inmates motivated and encouraged while confined. He'd only received a total of eight letters from his pen pal Marie and they always seemed to arrive on some of his worst days, when he was at his lowest and needed motivation and encouragement. The letters had been a beacon of hope against the injustices that had put an innocent man behind bars. They had kept him positive, and that optimistic attitude was the reason he had been released after serving only two years of a five-year sentence.

The guidelines of the program prohibited the pen pals from sharing personal information so Vaughn was fairly certain Marie was not even his pen pal's real name. The letters were delivered to him through the agency and when he wrote back, they were delivered to his pen pal the same way. He definitely owed "his Marie" a debt of gratitude.

And now his name was being cleared.

Vaughn drew in a deep breath, feeling like a heavy weight had been lifted off his chest. Knowing he couldn't get back to sleep, he eased out of bed. One of the first places he went was to the dresser where he kept a packet full of important papers. He knew just what he was looking for. The letters he'd received from Marie, which he still read on occasion.

Shuffling through the letters, he came to the last one he'd received, which was the one that had inspired him the most.

There are days that will seem hopeless.
And nights that seem filled with despair.
Always look forward to tomorrow.
Brighter days are coming, even when it appears they aren't.
You must believe.
Marie

He slid the letter back into the packet with the others and put them in the dresser before heading back to the bed. With his name cleared, he had reason to believe that for him brighter days were coming.

CHAPTER ONE

Three months later

Sierra Crane cringed every time her ex-husband called. Their marriage had ended almost two years ago, so why couldn't he get on with his life the way she had gotten on with hers? She hadn't heard from him since the divorce and now this was the second phone call in a month.

And why did he always manage to call her at the worst time? The dinner crowd was arriving at her soup café, the Green Fig, and she was short a waitress tonight. The last thing she needed to be doing was talking on the phone to her ex.

"What is it now, Nathan?" she asked, trying to keep her voice low to avoid being overheard by the customers coming in.

"You know what I want, Sierra. We rushed into our divorce and I want a reconciliation. We didn't even seek counseling."

She rolled her eyes. It wasn't as if counseling would have helped their marriage. She had put up with things for as long as she could, and had to remove herself from that toxic environment. His infidelity had been the last straw, and then there had been his total lack of sensitivity when her best friend Rhonda Andrews was dying.

"Why are we even discussing this, Nathan? You know as well as I do that no amount of counseling would have helped our marriage. You betrayed me. I caught you in the act. Look, I'm busy," she said when she saw customers waiting to be seated. "And do me a favor and don't call back. Our divorce is final, and I intend for it to stay that way. Goodbye." She clicked off the phone and, for good measure, she blocked his number.

Moving from behind the counter, she assisted her staff in seating customers and taking orders. It was an hour later when the dinner rush had ended that she found the time to go into her office and work on tomorrow's menu. The monitor screen on her desk was connected to a video camera showing the perimeters of the dining area. If she was needed to assist her staff again, she would know it.

She sat in the chair behind her desk thinking about Nathan's call. The nerve of him thinking they could get back together. Not only had he cheated on her but he had resented all the trips she'd taken from Chicago to Houston to spend time with Rhonda in her final days. It hadn't mattered to him that Rhonda was terminally ill and there had been so much to do and so little time left.

The main focus had been the well-being of Rhonda's four-year-old daughter, Teryn, who'd lost her father two years earlier in Afghanistan. Without family on both sides, Sierra was Teryn's godmother and Rhonda had made Sierra promise to take care of Teryn when the time came. Nathan, who'd never wanted children, had been resentful of that, too.

It had been one of those weekends she'd visited Rhonda in Houston and she'd returned home early to find another couple, namely her neighbors, in bed with her husband. That's when she'd found out about his swinging lifestyle. He'd confessed it was something he had tried during his college days but thought he had put behind him…until he had discovered their new neighbors had enjoyed doing that sort of thing.

When Sierra had filed for divorce, Nathan assumed if he kept sending her flowers, calling her all the time, and showing up unexpectedly at her new residence with chocolates, designer purses and jewelry, he could wear down her resistance and she would call off the divorce. He finally saw that wasn't happening.

An hour later Sierra left her office to return to the dining area. It was time for her only waitress on the floor tonight to take her break. Sierra had just stepped behind the counter when the sound of the bell above the door alerted her that she had a customer.

The Green Fig, which served lunch and dinner Mondays through Fridays, had been open for business for only a year. The restaurant closed every night at eight. Most of her customers were locals who'd known her grandmother and were happy that Ella Crane had passed her delicious soup recipes on to her granddaughter.

Sierra had a good staff. She'd hired Emma, who'd been a friend of her mother's for years, as head cook and Maxine, who'd graduated from the New Orleans cooking school last year, as Emma's assistant. Normally there were two waitresses, Iris and Opal, who handled the dining room, and Sherri took care of the take-out orders. On any given day there were more take-out orders than sit-down orders, especially during lunch.

She'd hired Levi Canady as the assistant manager. An ex-cop who'd retired early from the force due to an injury, he was also a good friend of Sierra's father from their elementary school days. Levi was a godsend and would take over for Sierra whenever Teryn came home from school. He managed the restaurant every night except on Wednesdays. He also opened and closed for her on Saturdays, when the restaurant was open only for lunch. Whenever Teryn had gymnastics practice Sierra would help out in the café until she got home. Today was one of those days.

Sierra glanced at the door and saw Vaughn Miller walk in,

dressed in a business suit. On any other man the outfit would probably look like just regular professional attire, but on him it appeared tailor-made. He was a very handsome man and looking good in anything he wore was just part of who he was.

Sierra didn't know Vaughn personally, although they had both been born in Catalina Cove and had attended the same schools. She hadn't had the right pedigree to be in his social circles since his family had been one of the wealthiest in town. They had come from old money, probably as old as it could get in the cove when you were a descendant of the town's founder.

When Vaughn Miller took a seat at one of the booths, she grabbed a menu out of the rack and headed to his table. He'd come in once or twice before, but it had always been for takeout. It appeared that today he intended to dine in.

"Welcome to the Green Fig."

He looked up when she handed him the menu. "Thanks."

This was the closest she had ever been to Vaughn Miller and she couldn't help noticing things she hadn't seen from a distance. Like the beautiful hazel coloring of his eyes. He had sharp cheekbones and she liked the way his nose was the perfect size for his face and the full lips beneath it. And speaking of lips…did his have to be of such sensual perfection? And then she couldn't miss the light beard that covered his lower jaw and how it enhanced those lips but didn't hide the dimple in his chin.

Vaughn's skin was a maple brown and he wore his thick black hair long. It wasn't down past his shoulders like Kaegan Chambray's, but it was long enough to touch his collar. To her the long and tousled hairstyle did much to highlight his French Creole ancestry.

The Creoles derived from free people of color from Africa, France and Spain, as well as other mixed-heritage descendants. Those blended races and cultures were a large population of Louisiana, and more specifically, New Orleans, Catalina Cove and other surrounding cities.

Sierra had to concur with the feminine whispers around town that Vaughn Miller was a very handsome man and a sharp dresser, yet she noted he had a definite rugged masculine appeal. Even dressed nicely in a suit, all you had to do was add a tricorne hat on his head and a loop earring in his ear and he would instantly become a dashing pirate. A look that no doubt would make his great-great-great-great-grandfather, the cove's founder, Jean Lafitte, proud.

She knew six years ago he'd been sent to prison for a crime he didn't commit. Three months ago, articles appeared in numerous newspapers reporting on his exoneration and how those who were guilty had been brought to justice. He had been cleared of all charges.

"What's the special for today?"

She blinked upon realizing she'd been standing there staring at him the entire time. Clearing her throat, she said, "Today's special is the broccoli and cheese soup and it's served with a half sandwich. Turkey or chicken."

He smiled up at her and that smile made his features even more beguiling and clearly showed that dimple in his chin. "That sounds good. I'd like a bowl with a chicken sandwich."

She wrote his order down on the pad and noticed his French accent. She recalled overhearing her parents say that his mother had been French and his father mixed French and African American, and that French had been the primary language spoken in the Miller household. She also remembered hearing while growing up he would spend his summers in France as well with his grandparents. That was probably the reason the accent was still strong after all this time.

"What would you like to drink?"

"Brown ale."

Sierra nodded. "Okay, I'll put in your order and get your ale."

"Thanks."

She turned and walked toward the kitchen. When she knew

she was out of his sight and that of customers and staff, she fanned herself with the menu. Vaughn Miller had definitely made every hormone in her body sizzle.

Vaughn watched the woman leave, taken aback by how attracted he was to her. He didn't particularly like the thought of that. He'd been attracted to women before but never with this much intensity and magnetism. The moment he had looked into her face, he'd been a goner and he sat there feeling stunned.

He was convinced it had to have been the beauty of her eyes that captivated him. They weren't just brown, they were a shade that reminded him of chestnuts. And damn it, he felt like one roasting on an open fire.

He'd noticed her before from a distance when he'd come in to pick up his order, but this was the first time he'd seen her up close. The male in him definitely liked what he saw. The moment she'd appeared with the menu and he'd looked into her eyes, he'd instantly felt something, something he hadn't felt in a long time—an intense physical attraction. There were some things that couldn't be helped. He was a man after all, but still he found it strange that he'd been back in the cove over four years now and he hadn't been this attracted to any woman before.

He forced his gaze away from her to look around. The place was busy. This was the first time he'd actually stayed and not done takeout. The only reason he was eating in now was that there was a zoning board meeting at city hall and there was no reason to go home only to leave an hour later.

His friend Kaegan Chambray had talked him into taking his place on the zoning board during the time Kaegan's wife, Bryce, was due to deliver the couple's first child. Although the little boy had been born six months ago, Kaegan had yet to reclaim his position on the board. Vaughn had a sneaking feeling Kaegan wouldn't be doing so anytime soon since being a new father was keeping him busy.

In a way Vaughn didn't mind since it gave him something to do other than going home to watch television before going to bed. He wasn't all that hungry, so instead of dropping by the Witherspoon Café for a full meal, he'd decided a bowl of soup and a sandwich would hit the spot.

"Here's your drink."

He met the woman's gaze as she placed the beer in front of him and thought she smelled good, and she had nice hands. He studied her face and saw how her hair framed her features like a pool of thick, glossy silk and how the dark brown coloring brought out the beauty of her eyes.

He cleared his throat and managed to say, "Thanks."

"Your soup and sandwich will be ready in a minute."

She walked off again and just like before, his gaze followed her every movement, appreciating the shape of her ass. There was something about the way she was dressed in a pretty blue silk blouse and tailored slacks that made him wonder when the last time was that he'd taken interest in what a woman was wearing.

He didn't recall her from when he was growing up in the cove. But then, he figured there had to be a good six-year difference in their ages, which meant she was just probably starting junior high school when he'd been leaving for college.

"Here you are."

A bowl of soup and a plate with a sandwich was put in front of him and he thanked her.

Just as she was about to walk away, he asked, "You're the owner, right?"

She turned and smiled. Why did that smile send a spike of heat low in his gut? "Yes," she said, extending her hand out to him. "I'm Sierra Crane."

He took it, and immediately full awareness of the warmth of her skin almost made him groan in male appreciation. His voice was raspy when he answered, "And I'm Vaughn Miller."

She nodded. "Yes, I know who you are."

Did she? He didn't really have to wonder how. Although no one had ever spoken to him directly about his past, he'd figured there had been discussion nonetheless. He hoped those same people now knew he'd been cleared. "And how do you know?" he asked.

"You probably don't remember me, but I'm Preston Crane's daughter."

He might not remember her but he did remember Preston Crane. Years ago, Vaughn's parents had owned the only gas station in town, as well as numerous others throughout Louisiana, Texas and Oklahoma. He recalled Preston Crane managed the one in the cove for years.

"I recall Preston, but I never knew his family," Vaughn said.

"You wouldn't have."

He agreed with her. He wouldn't have. His parents had frowned on mingling with the "hired help," as his father referred to his employees. The reason Vaughn recalled Preston was because Vaughn would often accompany his father when he would check on the gas supply at that station.

"I remember that you graduated from high school the same year Vashti and Bryce did," she said.

He nodded. "Yes, I did. When did you graduate?"

"Four years after you did."

That meant she wasn't as young as he'd thought. "I believe my sister might have graduated with you."

"Yes, she did. Zara Miller was Miss Catalina Cove High our senior year. She was also captain of the cheerleading squad. She was popular and friendly."

"Did you attend the school's Holiday Homecoming a couple of years back?" he asked. Vaughn didn't recall seeing her but then a number of people had returned for the event.

"Yes. That's one of the reasons I moved back to the cove. Reid Lacroix's offer of a low-interest loan was too good to pass up."

He knew what she was referring to. As an incentive to get

people to consider moving back to the cove, in memory of his son Julius, Reid had announced at the high school's Holiday Homecoming banquet that he would be offering low-interest loans to anyone who would return to the cove to open a business. Of course, to maintain the integrity of the town, it had to be a Reid Lacroix–approved business.

When the bell on the door sounded, indicating another customer, she said, "Well, I hope you enjoy your meal, Vaughn."

"Thanks, Sierra," he said, liking her name. He watched her hurry off to greet the couple who had entered.

He continued watching her, wondering why he'd let her get under his skin. She was definitely beautiful, but he'd encountered a number of beautiful women since returning to the cove. As part of Reid's executive team, he often traveled to attend social functions on Reid's behalf. At those events, there were always women who came on to him. Therefore, he'd had no problem finding a woman willing to share his bed for a night or two.

There was something about Sierra Crane that presented a temptation he wasn't ready for or even wanted. Since returning to the cove, he'd been a loner and had gotten used to it. However, there was no way he could deny his attraction to her, and wasn't even sure he'd be able to ignore it. Even now he was thinking of a number of things he wouldn't mind doing to her.

He noted she wasn't wearing a ring and he was glad of that. He would hate to be having these kinds of thoughts about someone's wife. But then her not wearing a ring didn't necessarily mean she wasn't spoken for. He honestly couldn't imagine a woman like her not belonging to some man. If she had graduated with Zara, that meant she was around thirty. Where had she lived and what had she been doing before moving back to the cove?

He began eating his soup and knew just the person who would know the answers to any questions he had about Ms.

Crane. Sawyer Grisham. As a former FBI agent turned sheriff, Sawyer made it his business to know about everyone living in the cove, especially anyone who had moved back. It just so happened Vaughn would be seeing Sawyer tonight at the zoning board meeting. He'd never made inquiries about a woman before, but he had no problem accepting that there was a first time for everything.

CHAPTER TWO

Sierra looked up when a very excited six-year-old Teryn burst into the room, followed by Velvet Spencer, Teryn's gymnastics coach. "Goddy, Goddy, I did good on my routines today!"

Sierra pushed away from her desk and extended her arms for her goddaughter to race into them. She gave Teryn a tight squeeze and closed her eyes, thanking her best friend for leaving her daughter in her care. Rhonda had still been mourning her husband Terry's death of barely a year when she'd been diagnosed with terminal cancer. After getting a second opinion and a third, Rhonda had opted out of chemo, saying she needed the quality, and not the quantity, of time to spend her last remaining days getting her business in order and being with her daughter.

Sierra finally released Teryn and saw her goddaughter beaming, looking every bit like her mother, although she had her father's eyes. Today had been her gymnastics lessons. It was something Rhonda had introduced her daughter to when she was only three.

"I'm glad to hear you did well, Teryn," Sierra said, matching her goddaughter's excitement before turning her attention to Velvet, who'd volunteered to deliver all the girls she coached home after each lesson, which were held three times a week.

Sierra's office was in an area between the restaurant and the staircase leading above. That's where Sierra and Teryn lived, in a spacious three-bedroom apartment. The living quarters had been a change from the six-bedroom, five-bath monstrosity of a home she'd moved out of when she left Nathan. However, that didn't bother her. She loved her home, and it was the perfect size for her and Teryn.

That way she could work in her office late at night and still be available if Teryn needed her.

"She is telling you the truth, Sierra," Velvet said with a huge grin on her face as she sat down in the other office chair. "Teryn was great today on all of her routines. She's a natural."

Sierra liked Velvet. They were similar in age and had moved to the cove around the same time. She and Velvet had become good friends. During the day, Velvet taught at the junior high school, and then three days a week she volunteered as a gymnastics coach. "Only because she has a great trainer," Sierra answered warmly, closing her book.

To give her goddaughter her absolute attention, Sierra's workday ended the moment Teryn came home from school or practice. If things got hectic in the café, Sierra would sit Teryn at a booth in the back, to do her homework, color or work on a puzzle, while she helped out.

She'd established a great routine for her and Teryn. Usually she got up every morning at six to start on soups, and then around eight while the pots were simmering she'd wake Teryn up and get her ready for school. After walking Teryn to school—which was only a few blocks away—Sierra would return to relax a minute before opening up for lunch.

There were five different soups served daily and one "soup of the day." That meant, with Emma and Maxine's help, she prepared six different soups daily.

In the evenings after dinner, Sierra would usually go over Teryn's homework with her before putting her to bed.

A few hours after Velvet left, Sierra found herself fighting back tears when Teryn's bedtime prayer to God was to relay a message to her parents that although she missed them, she wasn't sad knowing they were together again and were now angels watching over her. Teryn also told God to thank her parents for leaving her here with her Goddy, whom she loved a lot and who was taking very good care of her.

After kissing Teryn good-night, Sierra rushed from the room and threw herself across her bed. Teryn's prayer had left her so emotional. With no living family on Rhonda's or Terry's side, she had called on Sierra, who'd been her best friend since they were kids. Rhonda and Sierra had grown up in Catalina Cove and the two had left for college together in Texas where they had been roommates.

Even though Rhonda had known Sierra had decided not to have children of her own, Rhonda had asked her to raise her daughter. It wasn't that Sierra didn't like children, because she did and had always thought she would marry a man who wanted them as well. Unfortunately, she hadn't.

Nathan had told her from the beginning that he didn't want children. He had grown up dirt-poor and didn't intend to die that way. He wanted a woman who desired the same things out of life that he did, which was to be successful and wealthy. Kids, he'd said, would only weigh them down. He'd let her know up-front he'd gotten a vasectomy years earlier to assure there were no offspring in his future. That meant if she married him, she had to accept she would never be a mother.

He convinced her that the two of them could be a power couple. At the time she'd thought she was head-over-heels in love with Nathan and had bought into it. Against the advice of family and friends, she had forgone her own dreams to become a part of his.

Sierra and Rhonda had decided for the adoption to let Teryn keep her last name of Andrews as a way to always remember the parents who loved her. It would be up to Teryn if she wanted to change it when she got older. To Teryn, Sierra had always been *Goddy*, and she was fine with her calling her that and Sierra referring to her as her goddaughter. Both Rhonda and Sierra had felt the fewer changes Teryn had to make in her young life, the better.

Sierra missed Rhonda. She'd been the greatest best friend anyone could have. Each night she thanked God for having both Rhonda and Teryn in her life. She was letting out a good cry when her phone rang. She recognized the ringtone. It was her sister, Dani. Dani was four years younger and lived in Atlanta with her husband and three kids.

"Hello."

There was a pause. "What's wrong, Sierra?"

She fought back more tears. "What makes you think something is wrong?"

"The sound of your voice. Are you going to tell me or do I have to catch a plane to Catalina Cove tonight to find out?"

Sierra smiled. They both knew there was no way Dani would voluntarily catch a plane for anywhere since she hated flying.

"I'm fine, Dani. I just put Teryn to bed and her prayers got to me. She gave God a special message to pass on to her parents."

"Oh. And what was the message?"

Sierra told her and when she'd finished, she could hear her sister sniffling. "Now you see why I was crying," Sierra said, wiping her tears.

"Yes. Hold on, let me grab some tissues," Dani said.

Sierra was glad her tissue box was beside her bed, and she reached to grab a few more. When Dani returned to the phone, Sierra said, "I love her so much, Dani, and I appreciate Rhonda trusting me to take care of her."

"We both know Rhonda would not have wanted anyone

else to do it. Too bad Nathan couldn't have been understanding about it."

Sierra shrugged. "It didn't matter. By then I had found out
about his extracurricular activities and filed for a divorce."

"Yes, but what if you hadn't found out? You and I both know
he would not have welcomed Teryn into your home. Then
where would she be?"

"She would still have been with me. I would have hoped Nathan would understand."

Dani didn't say anything, and Sierra knew why. Nathan would
not have understood and would have made her choose. While
they were discussing Nathan, she decided she might as well tell
her sister the latest.

"Nathan called me today."

"What on earth did he want?" Dani asked. "And please don't
tell me he still wants the two of you to get back together."

"Okay, I won't tell you."

"Honestly, Sierra. The two of you are divorced. After what
he did, how can he even think you'd take him back? He was
caught in bed with two other people. One would have been
bad enough, but his freakish ass had two. Forget about Nathan
and focus on a new beginning, sis."

"That's the plan."

"Good. So how did your day go? Met a nice man yet?" Dani
asked, changing the subject.

Sierra chuckled. Her sister and parents never liked Nathan
and thought he was bad news from the start. Dani, in particular,
felt Sierra had gotten a raw deal during the seven years of her
marriage and was glad Sierra now realized that as well. However, Dani refused to accept Sierra's proclamation that she was
through with men and would never marry again.

"My day went just fine and no, I didn't meet a nice man."
Sierra then thought about Vaughn Miller and decided to add,

"One did come into the restaurant, and it was someone who grew up in the cove. I found him rather interesting."

"Interesting in what way?"

"Interesting in that I studied his features and liked what I saw. I kept looking at him when he was eating, too. It was like I couldn't take my eyes off him."

Dani laughed. "That's called an attraction. You were attracted to him. That's a start."

"No, it's not. Like I said, I found him rather interesting."

"Now I'm really curious. Who is he?"

"You probably won't remember him since he'd graduated years before us. His name is Vaughn Miller."

"Vaughn Miller? Umm… I vaguely remember him. I recall the Millers were some of the rich folks in town and owned the gas station that Dad managed."

"I know. I mentioned that to him."

"So, the two of you had a conversation?"

"A very brief one. I was short of help and waited on him."

"What do you know about him?" Dani asked.

"I know he returned to the cove a few years ago. I also know he spent two years of a five-year sentence in prison for embezzlement, but his name was recently cleared."

"That's good. I can't imagine a Catalina Cove Miller needing money enough to steal. His family was loaded. I recall hearing that his parents died in a boating accident in Paris some years back. I don't believe they sold their mansion in the cove, though. Is Vaughn living there?"

"I have no idea. Like I said, he came in for soup and a sandwich and we introduced ourselves, and I told him our dad worked for his."

"So, he was friendly?"

"Yes, he was friendly, why do you ask?"

"I was just thinking of how snobbish his parents acted at times. All that money went to their heads."

Sierra had never met Mr. or Mrs. Miller and doubted Dani had either. Her sister was probably recalling their parents' whispered conversations about the Millers and their uppity attitudes. "I graduated with his sister, Zara, and recall she was nice enough," Sierra said.

"I remember Zara and she was nice," Dani agreed. "If you recall in my freshman year, I became a cheerleader, and Zara was captain of the squad. Glad she never acted snobbish like her parents. I understand she now owns a slew of boutiques around New England and on occasion I see her name in fashion magazines. The rich continue to get richer."

Sierra knew Dani had a real problem with people who thought being wealthy was everything. That's one of the reasons Dani had disliked Nathan. Her sister thought in addition to being too controlling, he was also obsessed with being rich. She was worried that his obsession would eventually rub off on Sierra. After all, he had convinced Sierra that she didn't need to be a mother.

Sierra and Dani talked for another half hour as Dani told her she had talked to their parents earlier that day. After Sierra and Dani had left home, Preston and Beatrice Crane had sold their home in the cove and purchased a large RV. Their goal was to travel all fifty states, and it seemed they were enjoying doing it and were making a number of like-minded friends along the way. They were living the life, fulfilling their dream, and Sierra and Dani were happy for them. They also appreciated their parents for calling them every week, letting them know where they were and how they were doing so their daughters wouldn't worry about them. This week they were in the Rockies and would be there the rest of the month.

Dani also told Sierra how much she missed her husband, who was away on a business trip. Emory worked for a company that sold medical equipment to doctors' offices and hospitals and often did a lot of traveling. Dani shared with Sierra her plans to jump Emory's bones the minute he walked through the door on Friday.

Sierra couldn't recall a time she had "jumped" Nathan's bones or even wanted to. There had never been that much passion in their marriage. In fact, he'd always come across as very conservative in the bedroom when it came to sex, and he wasn't into trying new and different things. Boy, had she been fooled.

Dani thought she should focus on a new beginning. It was her desire for that very thing that made her decide to move back to Catalina Cove with Teryn. She had wanted to make a home for them. That's why for the past year she'd worked hard to make the restaurant successful and build a stable life for Teryn.

If nothing else, being married to Nathan had taught her an important lesson. Never again would she depend on anyone for her happiness. Over the past two years, she had become a strong, independent woman and intended to remain that way. Teryn was now her main priority. The last thing Sierra needed in her life was a man shifting her attention.

Nathan had shown her how men could be controlling and couldn't be trusted most of the time. His betrayal had done more than hurt, it had nearly destroyed her. Their marriage hadn't been perfect, but she never thought he would cheat on her. She'd thought better of him. The realization that he wasn't the man she believed him to be would have devastated her if it hadn't been for Teryn.

Losing Rhonda had been terrible enough, but it meant Teryn needed her. In essence, they had needed each other. What Dani had said was right. Nathan would never have welcomed Teryn into their home. And had he done so just to appease Sierra, he would have outright ignored Teryn. Sierra would not have brought her into that kind of environment.

The two times Nathan had contacted her since their divorce, not once had he asked about Teryn, when he was well aware she had officially adopted the little girl, as Rhonda had asked her to do.

An hour later, Sierra showered and got ready for bed. When she finally closed her eyes, an image of Vaughn Miller filled her mind, and he was smiling at her.

Shifting in bed to a comfortable position, she couldn't help but smile back as she drifted to sleep.

"Hey Sawyer, wait up a minute," Vaughn said, jogging to catch up to Sheriff Sawyer Grisham.

Sawyer, who had been walking toward the parking lot after the zoning board meeting, turned around. "Yes, Vaughn?"

"If you're not in a rush, I need to talk to you about something."

"Sure thing, what's up?" Sawyer asked, tightening his jacket around him against the strong October wind.

"I met someone today and I'd like to get to know her better."

Sawyer nodded, smiling. "I'm glad a woman has finally caught your eye."

"Women have caught my eyes before, Sawyer."

"I mean a woman living here in the cove."

Sawyer had once shared with Vaughn how when he first moved to the cove with his teenage daughter, he hadn't wanted to date any of the single women in town because it was too close to home. Catalina Cove was a close-knit community where a lot of times your business wasn't your own. He had been lucky enough to have a friend with benefits who lived in New Orleans and the two of them would hook up there.

Vaughn had pretty much felt the same way about dating any of the local women. A few different women had approached him, and he'd thought they were pretty enough. However, he always held back. So why was he changing his mind when it came to Sierra Crane?

"Who is she?"

Sawyer's question intruded into his thoughts. "Sierra Crane."

"Sierra makes the best soup in town," Sawyer said grinning.

"What else can you tell me about her?"

Sawyer leaned against the light post. "What exactly do you want to know?"

Vaughn shrugged. "I didn't see a wedding band on her finger, so I take it she's not married."

"Not anymore. She's divorced and I understand she has been for a couple of years now. And she is raising her goddaughter. The child's mother also grew up here in the cove and passed away."

"Where did Sierra move from?"

"Chicago. She did some high-powered computer-related job there," Sawyer replied. "I don't know her that well, but she seems nice. I haven't given her a ticket yet. That's all I can tell you. If Sierra Crane really interests you then I suggest you stop rushing home every day to that empty house and start hanging out in town more. Namely at the Green Fig. Your name has been cleared, Vaughn, so what are you waiting for?"

Vaughn knew why Sawyer was asking him that. He'd once told Sawyer that he didn't want to get serious with anyone until his name had been cleared. "Sierra's very pretty."

Sawyer chuckled. "Since I only have eyes for my wife, I'll take your word for it. If you're interested in her, why not ask her out?"

Vaughn cleared his throat. "It's been a while since I've been on a date." He didn't count the occasional hookups he had at the work-related social functions he attended.

"It's just like riding a bicycle. Once you do it again, everything will come back to you."

A half hour later Vaughn entered his home. At some point he and Zara needed to decide what they would do with this monstrosity of a house. The estate was way too big for one person. There were days he never ventured upstairs, since he'd taken one of the bedrooms downstairs. Ms. Baker, the housekeeper, was still working here.

That was the only decent thing his parents had done, namely made sure in their will that the household staff—the housekeeper, cook and gardener—were taken care of for life. Mrs. Jones, the cook, had moved away temporarily to take care of her older brother in Baton Rouge who had health issues. Otherwise, Vaughn would have used her services instead of eating takeout every day. Mr. Connors still maintained the yards and at sixty-five said he enjoyed doing so. Ms. Baker came twice a week to dust and change bed linens and whatever else needed to be done. From the aroma of citrus that had met him when he entered his home, this had been her cleaning day.

As Vaughn headed for his bedroom, he thought about Sierra Crane. She had stirred something to life within him that wasn't just sexual. There was just something about her that he couldn't walk away from, even knowing it was probably in his best interest to do so. It wasn't like he had a lot of extra time on his hands.

Just today Reid had called him to his office to discuss an important matter. Larson Barrows, who owned Barrows Bank, was retiring. Catalina Cove's only bank had been bought out by the Colfax National Bank, a group of family-owned banks with branches in Arizona, Texas and Oklahoma. This would be the first Colfax bank in Louisiana. The Colfax family had agreed to retain the present employees so no one would be losing their jobs in the process.

Barrows Bank handled all of Lacroix Industries' business dealings, including payroll for the blueberry plant. It was important to Reid that the people taking over the town's bank were capable of providing the cove with what it needed financially.

In addition, because of Vaughn's expertise in the financial arena, Reid wanted him to handle the influx of applications for the low-interest loan program. The funding came from Reid and he vetted the recipients, but the loans were handled through the bank.

Next week Vaughn would be flying to Arizona to meet the Colfax family. It would be Vaughn's job to make sure Reid's funds were invested wisely and the low-interest loan program continued to run smoothly. Plans were for the bank to change its name the first of the year. So far, no official announcement had been made. That would be done during a town hall meeting in December.

His thoughts shifted back to Sierra Crane. Whether he wanted to be or not, he was interested in her. He didn't want to rush her into going out with him. And if they did, where would they go? There were a lot of nice restaurants in New Orleans, but then he didn't want to give her the impression that he wouldn't want to be seen with her in the cove. He would let her decide. She might know about his past, and although his name had been cleared, she still might not want to go out with him because of that.

As Vaughn stripped to take a shower, he decided not to go into the Green Fig for the next few days. He needed to plan a strategy and when the timing was right, he would ask her out.

CHAPTER THREE

Three days later, Sierra felt a jolt of sexual energy all the way to her bones the moment Vaughn Miller walked through the door of the Green Fig. She didn't know where that jolt had come from. She'd never responded that way to a man before. But then few men were as handsome as Vaughn Miller, she thought dryly. Definitely not Nathan and not even Mervin Price, the guy she thought she was head-over-heels in love with while in college.

And it didn't help matters just now when their gazes connected, and she could almost feel herself drool. Holy moly, how crazy was that? She figured it wasn't any crazier than the fact that when he'd entered the restaurant, his gaze had gone straight to her instead of glancing around for a table. Should she be flattered or worried that something was happening that she might not be able to control?

And she *was* finding it hard to control. She wasn't imagining the fact he was still holding her gaze or the heat it was stirring inside of her. Nor did she imagine the smile he gave her before finally turning his attention away when one of her waitresses approached him. It was only then that she exhaled a deep breath. Another thing she hadn't imagined was that she'd gone to bed thinking about him every night since the last time he'd been to her restaurant.

"He's a looker, isn't he?"

Sierra looked at the woman now standing beside her. She raised a brow at Emma's comment. The happily married woman was the same age as Sierra's mother. "Why, Ms. Emma, I wonder if Mr. Frank knows you're checking out other men."

Emma chuckled. "He knows I'm not blind and that says it all. Catalina Cove is a lucky place for a young, unattached woman with so many good-looking single men around. Unfortunately, most aren't staying single long. So, if you're interested, you might want to strike while the iron is hot."

Sierra reached out and straightened the menus in the rack. "I'm not interested. Have you forgotten why I'm here?" Although she hadn't gone into details with anyone about why she'd gotten divorced, everyone knew that she had. And since Emma was one of her mother's good friends, she figured her mother had expressed her dislike of Nathan.

"No, I haven't forgotten and I'm glad you came back home to the cove. This is the best place to heal and find love again."

Sierra agreed with the healing part but not so much with the finding love again. "It's not easy when your heart has been broken."

Had her heart been broken, or was it just her pride that had been damaged? During the last three years of their marriage, Nathan had been competing for a key promotion in his company, which had caused a lot of stress. A stressed Nathan had turned into a mean Nathan, and he'd found fault in practically everything she'd done. He'd even been jealous when she received a big promotion at work.

"Your parents and grandparents would be proud of you for coming back to the cove," Emma said, puncturing Sierra's thoughts. "Now if we can only get Dani to come back."

Sierra grinned. "You can forget that. She loves living in Atlanta and is satisfied just to come back and visit like the folks are doing."

"Your parents got wanderlust. They will eventually come back and settle down again. In the meantime, I am happy for them. Well, break time is over. I'm needed back in the kitchen."

When Emma walked away, Sierra told herself she would not look to see where Vaughn was seated. The waitress who'd seated him was now headed to the kitchen to put in his order and prepare his drink.

Would he want brown ale again? Not able to resist temptation any longer, she glanced over at him and saw he was staring at her, as if he'd been waiting for her to look his way. As if he'd known she would.

She wasn't sure how long she stood there exchanging stares with him, or if he felt the same thing she was feeling in that moment—a surge of yearning and acute awareness erupting and tying her insides into knots. The peep of her wristwatch finally made her break eye contact with Vaughn. Glancing down she saw it was a text message from Velvet saying the girls had done so well at gymnastics practice, she wanted an okay to treat them to burgers and shakes at Spencer's before returning them to their parents.

It was a Friday night and with no school tomorrow, Sierra got her phone and texted Velvet that it was fine. Besides, one of the other little girls getting lessons was in Teryn's first-grade class. Teryn and Chelsea had become the best of friends and since they wouldn't be seeing each other again until Monday, they would probably enjoy that.

She had slipped the phone back in her pocket when she felt a presence in front of her. Across the counter from her was Vaughn. His appearance surprised her. "Is anything wrong?" she asked, fighting back the nervousness in her voice.

He shook his head. "No. I was just wondering about something."

She regarded him inquiringly. "Wondering about what?"

"I prefer not eating alone and wondered if you would join me."

Join him? Why would she do that? And would that constitute a date? Something she wasn't ready to do? *Of course it's not
a date, Sierra. He's merely asking you to sit with him while he eats. No
biggie, so you shouldn't blow his request out of proportion. But still…*

Sierra was about to tell him that she was too busy to sit with
him when she studied his eyes, and those beautiful hazel depths
seemed to reach out to her with mesmerizing force. And she
was aware of it in every part of her body.

She shouldn't be drawn to him this way, yet she was. That
made her curious as to why. It would be a while before Velvet
brought Teryn home, and it was time Sierra took a break anyway. There was no reason she couldn't give Vaughn fifteen minutes of her time. Fifteen minutes and no more.

She finally nodded and said, "I was about to take a break, so
yes, Vaughn, I'll join you."

Vaughn looked at the woman sitting across from him in the
booth. Even though he hadn't seen her in three days—and he'd
tried not to be—he couldn't deny that he was still attracted to
her. He could tell she was nervous and he didn't want her to be.
So, he tried making her feel relaxed by asking, "Would you like
something to drink? It will be on me if you do."

She smiled and like before, that smile did something to him. It
was the same smile he remembered every night when he closed
his eyes before falling asleep.

"Although I'd love to have what you're drinking, I'd better
settle for iced tea instead. After all, I'm still on duty."

He wanted to tell her in that case he needed to make sure
they shared a drink somewhere when she wasn't on duty, but he
knew it was too soon for that. Instead, he said, "I take it you're
a fan of brown ale, too?"

She chuckled, and the sound sent sensuous shivers flowing to his groin and he had to shift in his seat.

"Of course, especially since it's manufactured right here in Catalina Cove," she said. "Demetri Langston returned to town the same time I did to open that brewery, thanks to Reid Lacroix's low-interest loans. Even my attorney had a hard time believing how great the terms were."

Vaughn could believe that. Reid had more money than he knew what to do with and Vaughn was glad he was using it to grow Catalina Cove into the kind of place everyone would be proud of. In reality, what he was doing was home growing their own. Vaughn had looked at the stats just that morning and over twenty new businesses had opened in the cove. All were owned by those who'd been born in the cove but moved away for college with no intention of returning.

Reid had found a way to lure them back with a strategic plan that benefited the town. And to accommodate all that required more housing. Already Reid was working on a project to tackle that issue.

Vaughn nodded. "The terms are hard to believe, but it's serving a purpose. He wants the cove to flourish for future generations, especially now that he has grandchildren."

"His granddaughters, right?"

"Yes." Vaughn smiled. "His granddaughters." He would never forget the first time he'd seen Julius's daughters. His best friend had died not knowing that he'd fathered two beautiful baby girls who were now in college.

"I understand that you and his son, Julius, were good friends."

Vaughn nodded as he took a sip of his ale. "Yes, Julius was my best friend." Vaughn had known Julius's secrets. He had also known his pain and the guilt that had eventually destroyed him. He had chosen social class over love and he had lived to regret it. Vaughn didn't intend to make that mistake. If he had to, he would choose love and not wealth.

"I was sorry to hear about the car accident that killed him."

"So was I. I miss him," Vaughn said.

One of the waitresses came up to take Sierra's order and she asked for iced tea.

When she glanced over at him, he said, "You might want to try the special for today. I heard that the black bean soup with crab meat and andouille sausage is to die for and would make you want to slap your mama."

Another grin lit up her face. "And just who told you that?"

"A number of people, but those words came from Sawyer."

She laughed in delight, and he thought it was a beautiful sound and wondered if she did it often. "I can believe you," Sierra said. "The sheriff never misses a chance to come in whenever I serve it. He's been in already today for family takeout."

"I think the kegs you use to put takeout orders in was a novel idea. How did you come up with it?"

"It was my grandmother's idea actually. Whenever she made the soup for the neighbors, she would give it to them in a cute miniature keg my grandfather made. That way, when it was time for a refill, people brought their kegs back for more. Of course, due to health department restrictions we can't refill them, but it's a cute keepsake."

"It is. Some of the ladies in my office use it as a pencil holder."

At that moment the waitress returned and set his bowl of soup in front of him with a chicken sandwich on toasted bread. His mouth was watering from the aroma. He thanked the waitress and looked over at Sierra. "Would you like to try some of this?"

She chuckled. "No thanks. I know exactly how it tastes. The crabs came off one of Kaegan's boats this morning. You can't get it any fresher than that."

"You're right about that." He spooned up a taste, which caused him to moan in pleasure and lick his lips. "This is the best. I don't know what you did before moving back to the cove and opening this restaurant, but I'm convinced being a soup-maker is your calling."

"Thanks, but I'm not sure my former boss would agree. Before coming here, I worked in Chicago's business district as a software development manager for Smithfield and Tyler."

"I've heard of them. They are a well-known and respected company."

"I know. I got hired by them right out of college and enjoyed working for them."

"What made you want to move back to the cove?"

She didn't say anything for a moment and Vaughn wondered if he was asking her to tell him too much too soon. He wanted her to feel comfortable with him, to feel that she could talk to him about anything.

Instead of answering, she checked the time and then said, "My break is over, and I need to get back."

He knew she didn't really need to get back, but if she felt she needed to end her chitchat with him then he would not stop her. "Thanks for sitting with me for a while."

"No problem. I enjoyed it."

He held her gaze when he said, "Then we must do it again."

She smiled as she stood. "Sure. Anything to please the customers. Goodbye." She turned and quickly walked off.

Vaughn watched her leave, determined that one day he would be more than just a customer to her.

"How many more days, Goddy?"

Sierra smiled at Teryn as she helped her goddaughter into her pajamas. Rhonda had warned her that Christmas was Teryn's favorite day of the year. This would be the second one the two of them shared together.

"There are seventy-four more days left until Christmas, Teryn. Are you getting excited?"

"Yes!"

Usually on Friday nights, Sierra allowed Teryn to stay up later than normal and they would watch a movie together. However, she could tell by Teryn's yawning and drowsy eyes that school, gymnastics practice and dinner with Velvet and some of the other kids had worn Teryn out and she was ready to fall asleep.

Teryn's question had Sierra thinking about Christmas.

Last year Dani had talked Sierra into spending the holidays with her, Emory and their kids—eight-year-old twin boys, Tucker and Turner, and their six-year-old daughter, Crane. She had gone along with it, thinking being around other kids would be good for Teryn. It had been, and Sierra was glad she'd made that decision, but this year they would spend Christmas here in the cove. And Sierra had already volunteered to be a part of the cove's Christmas planning committee, which consisted of local business owners.

Catalina Cove had always been such a beautiful place during the holidays, and she couldn't wait to introduce Teryn to it. The lighting of the Christmas tree in the town's square would kick off the holiday season the first Saturday in December.

There was also Christmas on the Main, an annual event where everyone was encouraged to visit all the stores, restaurants and shops on Main Street. That night, the best decorated storefront was given an award. Since the Green Fig was on Main Street, Sierra intended to participate.

Then there was Christmas Wonderland. It rarely snowed in the cove, but that didn't stop the locals from bringing in their own fake snow and creating a section of downtown that looked like the real thing.

The people in town were known to go overboard when decorating their homes, and even decorated their boats for a boat parade. It was fun to see all the various boats decked out in Christmas regalia to parade in the gulf, with holiday lights flashing. There was even a prize for the most decorated boat.

"Is there anything in particular you want Santa to bring you this year?" Sierra asked as she pulled back the bedcovers for Teryn to slide under.

"Yes. I will be giving you my wish list to send to him soon."

Sierra nodded, thinking that was good to hear, and she intended to make sure Teryn got everything on that list.

"What about you, Goddy? Do you have a wish for Santa? You only get one."

Sierra gazed at Teryn as she adjusted the pillow beneath her head. "Oh, really? And why do I only get one Christmas wish?"

"Because you are a grown-up. Mommy said grown-ups don't need as much stuff as kids."

Sierra smiled. Yes, she could certainly see Rhonda saying something like that. Her friend always thought of others before thinking of herself, which is why for years she'd worked at a nonprofit agency that handled multiple charities and foundations. "If that's what your mom told you, then that's the rule. I will only get one Christmas wish."

"Do you know what it is yet?" Teryn asked, her eyes widening with excitement.

"Nope, not yet. But I will think of something."

"It has to be something you truly want, Goddy, and then you need to write your own letter to Santa. Remember, you only get one wish."

Sierra hugged Teryn. "I'll remember."

A short while later, Sierra was in her office, curled up on the sofa in front of the fireplace with a glass of wine. Dani had called every night while Emory was out of town on business, and this was the night he was to return home. Sierra hadn't heard from Dani, so she could only assume her sister was jumping her husband's bones, like she said she would be doing the moment he got home.

She took a sip of wine and her thoughts went to Vaughn Miller.

She would admit after he'd visited her restaurant on Tuesday, she had gone to sleep every night thinking of him. When he hadn't come back over the next few days, she figured he had returned to his regular routine of dropping in every so often for takeout. She definitely hadn't expected him to walk into the Green Fig this evening.

She hoped joining him while on her break had not been a mistake. The last thing she wanted was to give him the impression that she was interested in dating, because she wasn't. She was way too busy and her main focus was Teryn. But she had enjoyed sitting across from him, hearing the sound of his voice, watching him enjoy his meal. She rubbed her hand down her face. Dani was right. She was attracted to the man. Was that pathetic or what?

Vaughn wasn't the first man to show interest in her since she had returned to Catalina Cove. Several of the single guys she'd gone to school with had asked her out, including Demetri Langston—back in the day, he'd taken her to her high school prom. In the beginning, she always held back because she was taking care of Teryn. Now Teryn was getting older and Sierra wasn't as protective of her. Several of the women in town had shared the names of teens they used as babysitters who were responsible and dependable. One just happened to be Emma's granddaughter, Jacquelyn, who was a junior in high school. On a few occasions, she had hired Jacquelyn so she could attend a committee meeting or join Velvet for a girls' night out. Jacquelyn had worked out wonderfully. But still...

Sierra knew that staying busy was key, and she was doing just that. However, tonight, while she sat across from Vaughn Miller, he had been able to do what all those other guys hadn't. He had reminded her that she was not only a woman, but she was a woman with needs.

CHAPTER FOUR

"Well, that about does it," Vaughn said, snapping closed his briefcase. He had left Catalina Cove to fly to Phoenix, Arizona, almost a week ago. He'd met with the Colfax Group that consisted of the father, Jack Colfax, and his three sons, Jack Colfax Jr., whom everyone called Jaye, Dean and Franklin.

Over twenty-five years ago, Jack founded the Colfax National Bank, opening the first one in Phoenix, Arizona. Since then, more than seventy branches had opened, not only in Arizona but in Texas and Oklahoma. And now they were expanding to Louisiana. Specifically, Catalina Cove.

As the biggest employer in town, Reid Lacroix had sent Vaughn to make sure the acquisition of the cove's only bank by the Colfax Group went smoothly. After meeting with the father and son team, Vaughn had no doubt that it would. According to Jack Colfax, the suggestion to acquire Barrows Bank had come from Jack's oldest son, Jaye. Vaughn discovered that he and Jaye were about the same age and both were part of the same Greek fraternity.

While in Phoenix, Vaughn had spent most of his time in business meetings with Jaye. It didn't take long for Vaughn to see that he was a sharp, highly intelligent and enterprisingly successful businessman who planned to expand the family's bank-ing business not only into Louisiana but to other states as well. However, Vaughn had a feeling the acquisition of Barrows Bank was very important to Jaye. Vaughn just hadn't figured out why.

"Are you flying out today?" Jaye asked, coming from around his desk and breaking into Vaughn's thoughts.

"No, I fly out tomorrow since I wasn't sure we would con-clude all our business today."

"I'm glad you flew out here. I could understand Mr. Lacroix's concerns since he's the bank's biggest client."

Vaughn nodded. There was no need to tell Colfax that if Reid hadn't wanted his bank to expand to Catalina Cove, they would not have. "Your team did an excellent job in providing all the information I needed. Do you know yet the name of the person who will manage the branch in Catalina Cove?"

"For the first six months or so, I will."

Vaughn raised a brow. Since the Colfax Group would be ex-panding to other cities and states, Vaughn expected that Jaye Colfax's expertise would best be used elsewhere.

"You will be moving to the cove then?" Vaughn asked.

"Yes. My personal assistant is looking into housing for me now. Hopefully, rental property won't be hard to find."

"It shouldn't be this time of the year. For the bank to open the first of the year, I assume you'd want to move to the cove sometime before the holidays."

"Those are my plans."

It wasn't what Jaye Colfax said but how he said it that gave Vaughn pause. Did the man have an ulterior motive for moving to the cove and opening a bank there? And why did Vaughn have a deep sus-picion it had something to do with a woman? If that was true, then the man was putting a lot of time and effort, not to mention capital, in this business venture just to be in the cove to pursue someone.

But on the other hand, he could see acquiring Barrows Bank was a win-win situation for the Colfaxes. Reid might be their largest client, but there were a number of other businesses that channeled their money through the only bank in the cove. Unlike Larson Barrows, who'd always been tight with his money when it came to a number of things, the Colfax Group planned to put money back into the community and the people they served.

"Well, your takeover of the bank will be a plus for Catalina Cove, and I wish you success with all your business ventures."

Jaye chuckled. "Thanks, but the business end is not what I'm worried about, it's the personal piece."

Personal piece? Vaughn nodded. "Then I wish you the best with that as well."

"Trust me, I'm going to need it. And another thing—"

"Yes?"

"I'd appreciate it if the news that Colfax Group will be taking over the bank isn't leaked to anyone," Jaye said. "At least not until the announcement is made at the town hall meeting in December."

Vaughn didn't say anything at first, thinking the man's request was an odd one. Most people in Catalina Cove knew that Barrows was retiring and were probably wondering who would be taking over. "Alright, but what about Barrows? Does he know of this request?"

"Yes, he knows and won't be saying anything." Jaye paused a moment and then asked, "By the way, do you know a woman living in the cove by the name of Velvet Spencer?"

Vaughn shook his head. "No, sorry, the name doesn't ring a bell. Is she someone you know?"

"Yes, she's someone I know. I believe she moved there around two years ago."

Just as Vaughn had suspected, Colfax's interest had to do with a woman. "The only people I can say I'm acquainted with are those I knew before leaving the cove for college. I've only been back a few years, but I don't recall our paths ever crossing. What does she do there?"

"I understand she's a teacher at one of the schools."

"I see."

As if Jaye Colfax figured Vaughn might be seeing too much, he looked at his watch before saying, "Since you're not leaving tonight, I'd like to invite you over to my place. I'm getting together with a few friends to watch the game. There will be plenty to eat and drink."

Vaughn smiled. "Thanks, and I'd love to."

After Vaughn Miller left his office, Jaye Colfax went to the window and looked out. The weather was typical for mid-October in Phoenix, and he was looking forward to moving to Louisiana for a while. According to Vaughn, although the town was located on the gulf, Catalina Cove rarely had real cold days. Like Phoenix, most days in October, the highs could reach the low eighties and the lows in the sixties. What he was looking forward to was the ocean being so close. He would definitely enjoy that.

His plans were falling together nicely and acquiring that bank in Catalina Cove was icing on the cake. That gave him hope that he could have a real chance at getting Velvet back.

When it came to business matters he was a born strategist, a trait he and his brothers had acquired from their father, but when it came to matters of the heart, he was the first to admit he'd failed. Mainly because he hadn't recognized love until it had been too late.

So now he had to plan an entirely new type of acquisition. Jaye knew it wouldn't be easy, but he intended to do whatever it took to prove to Velvet Spencer just how much he needed her in his life, and how wrong he'd been for taking what they had for granted and not realizing until she'd left just what she meant to him.

He knew Velvet, and for her to leave the way she had meant she didn't believe he could change, that he would always be a man totally against falling in love, settling down and marrying. Hell, they'd been together, dating exclusively for over three years and he still hadn't changed his mind about marriage.

For years the reason had been simple. Jaye never wanted to marry someone who would hurt him the way his mother had hurt his father, leaving him and their three sons to run off with another man. He would often see the pain in his father's eyes, especially around the holidays. It had been years before his father opened himself up to love someone again, and Jaye was glad when Arlene had come into not only his father's life, but his and his brothers' as well. She was just who their father needed, and he was smiling again.

Jaye turned when he heard the buzzer on his desk. He went to his desk and pressed the button. "Yes, Kim?"

"Mercury Steele is here to see you."

"Please send him in."

Mercury was his best friend and had been since grade school. They had also been roommates in college. Mercury knew him better than anyone, even his own brothers. He and Mercury were just that close. Last year Mercury had surprised the hell out of everyone and met a woman, fallen in love and married.

Mercury walked into Jaye's office smiling. Jaye noticed his friend smiled a lot these days, but this smile was even brighter than usual. "Any reason you're in such a happy mood?" he asked.

"Yes, there's a reason," Mercury said, dropping into the chair in front of Jaye's desk. "Sloan is pregnant."

A smile spread wide across Jaye's face. "I am happy for you. Truly happy. Has anyone told Eden yet?" Everybody knew that now that Mercury's mother had gotten her six sons married, she was looking forward to grandbabies. And it seemed she was getting them left and right. Two had been born this year from Mercury's brothers Tyson and Jonas and their wives.

"Yes. We told her last night at our regular Wednesday night get-together. Both she and Dad were happy."

"I can imagine."

"So, tell me, how was your meeting with that guy from Catalina Cove?"

"It went well. I plan to go there in December to check things out."

"Cut the BS, Jaye. The real reason you're going there is to see Velvet."

Jaye nodded. "I want to do more than see her, Mercury, although seeing her is a first step. It's been two years since she left me." And left him, she had. She'd moved away without telling him where she'd gone. All his friends, including Mercury, had warned him that one day Velvet would get tired of being just his bedmate when she deserved to be his wife. He'd been stubborn and refused to see it that way, and his friends had been proved right. It took losing her to make him realize that he loved Velvet. He regretted thinking their relationship had only been about sex. Boy, had he been wrong.

She had given him plenty of chances and he'd blown every one of them. He had hired a private investigator to find her and now, he planned on getting her back.

"You're right. It's all about Velvet and I need her in my life."

"Yes, you do. After being married to Sloan this past year, I can't believe I fought it for so long. I love being married and you will, too. I wish you the best on your plan."

"Thanks." Jaye knew telling Velvet that he loved her wouldn't cut it. He would have to show her.

"By the way, that guy from Catalina Cove will be in town until tomorrow so I invited him to tonight's party at my place. His name is Vaughn Miller, and I like him."

"Did you ask if he knew Velvet?"

"Yes. He doesn't know her."

Mercury stood. "I need to get going. I promised Dad I'd drop by and help him hang another painting Mom purchased. I'll see you later tonight."

"Will do."

After Mercury left, Jaye sat at his desk thinking. He needed Velvet back in his life and intended to make her his wife.

★ ★ ★

"Can you walk, Dani?" Sierra's question brought on a fit of laughter from her sister, who knew just why she was asking.

"You are so funny, Sierra. Of course I can walk, but I suggest you direct your concern to Emory. I plumb wore him out."

Sierra could believe it. She was convinced when they were giving out passionate bones, they overlooked her and gave double to her sister. Dani and Emory were two of the most passionate people she knew. They could never keep their hands off each other and were always touching. Even when they were out in public they held hands or he walked with his arm around her shoulders.

"The kids are okay?" she asked.

"Yes, they weren't here the night Emory got home since I wanted him to myself. My in-laws kept them through the weekend. What's going on with you? Any more action between you and Vaughn Miller?"

A part of Sierra wished Dani hadn't brought up Vaughn since she'd been trying to keep him out of her thoughts. She hadn't seen him this week so keeping him off her mind should have been easy, but it wasn't.

She eased down in her favorite spot on the sofa in a pair of her favorite pajamas. Instead of a glass of wine, tonight she'd settled on a cup of herbal tea. Normally she would have been in bed by now, but she wasn't sleepy. In reality, she just wasn't ready to close her eyes and see *him*. Even after a week of not seeing Vaughn, she saw him aplenty in her dreams.

"Sierra?"

"Yes," she said, when her focus was snatched back by Dani.

"I asked if there's been any more action between you and Vaughn Miller?"

That was easy enough to answer. "No. In fact, he didn't drop by the restaurant for soup this week."

"And how do you feel about that?"

A slight frown touched Sierra's lips. It sounded as if she should be lying on a couch with Dani as her therapist. "Am I supposed to feel some particular way?"

"You tell me. Do you feel indifferent, concerned, disappointed? Only you know how you feel, and I'm merely asking."

Sierra sipped her tea. Not only had Dani inherited all those passionate bones, she had nabbed quite a few of the perceptive ones as well. It had always been that way with Dani. Even when Sierra had tried putting her best face on the outside, Dani always detected how she was really feeling on the inside.

"I don't know how I'm feeling, Dani, and that's the thing. When Vaughn came into the restaurant last Friday, he invited me to share a meal with him. I was on break, but I did sit with him and had a glass of tea while he ate."

"And?"

"And it was pleasant…and I felt things."

"What sort of things?" Dani asked.

"Vibes. I actually felt vibes between us. I got turned on just looking at him. Whether it was watching him eat, drinking his ale, talking. Any time he moved his mouth I got hot. I mean burning hot."

"Wow."

Sierra had a feeling she should not be sharing this with Dani of all people. Dani with all the passionate bones and an overabundance of perceptive ones. But Sierra wanted to talk to someone about these strange sensations she'd felt that night and every night since. If Rhonda had been alive, she could have talked to her, but her best friend was gone, so Dani was it.

"Yes, wow. For a moment I actually knew how it felt to want to jump a guy's bones. Vaughn Miller is so sexy, so good-looking, so fine and masculine."

"So, what's the problem, Sierra?"

Sierra rolled her eyes. "The problem, Danielle," she said, calling her sister by her given name, "is that I don't have time for such stuff. I have a little girl to raise and—"

"Whoa. Don't use Teryn as an excuse not to get some. How long has it been since you slept with a man and I don't mean lie beside one or make love and pretend to have an orgasm. I mean, made love with to the point where you enjoyed it. To the point where you began riding him when he's finished riding you."

Dani's words had Sierra choking on her tea. "What!"

"Umm, just what I thought. You need to get laid, Sierra."

"I do not."

"Yes, you do. However, I'm not sure Vaughn Miller is the man for the job."

"Why not?" she asked, not that she thought any man would be the right one.

"Too rich. Rich guys can be selfish, overbearing and out-right controlling."

Sierra had news for her sister. Guys vying to be rich acted the same way. Dani had just described Nathan to a T. "If not Vaughn, then who?" she asked, curious to hear what Dani would say.

"I don't know, Sierra, but I'm sure there are other eligible single guys in the cove who aren't filthy rich."

"First of all, there's nothing wrong with filthy rich if you're a decent person. Second, I don't need to get laid, but if I did, I would think I would turn my attention to the guy who can push my buttons. Otherwise, I would feel nothing and he will feel everything."

What she didn't add, but what she figured Dani suspected, was the resentment in her words was aimed at Nathan.

"Okay, you have a point. But when and if you do hook up with Vaughn Miller, keep your senses intact. I recall he was pretty good-looking years ago, and—"

"I thought you didn't remember him." How could Dani remember him when she didn't?

"I didn't at first, then I recalled Zara's brother who would pick her up after cheerleading practice whenever he was in town from college, and how all of us would drool."

Sierra could see teenage girls drooling over a college-age Vaughn. She drooled over the adult version. She glanced at her watch. She and Dani had been talking a half hour already. That would have been fine if Emory wasn't in town, since Sierra had no problem keeping her sister company.

"Where's Emory tonight?"

"Thursday night football over at his folks' house. It's better for them to have the hoopla there since they make too much noise, whether their team is winning or losing. The kids need to sleep and not hear a lot of cursing and swearing. He should be home in an hour or so."

"And you will wait up for him."

"Of course."

Sierra couldn't help but smile. Although she teased Dani a lot about it, she was happy for her because one of them had hit the jackpot when they'd married. Emory and Dani were perfect for each other and they loved each other a lot.

"Sierra?"

"Yes?"

"You're going to find that special someone who is meant to be yours and no one else's. Don't give up. Who knows, it just might be Vaughn Miller. Who am I to say?"

Then, as if Dani sensed she was ready to change the topic, Dani smoothly shifted to Teryn, asking how she was doing, how she was handling first grade and her excitement for the approaching holidays.

"She told me last week she is working on her wish list for Santa." After taking another sip of her tea, Sierra added, "And she told me to make sure I did mine. However, I only got one wish because I'm an adult. So, I guess what I wish for better be a doozy."

Dani chuckled. "Yes, and I hope whatever you do wish for comes true."

CHAPTER FIVE

Vaughn stepped into the Green Fig as he loosened the collar of his jacket. It was an unusually cold October day and the breeze off the gulf was making it worse.

Due to a bad storm causing flight delays, he had returned from his trip to Phoenix late Saturday, and with the Green Fig being closed Sunday he'd had to wait until today. It was the start of a new week and he hoped it would end well.

Vaughn had enjoyed the gathering Thursday night at Jaye's house. The food was great and so were the drinks. He'd met some of Jaye's close friends, the Steele brothers. All six guys were happily married. Mercury Steele was Jaye's best friend and was overjoyed that he and his wife were expecting their first child.

He looked around the café before taking a seat at the same booth he'd sat in the last time he was here. A waitress quickly came to take his order. "I'll take a brown ale. And is your black bean soup with crab meat and sausage on the menu today?" he asked. "I had it the last time I was here and liked it."

"Sorry, it's not on the menu today but it will be on Thursday."

He nodded. "Okay, then what soup do you recommend?"

The waitress smiled, as if for him to suggest that she recommend something meant a lot. "Our special for today is corn chowder and it's being served with hot garlic rolls, right out of the oven."

"That sounds good. I'll take a bowl." Before the young woman could walk off, he said, "Is Sierra working today?"

"Yes, she's probably in the kitchen. Do you want me to tell her that you'd like to see her?"

Vaughn refrained from telling the woman he wanted to do more than see her. He had actually missed her. No matter that the closest he'd gotten to her was to shake her hand. "No, that's not necessary. Hopefully, she'll come out of the kitchen before I leave."

An hour later, he wasn't so sure of that. He had done everything—eaten slow, ordered another ale and checked the news on his phone—and still no Sierra. He was about to signal for the check when Sierra finally came out from the back.

He knew she didn't see him at first and she went to straighten up the menus in the rack. And then, as if she detected she was being watched, she glanced over to where he sat.

The moment their gazes connected he felt something right in the center of his gut. It was more than a sexual hunger or a spike of heat that stirred to life. It was something more profound. He didn't want to try to figure out what it was right now. All he knew was that it was powerful enough to play on his senses and make its presence known. He was about to get to his feet to go to her when he saw she had started walking toward him.

When she reached him, she smiled and said, "Hi. Welcome back."

His gaze slowly raked across her face, taking in the beauty that was uniquely hers, while little bubbles of want and need continued to burst to life in the pit of his stomach. It was then that he realized what her greeting had meant. Was that her way of letting him know she had missed seeing him...as much as he'd missed seeing her? "Hi yourself, and I'm glad to be back."

"That's good to hear. I had begun wondering if perhaps you didn't enjoy your last bowl of soup. Or even perhaps, my company, Vaughn."

He loved the way she said his name. However, her comment had him wondering if she was flirting with him, or was it a clear signal of interest on her part? He had no problem with either, although he really liked thinking she was interested in him like he was in her. "I enjoyed both, especially your company. Will you join me again?"

She studied his table. "You've eaten already."

"Yes, I got here a little earlier. I was about to order a cup of coffee. Will you join me?"

He watched her nibble nervously on her bottom lip and knew she was deciding. Even though joining him like she'd done the last time did not constitute a date or anything, it did indicate the building of something, of friendship or a relationship. He preferred the latter and definitely wanted to get to know her. There was a reason why she, of all the women he had met since his breakup with Camila, had this effect on him.

Considering how Camila had dumped him when he'd needed her the most, it would stand to reason that he should be putting the brakes on anything developing between him and Sierra. Yet it was just the opposite. It had taken years to realize not all women were like his ex-fiancée. Being around Sawyer and Vashti, Ray and Ashley, and Kaegan and Bryce had shown him a solid relationship was possible with the right person. He had accepted that Camila had been all wrong.

Sierra glanced at her watch and said, "My goddaughter is on her way from gymnastics practice and will be here any minute."

He nodded. "Until she arrives, will you sit with me and let me know how you're doing? I've been out of town for a week on business."

When Vaughn saw the look in her eyes it made him think she was glad the reason she hadn't seen him was due to business. He really wanted her to know that nothing else would have kept him from stopping by. "I thought of you while I was gone," he said, deciding to be honest with her.

She tilted her head and with a huge smile said, "Are you sure it was me and not the black bean soup with crab and sausage you had the last time you were here? You really seemed to enjoy it."

He returned her smile. "I did enjoy it, but I enjoyed your company more. So please join me, even if it's for a little while."

She nodded and he stood as she slid into the seat across from him. He sat down, getting caught up in the rare sexual energy that encompassed them. He felt it and had a feeling she felt it as well.

"So, you were away from the cove on business," she said, as if she needed to hear herself repeat his words.

"Yes, in Phoenix."

They paused when a waitress appeared to clean off the table and to see if they wanted anything. "Coffee for me," he told her.

"A cup of herbal tea for me, Opal," Sierra said to the waitress.

When the young woman walked off, Sierra looked up at him and said, "Do you enjoy working for Lacroix Industries?"

"I do. There is so much more under their umbrella than just the blueberry plant. Reid has quite a number of projects going and all to benefit Catalina Cove. It's true that he hates change in the cove, but he has unselfish reasons for it. He loves this town and knows what can happen if we lose what we have here."

He paused when the waitress delivered his coffee and Sierra's tea and then asked, "Are you glad you moved back?"

"Yes, what about you?"

"I'm glad I moved back, too. I lived in New York for years and soon discovered how much I missed living in the cove, where people were friendly and looked out for each other."

She nodded. "I never knew how much I appreciated Catalina Cove until now. That's the reason I returned to raise my goddaughter. Her mother, Rhonda, and I were best friends while growing up here in the cove."

He lifted a brow. "Rhonda? Was she related to Inez Boyer?"

He saw surprise flicker in Sierra's eyes. "Yes."

"Then I remember the Rhonda you're talking about. Ms. Inez used to do all the ironing for my family, and whenever she came to pick up the items each week, she would bring this young girl with her. She introduced her as her granddaughter, and I recalled her name was Rhonda."

Sierra smiled. "She's one and the same. After graduation, Rhonda and I left to attend college in Texas together. We even got married the same year. She was my maid of honor and I was hers. Sadly, Rhonda passed away two years ago from ovarian cancer, barely two years after losing her husband in Afghanistan. That left her little girl, Teryn, with no family on either side. Before she died, Rhonda asked me to take care of Teryn after she was gone. I promised that I would."

"It's admirable that you kept that promise."

"There was no way that I could not. Since the day we were born, Rhonda and I had been best friends. Our mothers had been best friends, so had our grandmothers. It just seemed natural that we would as well."

"Goddy! Goddy! I'm home!"

Hearing the happy voice, Vaughn turned his head to see this little sprite of a girl, with pigtails bouncing all over her head, race toward where he and Sierra sat. Sierra laughed and said, "Speak of the angel, here comes my goddaughter."

Sierra stood as Teryn raced into her outstretched arms. She doubted she would ever tire of this, showing and giving love and receiving it in return. More contentment than she ever thought she could feel filled her heart. Teryn was a gift from Rhonda that she would cherish forever.

Like her mother, Teryn had an overabundance of friendly

genes, having never met a stranger she didn't like. Once Sierra had released her from their hug, she smiled and said to Vaughn, "Hello, I'm Teryn."

Vaughn smiled. "Hello, I'm Vaughn."

"Hi, Vaughn," Teryn said, waving happily.

"That's *Mr.* Vaughn, Teryn," Sierra said.

Teryn nodded. "Oops. Mr. Vaughn."

Vaughn stood and extended his hand to the little girl. "I'm happy to meet you."

A radiant smile spread across Teryn's face and she said, "And I'm happy to meet you, too."

Out of the corner of her eye Sierra saw Velvet quickly cross the room to where they were. She glanced up at Velvet and smiled. Then Velvet said, "Sorry about that. The moment I entered the restaurant Teryn raced off to find you to share her good news."

"No harm done, Velvet." She turned to Vaughn—was she mistaken or was he looking at Velvet strangely? If he was, it wouldn't be the first time a man reacted to her. Sierra thought Velvet was gorgeous and radiant all rolled into one. She knew since she'd moved to the cove a number of men had tried asking Velvet out and so far, she had refused. That made Sierra wonder about the man who'd broken her friend's heart. Maybe one day he would be smart enough to know what he'd lost.

"Velvet, I'd like you to meet one of my favorite customers, Vaughn Miller. Vaughn, this is Velvet Spencer. Velvet is a teacher in town and she's also Teryn's gymnastics coach."

Vaughn extended his hand. "Nice meeting you. Velvet is an unusual name."

Velvet chuckled. "Not if you had a grandmother who was an Elizabeth Taylor fan and *National Velvet* was her favorite movie. It's nice meeting you, Vaughn." Velvet turned to Teryn. "Now tell your godmother your good news."

Teryn's face was a vision of excitement. "They picked me!"

Sierra smiled. "Who picked you and for what?"

"To sing. They liked the way I was singing."

"Oh."

Sierra looked up at Velvet, who explained further. "Mrs. Mayes from church came to pick up her granddaughter from practice and asked any of the kids if they wanted to be part of the youth carolers this year. They will make their debut at church during Youth Sunday in December, and then the following week they will be going around the neighborhood singing Christmas songs."

Velvet grinned and then added, "Although Teryn readily volunteered, I told Mrs. Mayes I would mention it to you and that you would have to decide."

"May I, Goddy? May I?"

Sierra smiled down at Teryn and wondered if she would have to audition. Granted, she'd never heard Teryn sing a song, but she wouldn't dare tell her it was a standing joke when they were kids that the best thing Rhonda had done for their church was to get out of the youth choir and join the usher board instead. Lord knows, her best friend couldn't carry a note.

She looked at Velvet. "Will they have to audition?"

"That was done tonight. Teryn sang 'Silent Night' for Mrs. Mayes and sounded beautiful."

Sierra was glad and decided Teryn must have gotten her singing talent from her father. Definity not her mother. "Then there's no reason you can't. When are the rehearsals?"

"They won't start until next month," Velvet said.

Sierra turned to Vaughn with regret. "Sorry, I need to get Teryn fed and up the stairs to help her with any homework before she goes to bed."

Vaughn's brows rose in question. "Up the stairs?"

"Yes, I have an apartment upstairs," Sierra said. "Hopefully, we'll be able to chat over drinks another time."

"I'm sure we will, Sierra. Enjoy the rest of your evening." And then to Velvet, he said, "It was nice meeting you."

"Same here, Vaughn."

He turned his attention to Teryn and gave her a huge smile and said, "It was nice meeting you, too, Teryn. And congratulations for making the carolers."

"Thank you, Mr. Vaughn."

Sierra, Velvet and Teryn then walked away. It took everything within Sierra not to look back.

An hour later, Vaughn eased down at his kitchen table with a cold beer. Although he hadn't spent as much time with Sierra today as he'd liked, at least he had seen her and talked to her a little. His eyes hadn't been playing tricks on him. She was as beautiful as he'd remembered, and he had missed her. He had no problem telling her that he'd thought of her.

He took another swig of his beer, remembering he'd just told Jaye Colfax last week that he didn't know a Velvet Spencer, and then was introduced to her this evening. Vaughn was certain she was the same woman Jaye had asked about. The name and the occupation fit. He didn't know the story between them but figured there was one. There was no doubt in his mind that Colfax's decision to live in the cove for a few months had something to do with Velvet Spencer. Hell, he wouldn't be surprised if the man's decision to buy Barrows Bank centered around Velvet Spencer somehow. Time would tell.

Vaughn shifted his thoughts to Sierra's goddaughter, Teryn. He couldn't help but smile when he thought of how excited she'd been at being selected as a caroler. The little girl had been bubbling over with happiness.

He took another sip of beer as he thought about Sierra. She was wearing a pair of slacks and a printed blouse and she had looked good in them. As far as he was concerned, she looked good in whatever clothes she wore. He wished he could have spent more time with her but understood she had more important things to do. Besides, he didn't want to rush her into anything. He wanted to take his time to get to know her and wanted her to get to know him.

However, what he wouldn't do is go to her restaurant every single day, although he would like nothing better than to see her whenever he could. He didn't want her to feel uncomfortable or pressured by his presence. He wanted things to progress naturally between them.

A short while later, before going to bed, he pulled out some of the letters he'd gotten from Marie and read them. And as always, they gave him encouragement and hope.

CHAPTER SIX

"Good morning, Sierra. I'm surprised to see you here."

Sierra recognized the deep, husky voice even before looking up. Her lips spread into a smile, determined to focus on his features and not his voice. But then the man was handsome as sin, so that wasn't a good option either.

"Good morning, Vaughn. I just walked Teryn to school and decided I had a taste for some blueberry muffins, so here I am, in the place that makes the best."

The Witherspoon Café was a favorite with locals and served the best omelets, pancakes and blueberry muffins for breakfast, sandwiches for lunch and delicious meals for dinner. Every once in a while, on her way back home from walking Teryn to school, she would stop at the café to grab a muffin and a cup of tea. Usually, she got it to go, but this morning she'd decided not to rush and to just sit and enjoy both.

Catalina Cove was considered the blueberry capital of the country, and every time she bit into a muffin she liked that the blueberries were homegrown. She had eaten the blueberry muffins in Chicago and other places, but there was nothing like a muffin from the Witherspoon Café.

"Do you mind if I join you?"

"Sure." There was no reason she should mind, other than the fact she was attracted to him when she shouldn't be.

She noticed a number of eyes on them. There had been curious looks when she'd sat with him at her restaurant, too. Some of the good people of the cove had always been busybodies. She couldn't see that changing anytime soon. She figured Vaughn had to have noticed the gawkers, but he didn't seem bothered by the attention they were getting.

"What would you like, sir?" a young waitress came up to ask him.

He smiled up at her. "I'll have coffee for starters and an omelet. Just tell Chester it's for Vaughn Miller and he'll know how to fix it."

The waitress smiled. "Sure thing." And walked off.

He glanced over at her and asked, "Is it good?"

She swallowed. "Is what good?"

"That blueberry muffin you're eating."

She nodded and then after she had finished chewing and swallowing, followed by a sip of tea, she said, "It's delicious, but then they always are."

For the past couple of weeks, he had dropped by the Green Fig, although she hadn't had a chance to sit and chat with him again. Business had picked up and she'd been needed to help out her staff.

He hadn't come to the restaurant for the past few days, not that she expected him to come by every single day. However, she had missed seeing him. Of course, she wouldn't tell him that. The last thing she wanted was for him to assume she was looking for him every day.

"I'm sure you don't miss the Chicago weather this time of year," he said.

"You're right. All that snow took getting used to and now I don't miss it at all. As a software development manager, I did get to work from home on the real cold days, but I honestly preferred being in the office."

"You enjoyed what you did?"

"Yes, but it was taking over my life and there was no way I could have kept up all the hours required with the adoption of Teryn. Raising her and giving her the time she needed was more important to me. I hired a good staff, so I can make my own hours. I enjoy walking her to school every day and being there when she comes home."

At that moment the waitress brought his coffee, and Sierra watched as he took a sip, fascinated by how his lips fit on the rim of the cup. She thought it was really crazy for a woman to get turned on just from seeing a man drink coffee.

"That's good. I'm convinced they make the best coffee."

"I'm not a coffee drinker but I enjoy their selection of teas," she said, sipping her tea before taking another bite into her muffin. She decided since he was always asking her questions, now was her turn.

"You've never been married, have you?" It was only after she'd asked that she wondered if perhaps her question had been too personal.

"No, I've never been married. I take it you have, though."

She wondered how he figured that. And then as if the question was in her eyes, he reached out and touched the third finger of her left hand and said, "The imprint where you wore your ring is still there."

Sierra looked down at her hand and saw that it was. She had worn her wedding rings for seven years and had taken them off the night she'd caught Nathan cheating. "Yes, I was married before. Nathan and I were married for seven years."

He nodded, and because she figured he was too much of a gentleman to ask, she said, "I caught him cheating."

"I'm sorry that happened," he said lightly. She felt his words were sincere.

"So am I. After it happened, there was no way I could re-main with him."

He nodded. "I understand. I believe trust in a marriage, as well as in a relationship, is very important."

She thought so, too. Entwining her fingers together she placed her elbows on the table and asked a question she needed to know the answer to. "Why aren't you seriously involved with someone?"

He tilted his head and gave her a smile and asked, "What makes you think that I'm not?"

Vaughn's question gave her pause and for a moment she didn't know what to say. Then she decided to be up-front with him. "I believe you're a man of good character. One who wouldn't be seriously involved with one woman while talking to another."

He shrugged. "There's nothing wrong with a man talking to a woman, Sierra. I guess what you could have said is that I'm not the type of man who would be seriously involved with one woman while *pursuing* another."

Her brows drew together questioningly. Was he pursuing her? "If that's a hint that you're pursuing me, Vaughn, then maybe now is the time I should warn you off. I am not interested in being pursued. Marriage left a bitter taste in my mouth."

Vaughn nodded again. "I should say my last serious relation-ship left a bitter taste in mine as well. I thought Camila loved me as much as I loved her. But she broke things off with me the day I was arrested. She didn't even ask if I was innocent or guilty."

He took a sip of his coffee and then said, "Just the thought that she'd been involved with me was an embarrassment for her. In fact, it was more than a mere involvement. We were engaged to be married."

"Oh, no. I'm sorry that happened, Vaughn. Why do the peo-ple we love hurt us sometimes?"

"Maybe it's because they aren't as deserving of our love as we thought. Sounds like we both picked a couple of losers."

"Yes, it certainly sounds like it."

The waitress brought out his omelet and gave her a refill on her tea. Sierra could have easily told the young woman she didn't need a refill because she was about to go, but something made her want to stay. She discovered she liked talking with Vaughn. Even when they broached subjects she'd rather not discuss, he had an easygoing demeanor and a pleasing personality.

"How long were you and your fiancée together?" she asked, curious to know.

"Three years. I worked on Wall Street and so did she, but for different companies. When she broke off with me, she said that she had a reputation to protect."

Sierra frowned. "Like you said, we picked a couple of losers."

Vaughn liked Sierra. He really liked her. Not only was she pretty but she was a great conversationalist. The more he talked to her, the more he found out about her.

He hated hearing that her husband had cheated on her. He couldn't imagine anyone doing that to her, but then he knew some men, as well as some women, were never satisfied with who they had.

She had finished her muffin and as time slipped by, she declined any more refills of her tea. However, she didn't make any attempt to leave, which meant she was enjoying spending this time with him as much as he was with her.

They chatted a lot, about all the activities that would be going on in the cove during the holidays, and she told him she was on the committee for planning Christmas on the Main. He could tell she was excited about that.

She checked the time. "I must be going. I open for lunch in a couple of hours."

"You make the soup every day?" he asked.

"Yes. It's made fresh daily. I usually get up at six and get started. Then while it's simmering I get Teryn up and ready for school. Before I leave the house, everything is done."

"Has there ever been an instance where you ran out?"

She chuckled. "Heck yes. That time that large group of boaters came through here. We sold out the place before dinner. I had to remake pots of everything."

"Your restaurant is successful."

"I have my regulars and I have newcomers all the time. I appreciate all of them." She glanced at her watch again. "I hate to run, but I have to go."

"I understand. I'm finished up here, so I'll walk you to your place."

"You don't have to do that, Vaughn."

"I want to."

She leaned in and in a low voice said, "I guess I don't have to tell you that we're drawing interest."

"Does that bother you?"

She shrugged. "No, but there was a time in Catalina Cove when a Miller wouldn't be caught socializing with a Crane."

"Well, I'm glad those days are over, aren't you?"

She smiled at him and his guts clenched. "Yes, I'm glad."

Although she'd told him it wasn't necessary, he paid for both their meals. Debbie and Chester Witherspoon called out to them to come back again as they were walking out. "They are good people," he said to Sierra.

"I know. I was four years younger than their daughter Bryce and she would babysit me when I was a kid. She was the best. She would always bring treats her parents had baked. I loved it."

"And now Bryce is married to Kaegan and is a mother of a little boy."

"I can't wait to see him. I'm told he looks just like Kaegan."

"He does. He already has a head of black hair."

"Sounds like the name Kaegan Junior fits him," she said.

"I think it does," he said.

They walked side by side on the sidewalk. He loved this section of Catalina Cove. The entire downtown area was a close replica of New Orleans's French Quarter, a deliberate move on Jean Lafitte's part. According to history, the cove was where the pirate would return to when he and his band of smugglers needed downtime.

Like where Vaughn lived, the scent of the sea was prevalent with the shipping district just blocks away. Since returning to the cove, he often wondered why he'd left. When he had arrived in New York he had looked upon it as a great new adventure. All he'd found were tall buildings, congested streets and sidewalks, and a slew of people who always seemed in a hurry. It had been the complete opposite of Catalina Cove.

They kept walking on the wide sidewalk and passing all the historic buildings that were now various shops and cafés. No matter what type of business you had going on inside the building, the outside remained the same. The zoning board had strict laws against architectural changes.

As they continued to stroll toward Sierra's café, Vaughn noticed she was wearing a long, flowing skirt and boots and loved how the skirt would swish around her legs when she walked. She was also wearing a mid-length leather jacket. "Do you walk Teryn to school every morning?"

"Just about. If it's raining then I'll drive her. I prefer walking so I can get my exercise. There's nothing like walking and smelling the scent of the gulf. Sometimes I wonder why I ever left here."

He looked at her, recalling he'd been thinking that same thing just moments earlier. "I'd like a stab at answering that. At least I can tell you the reason I left."

"Okay."

"I felt suffocated. Other than New Orleans and the states where my family's gas stations were located, we didn't visit much. Most of our travels were out of the country. That was nice, but there was so much here in the States I hadn't seen. I felt there had to be a life outside of Catalina Cove and I wanted to see it."

"Did you ever think you'd come back?" she asked.

"No. When I left, I left for good, although I would return on occasion to visit my folks. And then when they moved to Paris, I would return to visit Julius."

"Here we are," she said, coming to a stop in front of her restaurant. "Thanks for walking me home."

"It was my pleasure. What's the soup special of the day?"

She tilted her head to look up at him. "Black beans with crab and sausage."

He couldn't help the smile that touched his lips. That was his favorite. "Then you'll definitely see me later. Have a good day, Sierra."

"You do the same, Vaughn."

She opened the door to her shop and went inside. He walked off, counting the hours until he would see her again.

CHAPTER SEVEN

"So, I heard you had breakfast with Vaughn Miller this morning."

Sierra glanced over her shoulder at Emma as she opened the refrigerator to pull out the huge pot of soup she had made that morning. "Boy, news travels fast around here."

Emma chuckled. "In Catalina Cove, it always does and always will. But I only heard good things. Both you and Vaughn are well-liked, so of course everyone is wishing you the best."

Sierra shook her head as she set the pot on the kitchen counter. "I hate to disappoint everyone, but it's not like that."

"Then how is it, really?" Emma asked, turning from the sink.

Sierra paused. She honestly didn't know. What she did know was that they were attracted to each other. She also knew that she missed seeing him whenever he didn't come into her restaurant on a regular basis…like the week he was out of town on business. She also knew she thought about him at night and even went to sleep with his features etched in her mind.

"Sierra?"

Hearing Emma, Sierra realized that she'd just been standing

there and staring into space. She looked over at Emma. "I think he's a nice guy."

"I think so, too. And I've seen the way he looks at you and I've also seen the way you look at him."

"You're imagining things."

"I'm not imagining the fact that you're the only woman in town he seems to want to spend time with."

"He's not actually spending time with me," Sierra pointed out. "I haven't even shared a meal with Vaughn. I've merely kept him company while he ate. And I don't consider this morning at the Witherspoon Café a real meal."

"Like I said, that's more than any of the other women in town have done. Since returning he's made a point to be a loner. Heck, he didn't ever dine inside any restaurant. He always did takeout and went home and ate alone. I figured he didn't want people asking him questions about the time he was in jail. But now it was announced he is an innocent man, and that's a good thing."

"Yes, that is a good thing," Sierra agreed.

"Well, just so you know, rumor has it that Laura Crawford is interested in him. I understand she had a thing for him in high school."

Sierra wouldn't be surprised that Laura had had a thing for Vaughn years ago. She didn't know Laura that well; however, she was aware that the woman's family still owned several businesses in town, and she was a divorcée. She'd also heard that because of her family's wealth, Laura liked having things her way, and to keep the peace, people usually gave in to anything she wanted.

"Well, if Laura is interested in him I'm sure she will let him know it sooner or later. She might be more to his liking and the woman he wants," she said, breaking eye contact with Emma.

"I doubt he cares that she's interested, especially now. She could have made a move when he first came to town and didn't because she probably believed he was guilty of whatever he'd gone to jail for. Now that his name has been cleared, she wants him. I believe Vaughn Miller is smart enough to see through that BS."

Wanting to change the subject, she said, "I'm hoping Jacquelyn will be able to keep Teryn tomorrow night. There's a Christmas committee meeting. It's the first one and I really want to attend."

"I'm sure my granddaughter will be available tomorrow. I will call her when school is out."

By the time the Green Fig opened for lunch, Sierra wished she could say she'd been too busy to think about what Emma had told her about Laura Crawford's interest in Vaughn. But she hadn't. It would be just like the woman to want him now that he'd been exonerated. That was so sad.

Sierra recalled a few years ago when Rhonda had approached her about being a pen pal for prison inmates through a program her best friend had gotten involved with. At first Sierra had declined, but Rhonda had finally worn her down. Although letter writers were assigned to someone who was incarcerated, they never got to know them personally. The letters sent to the prisoners and their replies were brief and contained no identifying information and were screened through the agency that required you used a fake name. So she had used her middle name.

Sierra never knew the name of the person she wrote to, didn't even know if the person was male or female, the reason they'd been locked up, how long or at what facility. All they needed were words of encouragement. Because internet access was sometimes restricted, all the letters had to be handwritten.

The restaurant had a steady flow of customers for lunch and they only got a small break before it was time for the dinner crowd to arrive. When they parted that morning, Vaughn had mentioned he would be dropping by later. Although she was trying hard to downplay it, she was looking forward to seeing him again.

★ ★ ★

Vaughn leaned back in his chair while seated at the conference table. He'd been invited to attend the business meeting between Reid Lacroix and Ray Sullivan, another resident of the cove. If Reid was the wealthiest man in the cove then Ray Sullivan was probably the second wealthiest. However, few people knew that.

About six years ago Ray had moved to the cove after losing his memory to retrograde amnesia. The only thing Ray had remembered was his love of boats and being out on the water. So, it made perfect sense for him to be hired by Kaegan Chambray's seafood shipping company, and the two became the best of friends.

A year later, Ray had saved up enough money to buy a sight-seeing boat business that now included deep-sea fishing. A few years ago, Ray had gotten his memory back, remarried his wife, Ashley, and the couple had two-year-old twins, a boy and a girl.

What was so amazing was that in his former life—before the memory loss—the jeans-and-T-shirt-wearing, bearded ship captain Ray Sullivan had been Devon Ryan, a Harvard-educated, business-suit-wearing, suave, wealthy tycoon.

Although one and the same, Devon Ryan was the total opposite of Ray and even though his memory had returned, he preferred being called Ray.

Ray still had a knack for knowing how to make money. A couple of years ago, he had come up with an idea for a water-taxi service from Catalina Cove to New Orleans. Now, everything was set to go, with the official opening of the water-taxi service in the spring next year. When Ray had suggested the venture, Reid had immediately bought into the idea. So had Kaegan and Sawyer. Vaughn appreciated that he was able to buy stock in the company as well. He definitely saw it as something the cove needed. It would mean fewer cars on the road commuting to and from New Orleans, and traffic jams would be eliminated. The water taxi to New Orleans would take half as long as driving, and it would be a relaxing trip that would remove the stress of driving.

"Are there any questions?" Ray asked. In attendance were Reid, the mayor, Sawyer and several other local businessmen, including Kaegan and Chester Witherspoon.

Another benefit of the water taxi was a complimentary breakfast from the Witherspoon Café, something simple like their famous blueberry muffins and coffee. That would increase revenue for the Witherspoons as well as for blueberries produced by Reid's plant.

The mayor had questioned the possibility of adding additional taxis whenever Catalina Cove held their annual festivals. Ray assured everyone that would not be a problem. After a few more questions the meeting ended.

Vaughn looked at his watch. It was later than he'd thought, and he had told Sierra he would be by tonight. He knew her restaurant closed at eight and it was close to that time. If he left now, he could make it, although he would have to order takeout. He wouldn't have time to sit and eat there and talk to her like he would have liked, but at least he would see her again. He refused to question why that was important to him. He stood and closed his briefcase and after bidding everyone goodbye, he quickly headed for the door.

"Rushing to a fire, Vaughn?" he heard Kaegan ask.

"No, I'm trying to make it to the Green Fig before they close."

"You like their soup that much?" Sawyer asked, grinning.

Over his shoulder, he gave his friend a scolding glance. Sawyer knew why he was in a hurry to get there.

"I guess you can say that, Sheriff."

"Just don't speed on the way there," Sawyer said.

Vaughn ignored Sawyer's laughter as he left the room.

Although dinnertime had been practically nonstop, the last hour of the evening had become rather slow. In a way Sierra was glad that she and her staff had been able to take a breather. The closer it got to closing time the more disappointed she felt that Vaughn had not come by.

When the pot of the special for today got low, she had asked Emma to put enough aside for both her and Vaughn. She had been certain he would come and figured she would share a bowl of soup with him when he did.

She had fed Teryn, read her a story before putting her to bed. She had gone back downstairs hoping Vaughn would be sitting at one of the booths. He wasn't.

Sierra began thinking of a number of reasons he hadn't come by and for some reason Laura Crawford's name headed the list. In a way she wished Emma hadn't told her of Laura's interest in Vaughn. From the conversations Sierra had overheard since returning to the cove, the woman hadn't changed. She felt entitled to any man she was interested in.

She looked over at her staff. "You can all leave now since you've finished straightening up already. With just a couple of minutes before closing, I doubt anyone will be coming in this late."

No sooner had she said the words than the bell above the door chimed. She looked over her shoulder and met Vaughn's gaze.

"Sorry, I know you're about to close but my business meeting ran late. I'll be happy for takeout if it's available," he said.

She turned to her three waitresses. "I'll take care of his order. It's closing time so you can leave."

Giving her appreciative smiles they rushed toward the door. Sierra smiled at Vaughn. "I'll let my cook know to prepare you a bowl of today's special. I was just about to sit down and eat a bowl myself, so unless you're in a hurry, you can join me."

She saw the huge smile that appeared on his face that made that dimple in his chin stand out. "No, I'm not in a hurry, and I would love to join you," he replied.

"Okay, grab us a booth. Do you want brown ale as usual?"

"Yes, that sounds good."

She nodded. "I'll be right back."

As Sierra headed toward the kitchen, she figured there just might be some truth to the saying, good things happen when you least expect it. She honestly hadn't expected Vaughn to come tonight when it got close to eight. She figured he had changed his mind, had eaten somewhere else or was with Laura. She had no reason to be jealous of the woman or any amount of time Vaughn spent with her...if he ever did. She had no dibs on him and he didn't have any on her. In fact, she'd told him just that morning she was not interested in being pursued.

"Emma, Vaughn just walked in after getting detained at a business meeting. Tell me where the soup is, and I'll warm it up." Sierra was glad she had told Emma to put some aside when they were about to run out.

The older woman checked her watch. "The restaurant is closed. He's not doing takeout?"

"No," Sierra said, then walked over to the beer dispenser to pump Vaughn's ale into a glass.

She knew Emma's eyes were on her. "Sierra?"

She turned to the older woman. "Yes?"

"Earlier today you gave me the impression that what's going on between you and Vaughn Miller was not that serious. When you decide it's getting serious, please be sure to let me know. Nowadays, I prepare for weddings at least two years in advance."

Sierra rolled her eyes as she finished pouring Vaughn's ale and took it out to him. He turned when he heard her and the look in his eyes nearly made her miss a step. A part of her felt she shouldn't have suggested he join her. She should have prepared his takeout and sent him on his way. But the truth of the matter was that she enjoyed conversing with him whenever she could. Compared to how Nathan had been, Vaughn had such a calming presence.

Placing the drink in front of him, she said, "I'll be right back with our meal."

"Thanks."

She turned to walk off while feeling the heat of his gaze on her. When she reached the kitchen, Mrs. Emma was taking off her apron.

"That's it for me today," she said. "I'm certain you can handle things from here. I parked my car out back, so come let me out and lock the door behind me."

Sierra watched to make sure Emma was in her car and was driving away before she closed the back door and locked it. She then collected the soup bowls and arranged them on the serving tray along with the tea Emma had prepared for her.

It was a short walk from the kitchen to where Vaughn was sitting, but with his eyes on her the entire time it seemed to take forever for her to reach him, and she'd done so on shaky knees. He had a way of looking at her that made her body throb in unusual places. Like the nipples pressing through her bra and against her blouse.

Pulling herself together, she placed the soup and her tea on the table. "Sorry if I took so long."

He shook his head. "No, I'm the one who should be apologizing for even coming here late."

"We hadn't closed yet."

"No, but with only two minutes before closing I'm sure your employees were anxious to leave." He scanned around. "Everybody's left except your kitchen staff."

"Everybody's gone. Emma is my cook and I let her out a few minutes ago. She parked out back. Levi, my assistant manager, is off on Wednesdays."

She suspected she didn't have to come out and tell him they were alone, he probably had figured it out. But then they weren't really alone. Teryn was asleep upstairs. "Sounds like you had a busy day today," she said, after they'd said grace.

"Wednesdays normally are. They're our meetings day. We get together in person, by Zoom or telephone conferencing. We had all three types today."

He then told her about the water-taxi service. She had heard about it when she first came to town, but she figured it was sort of like a pipe dream and was surprised it was really happening.

"What about you? Did you have a busy day? And how is Teryn?" he asked.

She thought it was kind of him to ask about Teryn and told him she was okay and upstairs sleeping and thanked him for asking. "I would admit it seemed today was busier than usual, but I won't complain when business is good. Just so you know, when I saw we were about to run out of today's special, I had Emma put some aside for you."

"I appreciate that. I love this stuff."

She grinned. "I can tell." Their bowls had had the same amount of soup in them and already he'd eaten half of his.

They chatted for a good half hour while eating their soup and sandwiches. He told her about his plans to join his sister for Thanksgiving in Massachusetts this year and how she hated cold winters there.

"How long has she lived there?"

"Since college. She lives in Newton, which is less than ten minutes from downtown Boston. She owns a slew of shopping boutiques in Boston, New Hampshire and Vermont. I figure sooner or later she'll get tired of the cold and move back to the cove like I did."

She could hear the fondness in his voice when he talked about his sister. "Although my sister, Dani, comes back here to visit often enough, she's satisfied with making Atlanta her home with her husband and kids."

"How many kids does she have?"

"Three. Twin boys and a girl. Her daughter and Teryn are the same age so that's good whenever we visit them or they visit here. We spent Christmas with them last year and it was a good thing. We'd lost Rhonda a year earlier, and I figured Teryn and I didn't need to spend the holidays alone. There's never a dull moment in Dani's household."

He took a sip of his ale and said, "For the last few Christmases, Zara has come back to the cove to spend the holidays with me. This year she has informed me she plans to spend the holidays in Paris with friends."

They had finished eating when he said, "There's something I'd like to ask you, Sierra."

"Oh? What is it?"

"Actually, there are three questions."

"Okay, what are they?"

He met her gaze. "Are you going to the New Year's Eve Ball? If so, do you already have a date? If you don't already have a date, would you go with me?"

CHAPTER EIGHT

Vaughn finished off the last of his ale as he waited for Sierra to answer his questions. She had broken eye contact with him and was staring down into her teacup, but he refused to accept that as a bad thing. He was hoping she was merely giving his questions consideration. When she finally gazed back up at him she had an unreadable expression on her face.

"I haven't dated since my divorce, Vaughn. After officially adopting Teryn I moved here and opened the restaurant. That meant hiring staff, managing the remodeling of not only the restaurant but my apartment upstairs. We arrived in the middle of the school year, so I had to make sure Teryn was situated in school, and then I had to get acclimated with the community."

He moved his empty ale glass aside. "Sounds like you were busy."

"I was." She paused, then said, "But that wasn't the only reason I haven't dated. It was hard to accept the man I loved and who I thought loved me could betray me in such a manner."

She took another sip of tea before she said, "But I should have suspected something. Now that I think about it, I can see that the clues were there, right under my nose and in eye view.

I was too trusting and totally naive. But to be completely honest, our marriage began falling apart even before I discovered he was cheating."

Vaughn could hear the pain in her voice. He figured she was not about to share any details of what happened and that was alright, but he also didn't want her thinking she was the only person who'd been hurt by someone they thought they loved.

He said, "In a way I know how you feel. I told you about Camila and how she turned her back on me when I needed her the most. It didn't matter that we were engaged to be married. The one person I had expected to believe in me and to stand by me, did not."

He moved his eating utensils around as he thought about that time. "It took me a while to get over the pain. I had plenty of time while locked up. But still, I was hoping she would contact me, let me know she had freaked out initially and that she was good now and knew I was innocent and wasn't capable of doing the things I'd been accused of. But that never happened."

He stopped fiddling and met Sierra's gaze. "The reason I shared that with you was for you to see that things happen in life we don't have any control over. Things I'm sure we wish we could forget. But they are there with us, reminding us to be more cautious than we were before. But we can't let our past dictate our future. I like you, Sierra, and would like to get to know you better."

She hesitated. "I like you, too, but I'm not sure I'm ready to officially date again. I enjoy what we're doing now. Sharing drinks as friends. To answer your question, I had not planned to go to the New Year's Eve Ball."

"Can I ask you another question?"

"Yes."

"Are you still in love with your husband?"

Vaughn felt he could ask her that even after what the man had done because he'd still loved Camila for months after being incarcerated. He had honestly tried looking at things from her point of view, refusing to give up on her completely, although he'd not once heard from her.

He'd felt the need to cling to some kind of hope, even if it was one he'd fabricated in his mind. It was only when Zara visited him and broke the news that Camila had gotten married that he'd accepted her decision not to have anything to do with him as final. Just when he was about to give up, those pen pal letters from Marie had begun arriving. They had given him the encouragement and hope he needed.

"No, I don't love Nathan. Right now, I just want to protect my heart from further heartbreak."

He leaned back in his seat. "Will you do me a favor?"

Nodding, she said, "Depends on what it is."

He chuckled. "Fair enough. If you do decide to go to the ball, will you consider going as my date?"

"I probably won't change my mind, but if I do, Vaughn, I will let you know."

"I appreciate it." He looked at his watch. "It's getting late, and I don't want to take up any more of your time." He hesitated a moment and then asked, "Do you mind if I have your phone number?"

She seemed surprised and said, "No, I don't mind."

He stood to ease his cell phone out of his pocket. "Okay, what is it?"

Sierra rattled off her number and he punched it into his phone, and when her phone rang, he said, "Now I have yours and you have mine."

He slid his phone back in his pocket and pulled out his wallet to retrieve his charge card. "Do you need me to help you wash these dishes?" he asked, offering her his charge card.

She stood as well. "No, I'm good, and you don't have to pay for this. You treated me to breakfast this morning so tonight was my treat."

He returned his card to his wallet, put on his jacket and shoved his hands in his pants pockets. "Don't think it will always be that way, Sierra Crane," he said, stacking their bowls and gathering up the trash.

Tilting her head to look up at him, she asked, "What way?"

"That whenever I do something for you, that you feel the need to reciprocate."

Before she could respond, he asked, "Will you walk me to the door?"

She smiled. "Yes, I can do that."

Vaughn hadn't realized just how long the walk was from where they'd been sitting to the door. It was then that he realized he had unintentionally grabbed a table in the back. He had no complaints since he was in no hurry to leave, although he knew he had to.

He kept his hands shoved in his pockets so he wouldn't be tempted to reach out and take her hand in his. He could feel the distinct crackle of sexual energy flowing between them and if he were to touch her, he was certain he might lose control.

When they reached the door she said, "I enjoyed your company, Vaughn."

He definitely thought that admission was a start. "And I enjoyed yours."

They faced each other and said nothing as they gazed into each other's eyes. Then after several tense moments he had to touch her and withdrew his hands from his pockets and placed them on her waist. The moment he did so, a hunger stirred in his gut at the same time she instinctively leaned into him.

Vaughn didn't want to make the mistake of crossing any lines he would come to regret. But he had to do the one thing he'd wanted to do from the first time he saw her. He wanted to taste her to see if she was as sweet as she looked.

Unable to help himself, he lowered his head and captured her mouth and immediately thought that she tasted even sweeter than he'd imagined.

★ ★ ★

Sierra was certain she had never been kissed with so much passion and hunger in her life. Her arms automatically reached up and wrapped around Vaughn's neck as she angled her head for a better fit against his lips—lips that smiled at her each night as she drifted off to sleep, lips she had often thought of doing this very thing to.

All kinds of things started happening to her. She could feel the magnitude of his kiss in every pore, cell and pulse. Desire was warming her to her very soul. His masculine scent was enveloping her so much she felt light-headed, and she was certain her heart was skipping several beats.

Her arms tightened around his neck and the kiss deepened. His tongue was making urgent demands, which she reciprocated. They needed to breathe but neither wanted to end the kiss.

When breathing became a necessity they could no longer ignore, he broke off the kiss then pressed his forehead against hers, and they both drew in long, deep, ragged breaths. Then they were kissing again, and she was convinced this was some type of lovemaking he was doing to her mouth. She heard a low growl that erupted from his throat as he finally dragged his mouth away from hers, but not before planting some kisses around the corners of her lips.

"I better go, Sierra," he whispered against her wet lips.

She wanted to moan in protest but knew he was right. They couldn't stand there and kiss like this all night. All she could do was nod. If she were to open her mouth, she would be tempted to tell him that his kisses had awakened something inside of her that she hadn't thought she was able to feel. At least not of that magnitude.

Taking a step back, she drew in a deep breath. "Good night, Vaughn."

"You'll think about going with me to the New Year's Eve Ball, right, Sierra?"

She loved the way he said her name, doing something most people didn't do and that was to pronounce both *r*s. "I promise to think about it and let you know in a few weeks."

He nodded and then leaned in and placed a gentle kiss on her lips and whispered, "Good night." Then he opened the door and was gone.

Sierra locked the door behind him and then leaned back against it, drawing in long, deep breaths while wondering what in the heck had just happened to her. She licked her lips, convinced she could still taste him there.

She'd always joked about Dani having all the passionate bones and Sierra not getting any. Now it seemed she just might have to rethink that. Vaughn had kissed her in a way that even made her toes tingle, and she had liked it.

By the time she had taken her shower and gotten ready for bed she figured she would have reclaimed her senses. However, a part of her liked the feeling of experiencing something new and different. Vaughn's kiss had definitely been that. She hadn't known men could kiss like that. Nothing had been rushed. He had taken his time and pleasured her mouth while applying just the right amount of pressure to her lips.

At what point had his hands moved from around her waist to cup the back of her head to take her mouth for all it was worth? He had kissed her like it had been worth everything to him. Or he'd definitely made her feel that way.

She shifted in bed knowing she would enjoy the best sleep she had gotten in a long time. A very long time.

CHAPTER NINE

Vaughn sat at his desk, absently rubbing his bearded chin as his mind churned with thoughts of Sierra.

He stood and, shoving his hands into the pockets of his slacks, walked over to the window that overlooked the gulf. It was the first week of November and the sky was cloudy, the air cool and crisp, yet today's weather wasn't what was on his mind. The taste of one particular woman was. It didn't take much to recall just how delectable her mouth was, or how she felt being held in his arms while he kissed her with a need he'd sensed all over.

He had not expected their kiss last night to affect him so powerfully. Over the past couple of weeks, he discovered she was a woman a man could become addicted to if he wasn't careful. The problem with him was that he didn't want to be careful. He wanted Sierra.

Even after he got home last night, he'd been tempted to call her, just to hear her voice, but he hadn't. He was still determined to progress slowly with her. It was important that they got to know each other. He wanted to get to know Teryn as well. The little girl was a major part of Sierra's life and that meant she would be an important part of his.

If anyone had told him this time last year that he would be pursuing a woman, he would not have believed them. However, he would have to concur that Sierra Crane wasn't just any woman. When he'd pulled her into his arms last night, he had felt her hesitation...for just a quick second...and then he had absorbed her acceptance by giving her a long, deep kiss. But it hadn't been enough, not even when they'd gone a second round. Hell, he could have kept going all night.

The buzzer on his desk sounded and he moved toward it. He should have appreciated the intrusion since it wasn't like he didn't have any work to do. He had plenty, but he still felt annoyed at the interruption. "Yes, Kate?"

"Mr. Lacroix would like to see you, Vaughn."

He smiled. The woman who'd been working for Lacroix Industries probably for as long as Vaughn had been on this earth was still the ever-efficient and well-organized Kate Dorsett. She'd been Reid's personal assistant for years and made the lives of every one of Reid's executive team members much easier.

"Let him know I'm on my way."

A short while later, on his way to Reid's office, Vaughn paused when he reached Kate's desk.

"You can go on in, Vaughn."

"Thanks, and how's Brody?"

Her son Brody Dorsett had graduated from high school two years before Vaughn. Like others, Brody had left to go to college and eventually took a job elsewhere. When his father had taken ill, he returned to the cove to take over as fire chief investigator. He was officially given the job when his father had passed away a few years ago.

"Brody is doing fine. Staying busy. I'm just so glad he came back home."

Vaughn nodded. He liked Brody, most people did.

When he opened the door to Reid's office the man looked

up and smiled. "Come on in, Vaughn," he said, offering him the chair in front of his desk.

Vaughn thought he had a pretty nice office, but Reid's took the cake. It was large, spacious and had the best view of both the gulf and the blueberry fields.

"You got something for me to do, Reid?"

Reid leaned forward. "As a matter of fact I do. I've finally made a decision about something."

Vaughn's brows lifted inquiringly. "And what is that?"

"I'll be turning sixty in eight months and it's time for me to think about retiring."

Of all the things Vaughn had expected Reid to say, that wasn't one of them. "Retire? You?"

"Yes, sometime next year." He paused. "I've been working here since taking over for my father when I was thirty. That's almost thirty years, and long enough for anyone to be at any one job."

Vaughn chuckled. "You better not say that too loud, or Kate might hear you. I know for a fact she's been here almost thirty-five."

"Yes, she has. Dad hired her, but I'm going to try and persuade her to retire when I do. She's given this company a lot of good years. Claims she'll be bored at home, unless Brody marries and gives her a bunch of grandkids."

Reid paused again and continued, "There was a time I thought this company was my life, and because of that I didn't give my son and wife the time I should have. For years I thought making a profit was everything. When I lost Julius and then Roberta months later, I knew nothing was more important than those you love, and I regretted the time I spent here instead of giving it to them."

"I'm sure they understood, Reid."

"Yes, they understood and never complained. But I won't make that mistake with Gloria. I've been given another chance to get it right and I intend to. I want to give her more, especially more of my time. We want to travel. Go out on our boat more. Just plain enjoy life together."

Gloria was the woman he'd married two years ago. The two had gone to the same college but had dated other people, whom they later married. They had met up again years later after both had lost their mates, and began dating. Gloria was good for Reid. He was happy again.

"Well, if that's your decision, Reid, I am happy for you."

"Thanks. I just wanted you to know that when I do leave, Vaughn, I'll be passing the CEO position on to you."

Vaughn sat stunned, unable to believe what Reid had just said. He leaned forward in his chair and gave the man a penetrating gaze. "Are you sure you're making the right decision?"

He knew very few people questioned Reid about anything, but he didn't care. What the man was offering him was totally unexpected.

Reid gave him a confident smile. "I'm positive. The other members of my executive team are doing an excellent job, and I know all of them have worked for me a lot longer than you have. But for me it comes down to trust. Unconditional trust."

Vaughn didn't say anything, knowing that Reid had a lot to tell him. It was true, the other members of the team did an excellent job and, honestly, Vaughn thought he could trust any of them. Obviously, Reid knew better.

"I always thought when I reached sixty that I would be handing the company over to Julius. But that's not going to happen. I do intend to hand it over to Julius's daughters one day, whether I am alive or dead. Of course, I'm hoping I'm alive. But if I'm not, I need to know I've put someone in place who will carry out my wishes. You were their father's best friend from the time the two of you were toddlers. I know what that friendship meant to Julius, and I also know what it meant to you. You will do right by them and will be there to guide them and help them to make good sound business decisions along the way."

"Thank you." Vaughn had to fight back the emotion in his voice. Reid was right. His friendship with Julius had meant the world to him.

There was something Vaughn wondered if Reid had thought about. "What if your granddaughters choose another career after college?"

He knew they were both juniors at the University of Reno. "What if they decide they don't want to return to Catalina Cove to live?"

Reid thought on his question and said, "Then I hope and pray that, like a lot of the others, their decision will be short-lived. Even if they decide to live elsewhere, I'm praying that one day they'll realize the same thing I believe you and the others who left now know. Catalina Cove is a treasure and it's going to take people, the locals, to keep it sparkling. You can call it an old man's blind faith, but I believe they will come back here."

Vaughn nodded. "I'll admit I've heard Jade say more than once that she's going to be mayor of this town one day."

Reid chuckled. "And I'm sure you've also heard her say when she becomes mayor she'll approve that tennis resort and all those chain stores I've kept out of here for years. She might think that way now, but I have to believe that once she realizes there are times when change isn't beneficial, she will sing another tune. Plus, both of us, their grandfather, and you, their godfather, will help them to see it that way."

Vaughn grinned. "We can try, but remember they don't just have Julius's blood running through their veins, they have Vashti's as well."

He couldn't help mentioning that, recalling how Sawyer often joked about how stubborn his wife could be at times. As teens, Julius had loved Vashti, but instead of speaking up and proclaiming that love when Vashti had needed it the most, a sixteen-year-old Julius Lacroix had let her face a difficult time alone. Vaughn and Reid both knew Julius had never gotten over that period of weakness and had taken that guilt to the grave with him.

"Yes, but remember Vashti left Catalina Cove and stayed away for sixteen years. Like I said, you all might leave but you eventually come back."

Reid stood. "Are you going to accept the position?"

A huge smile spread across Vaughn's face. "Yes, I accept."

"Congratulations, Vaughn."

He grasped the outstretched hand Reid offered him. "Thank you for the vote of confidence and trust."

"I think it's wonderful that Vaughn Miller asked you to attend the New Year's Eve Ball with him, Sierra."

Sierra gazed across the table at Velvet. Not surprisingly, Dani had said the same thing when they'd talked that morning. Her sister had even gone farther and said that if Nathan ever heard she wasn't dating or hadn't dated since their divorce, it might send out an erroneous message that she was still pining for him, which of course was not true.

"And I'm going to tell you the same thing I told my sister. He might have asked but I haven't decided if I'm even going to that ball."

Velvet's eyes warmed. "Why wouldn't you go with him? He seems like a nice guy."

Sierra decided not to say that not only was he a nice guy but he was also a terrific kisser. Every time she thought about how he'd taken possession of her mouth, she experienced a tingly sensation all over.

"He is a nice guy, but you know my history." She hadn't told Velvet everything about her ex-husband, but she knew Nathan had cheated on her.

"Yes, and I shouldn't push it because it will be like the pot calling the kettle black, since I haven't dated since I moved here either. However, I have to admit you and Vaughn Miller look good together."

Sierra smiled. "You've only seen us together once."

"Yes, and I saw how he was looking at you and you were looking at him. I could feel the chemistry."

"That might be true, but I told you about my husband's betrayal. I'm not ready to start dating. I want to give all my attention to Teryn."

"You also need to give attention to yourself. We have needs just like men do."

Sierra recalled Velvet once shared that before moving here she had enjoyed a very active sex life with the guy she'd been exclusive with. There had been no complaints in the bedroom. Their problem was that after three years he'd still thought it was only about sex, although she'd fallen in love. When she'd seen he was not capable of returning her love, she knew it was best for her to move on.

"In my case, you can't miss what you never had. It was different with you and your guy," Sierra said.

Velvet nodded. "It's been hard, trust me. But I've never been one to have sex just for the sake of gratification." She leaned over the table and whispered to Sierra, "My hormones got out of whack so bad that one night I even considered paying a surprise visit back to Arizona just to have a one-night fling and then disappear again. I figure one real good roll-between-the-sheets night with him would take care of me for another two years."

"Maybe he's changed and when he sees you, he will—"

"Trust me, that's not possible," Velvet broke in to say. "Jaye Colfax wants a bedmate, not a wife. I knew it from the beginning. I'd honestly thought I could change his mind and found out I couldn't."

Sierra heard the pain and sadness in Velvet's voice. Although they'd encountered different sets of circumstances with men, they both had reason to not only keep them at bay but stand their ground for doing so.

In all honesty, Sierra enjoyed her independence from a controlling and unfaithful husband. It had taken her stepping away to see just what a toxic marriage she'd been involved in. She didn't need a man in her life. All she wanted was to forge a better life for her and Teryn. After what Nathan had done, right under her nose, she often wondered if she had the ability to fully trust another man again.

Although she had her share of fantasy dreams like other women, none had driven her to seek out a man for her sexual needs—especially not her ex who'd left a lot to be desired in the bedroom anyway. However, she had to think that if a kiss from Vaughn could spark a fire within her like the one they'd shared last night, she didn't want to think how it would be if they shared a bed.

She could just imagine his body straddling hers, her legs opening to him, and then him sliding inside of her while…

"Sierra?"

She blinked, realizing Velvet had been saying her name. "Yes?"

"The waitress wanted to know if you wanted a refill on your tea."

"No, I'm fine." Sierra checked her watch. Every third Thursday of the month the junior and senior high schools let out early, which was why she'd been able to grab lunch with Velvet at Lafitte Seafood House, located on the pier. They served a great variety of seafood.

Velvet had called from school and said she'd had a taste for shrimp. They had agreed to meet here, and now it was time to go pick up Teryn and return to the restaurant.

"Are you going to the committee meeting tonight?"

Sierra looked over at Velvet. "Yes. What about you?"

"Yes, I'll be there," she said. "Do you want me to pick you up? No need both of us driving separate cars when we live so close."

"Sure, that's a great idea."

For a fleeting moment, Sierra wondered how she would react when she saw Vaughn again after their hot and heavy kiss last night. If he dropped by the restaurant while she was at the meeting, they would miss each other. Maybe not seeing him tonight would be for the best. Then, when she did see him again, she would be better in control of her senses.

A half hour later, idling in front of the school to pick up Teryn, Sierra watched as her goddaughter raced to the car with a huge smile on her face.

"Goddy?"

"Yes, sweetie?" In the rearview mirror Sierra could see Teryn in the back seat, snapping her seat belt harness in place.

"I got my list to Santa all finished."

Sierra's face lit up. "That's great, Teryn!"

"I put ten things on my list. Do you have your list to Santa ready yet, Goddy?"

"No. My list isn't ready yet." Sierra thought maybe she should have been concentrating on her list instead of engaging in a kiss-a-thon with Vaughn last night.

"Oh."

Was that disappointment she heard in her goddaughter's voice? "What's wrong, Teryn?"

"I wanted us to mail our letters to Santa together."

"And we will, hon. Goddy has been busy. Besides, we have plenty of time. It's just the beginning of November."

"Yes, but you know what Mommy always said?"

Sierra had to fight back a grin knowing she was about to embark on one of those "Rhonda knows what is best" moments. She'd had to deal with it all while growing up and all through college and even later in years. Rhonda had always been the philosopher—or thought she was. She would always have a saying for something or make up her own.

"No, what did your mommy always say?"

"That you shouldn't put off for later what you can do now."

Sierra could definitely hear her best friend saying that. "I will remember that, Teryn."

"You only need to write down one wish, Goddy," Teryn said matter-of-factly, like such a thing shouldn't be difficult or time-consuming.

"I know, but I need to think real hard about what I want that one wish to be," Sierra said, bringing the car to a stop at a traffic light.

Teryn smiled. "Okay. I want you to be happy on Christmas Day when I'm happy with my twelve things."

Sierra cocked a brow. "I thought you had a Christmas list with only ten wishes on it."

A wide grin that made her look so much like Rhonda appeared on Teryn's face. "I did, but I just thought of two other wishes I want now."

Sierra figured she needed to get her list together so she could get those lists off to Santa before Teryn's wish list grew any more.

CHAPTER TEN

"Congratulations, big brother. I am so proud of you."

Vaughn grinned and tossed a paper clip on his desk as he told his sister, Zara, the news. She was the first person he'd called after leaving Reid's office. The older man's faith and trust in him was astounding and had meant a lot.

Even if he had remained working on Wall Street and living in New York, he would not have gotten the advancement in his career like Reid had given him today.

"Thanks, I got work to do and I'm sure you do as well," he said, straightening up in his chair. "You're still planning to travel to Paris for Christmas?"

"Yes, those are my plans. It's been a while since I spent Christmas there."

His parents had a beautiful home in Paris that he and Zara now jointly owned. Zara had gone there a couple of times since their parents' death ten years ago, but he hadn't.

"I'm glad we'll be spending Thanksgiving together. Will you be okay by yourself for Christmas, Vaughn?"

He smiled, doubting if she would ever stop worrying about him. "I'll be fine." No need to tell her that he intended to make special holiday plans of his own if a certain woman cooperated. "Goodbye, Zara."

"Goodbye, Vaughn."

He hung up and drew in a deep, satisfied breath. It was hard to believe a few years ago at this time he was sitting in a jail cell, wondering if he would ever get his life back. Not only had he gotten it back, he'd gotten a lot of blessings as well.

His thoughts went to Sierra. Did she want to see him as much as he wanted to see her? Had she thought about him as much today as he'd thought about her?

Since he hadn't put his phone away he decided to call Sierra, to let her know he would be dropping by after work. Hopefully, she would have time to sit with him for a while.

"Hello?"

She sounded breathless. Nearly as breathless as she'd been last night. "Sierra, this is Vaughn. I hope I'm not calling at a bad time."

"No, I was getting dressed."

Vaughn's brow rose in surprise. "You're going out?" he asked, and too late he figured he had no right to.

"Yes, I have a committee meeting. I told you I was on that Christmas committee, thanks to Vashti."

He chuckled. "Vashti is known to do stuff like that. I have good news to share with you."

"What?"

"I'd rather tell you in person," he said, not able to keep the excitement out of his voice.

"Okay. The meeting should be over around seven. Usually there's socializing afterward. Do you want to drop by the restaurant around seven thirty?"

Vaughn really didn't want to wait that long to see her but had no other choice.

"Okay, I will be there. Will you have your cook put today's special aside for me? What is it, by the way?"

"Lobster bisque."

He didn't remember her ever having that on the menu before. "That's new, isn't it?"

"Yes, but it's still one of my grandmother's recipes. Kaegan had an extra shipment of lobsters from Boston that he needed to get rid of and sold to me at half price."

"Then I can't wait to try it. I look forward to seeing you later."

On the drive back from the meeting Sierra glanced over at Velvet. Her good friend had been unusually quiet both going to the meeting and now on the return trip. They'd shared lunch earlier and she'd been in a happy mood. Sierra wondered what had happened since then. "I think the meeting went well, don't you?"

Velvet brought the car to a stop when the arms came down at a railroad crossing and looked at Sierra. Moments later a train rolled by. "Yes, I thought so, too. Although I would have preferred not being in the company of Laura Crawford. After the meeting she took me aside and felt the need to again make me aware her brother was interested in me and instead of playing hard to get, I should feel honored."

Sierra chuckled. "I got just the opposite kind of talk from her."

Velvet's eyes widened. "What do you mean?"

"She pulled me aside and said she heard rumors that Vaughn and I were seeing each other, and thought I should know that she has him on her radar."

"Wha—? She actually told you that?"

"Yes."

"And what did you say?"

"I told her that just because she has him on her radar doesn't mean he has her on his."

Velvet burst out laughing. "You told her that?"

"Yes," Sierra said, frowning. "Emma had already scooped me that word around town is that Laura has her eyes on Vaughn now that his name has been cleared. What Laura told me tonight pretty much confirms it. The nerve of her. She doesn't know me. Besides, Vaughn and I don't have that kind of a relationship."

"Umm, he has asked you to be his date to the New Year's Eve Ball."

"But I haven't decided whether I'm even going. However, I refuse to let Laura Crawford think she can give me a heads-up like that and think it means anything."

"She probably sees you as a threat," Velvet mused. "You're four years younger and definitely a lot prettier. And you're well-liked, which I can't say the same about her. That was obvious tonight. Did you see the other women's expressions whenever Laura spoke? She's pushy, argumentative and was against every suggestion anyone made."

"But Ashley wasn't having it." Sierra grinned when she re-called the number of times the committee's president, Ashley Sullivan, had put Laura in her place, reminding Laura that everyone, and not just her, had ideas that should be considered.

"I noticed. Are you going to mention what she said to Vaughn?"

Sierra shook her head. "I doubt it."

"I think you should. I would."

Sierra shrugged. "What difference does it make? If he wants her, I am happy for them."

"You don't mean that, and you know it. You like him, whether you admit it or not. And just like you told her, just be-cause she wants him doesn't mean he wants her. If he did, he would be dating her. I personally don't think she's his type."

Sierra didn't think Laura was Vaughn's type either, but men were known to fool you. She of all people would know that.

"Laura honestly believes she could have any man she goes after. Her brother has that same mindset when it comes to women. I think the only reason he's interested in me is because he sees me as a challenge."

"Excuse me, Velvet. The reason he is interested in you is because you are beautiful. Webb Crawford isn't bad-looking either, but I know his good looks are just on the outside. I went to school with him, and he'd always thought of himself as a rock star, superjock."

"Well, I have better things to do with my time than to deal with that."

Sierra didn't say anything as the two of them watched the train rush by. After a moment of things being quiet, Sierra said, "Is that what was bothering you earlier, Velvet? The thought of knowing Laura would be at the meeting?"

She didn't think that's what it was but knew something was bothering Velvet. She had picked up on it the moment Velvet had arrived to take her to the meeting.

Velvet didn't say anything for a minute and then she turned to Sierra. "No, that's not it. I got a call from Ruthie, right before I left home to pick you up. She wanted me to know Todd asked her to marry him."

Sierra smiled. "That's wonderful!" Then she studied Velvet's features. "You are happy for her, right?" Although she'd never met Ruthie, she knew that she and Velvet had been best friends since their college days.

"Yes, of course I'm happy for her," Velvet said. "It couldn't have happened to a nicer person and Todd is a very nice guy. But it just bothers me that after putting everything into a relationship for three years, it didn't get me anywhere in the end. Why did I have to fall in love with a man who wasn't ready to settle down and probably won't ever be?"

"And why did I fall in love with one who gave me the impression he was ready to settle down but truly wasn't?" Sierra countered. "I guess falling in love isn't for everybody. You try it and then when it doesn't work out you—"

"Move on," Velvet plugged in.

"Yes, you move on but at the same time you guard your heart," Sierra said.

She knew some guarded theirs more than others. With her, because of Nathan, it would be hard for the next man. It wouldn't be fair to assume every man she met was a lowlife, but if and when she was ready to test the waters again, it would be up to her to make sure he wasn't.

That made her thoughts shift to Vaughn. She didn't like drama and she could see Laura Crawford causing plenty of it. Maybe she should tell him tonight that she had decided not to go to the ball with him, and that the only thing the two of them could ever be was friends.

Sierra drew in a deep breath, deciding that's exactly what she would do. Tonight.

"I hope I didn't keep you waiting."

Vaughn looked up and saw Sierra standing by the table. She set a bowl of steaming hot soup in front of him, as well as another glass of brown ale. She placed another bowl of soup across from him and a cup of tea, then slid into the seat opposite him. "Where did you come from?" he asked, scanning her features.

Vaughn was convinced the more he saw her, the more beautiful she became. And he'd noted before she sat down what she was wearing—a long navy blue skirt and a light blue cashmere sweater. He thought the outfit looked good on her.

"I arrived a few minutes ago and came in through the back. That's where the front door to my home is located. I slipped up the stairs to tuck Teryn into bed. I was hoping I would get back in time to read her a bedtime story, but her babysitter had beat me to it. Anyway, all I got was a kiss and she dozed right off to sleep."

"You don't have to apologize. You didn't keep me waiting. How is she?"

She lifted a brow. "Who?"

He smiled. "Teryn."

"Oh, she's fine, although I think she's upset with me for not having my one Christmas wish ready to give Santa."

"Excuse me?"

"Long story. I'll tell you another time. I'm eager to hear the good news you have to share," she said, scooting forward and leaning over the table.

Vaughn doubted she realized just how close their mouths were now. It wouldn't take much for him to lean in for a kiss. That made him scan around the restaurant, and that's when he saw they were alone. "Where is everyone?"

Sierra tucked a curl behind her ear. "They've all gone. The restaurant closed ten minutes ago."

"Oh." He'd been so busy reading the stock information on his phone that he hadn't noticed people leaving.

"I got here before closing so at no time were you alone," she said as if that might be a concern of his. "I had Emma put aside bowls of the lobster bisque for us."

"Thanks. It smells good and I can't wait to try it."

He was about to pick up his spoon to dig in when she said, "Vaughn Miller, don't you dare eat that soup without telling me your good news."

Leaning back against his seat, away from her mouth and temptation, he laughed. "Okay, I won't hold you in suspense any longer. Especially since it will make the *Catalina Cove Tribune* in the morning."

Her brow lifted. "What?"

He smiled and decided the hell with temptation, he would move his mouth back close to hers. "Today Reid advised me he plans to retire in about eight months and named me as his replacement."

CHAPTER ELEVEN

Sierra's jaw dropped as she stared at Vaughn. He was smiling and she knew there was no way he was joking. "You will become CEO of Lacroix Industries?"

There was silence and she saw he was staring at her mouth, and it seemed his gaze was making her lips feel moist. Suddenly, she became aware just how close their mouths were and wondered when that had happened. Instinctively, she licked them and saw how his eyes followed the movement of her tongue. What was happening here? Why did the way he was looking at her mouth tempt her to lean in close and...

At the sound of a car backfiring, she blinked and realized at some point her focus, their focus, had shifted from the conversation and onto each other. She knew as much as she had enjoyed last night and their hot kiss, it couldn't happen again. Things were getting complicated and she didn't do complication well.

"Vaughn?"

"Yes?"

"Are you saying that you will become CEO of Lacroix Industries?" she asked.

As if he realized what she was doing, namely getting the conversation back on track, he switched his gaze from her mouth to her eyes, smiled and said, "Yes, that's exactly what I'm saying. He informed me today that he'll be turning sixty next year and wants to spend as much time as he can away from the office with his wife and grandchildren."

"That's wonderful, Vaughn. Congratulations."

"Thank you. And this calls for a celebration. What about dinner this weekend?"

Sierra was truly happy for Vaughn but knew what he was asking. If she said yes, it would constitute a date, and she wasn't ready for that yet. Granted, she'd been divorced for two years, but she still wasn't ready—especially with someone like Vaughn. If she wasn't careful, she could become putty in his hands, and she couldn't allow herself to be that way with any man ever again.

His intense gaze was on her again and, almost too late, she realized she'd been nibbling on her bottom lip. That's what had caught his attention. She quickly stopped and decided to counter his question.

"What if I invite you to dinner here," she said, easing her mouth away from his to settle back in her seat.

"Here?"

"Yes—I mean, no. Not here in the restaurant but upstairs in my apartment."

When she saw the flash of heat that flared in his eyes, she felt clarification was in order. "Teryn will be there to help us celebrate, of course."

His smile widened. "Of course."

There was no doubt in her mind he'd figured she was letting him know that so he wouldn't get any ideas. This wouldn't be a date. It would be a dinner to congratulate him on his success. It was something worth celebrating, and he didn't have any immediate family nearby and considered her a friend. She pushed the thought to the back of her mind that friends wouldn't have kissed like they'd done last night.

"So, it's settled. Teryn and I will prepare dinner for you this weekend. How about Sunday evening around four? Are you free?"

"Yes, I'm free and I look forward to dining with you and Teryn. Thanks for inviting me."

She nodded and replied, "You are welcome."

They finished eating and he told her just how good the soup was. "I'm glad you like it. I heard it was a big hit with a lot of the customers today as well. That's good. You never know how something new will go over, but I think it was the lobsters. There's nothing like freshly caught lobster," she said.

"I happen to think it was all the other ingredients. I admit the lobster was tasty, but it's the combination of everything that sets it off."

His compliment made her smile. "Thanks."

"How did things go at the committee meeting tonight?" he asked.

She was glad to change the subject and grateful he wasn't making a big deal of her backing out of going out with him and inviting him to dinner instead. "It was great. Good ideas were floated around. There are nine of us, but the only two guys on the committee didn't make it. They'd left town for a hunting trip. However, I think you probably know everybody who did come," she said. "It was at Ashley Sullivan's home. Velvet was there, so were Vashti and Bryce. Then there were Donna Elloran and Laura Crawford. I think you went to school with most of the ladies there." She watched his features when she mentioned Laura and he hadn't shown any reaction.

"Yes, I did. Did Bryce have the baby with her?"

She shook her head. "No, he was home with his daddy. Bryce said this was the first time Kaegan had kept him without her, but she didn't seem at all nervous about it. I remembered the first time I let Teryn out of my sight to spend the night elsewhere. It was a pajama party for one of the girls in her class and I was a nervous wreck. I doubt I got any sleep that night."

He smiled. "My mom was like that, too. It wasn't so bad for me since I got to spend just as much time over at the Lacroix's place while growing up as I did my own house, and it was vice versa for Julius. But with Zara my parents watched her like a hawk, because she was such a rebel."

Sierra couldn't help but grin. "I don't recall Zara being a rebel. Like I told you, she was pretty popular and well-liked."

He paused in thought and then said, "I think that's the part of my childhood I most regret."

"What?"

"Allowing my parents to pick my friends for me. At the time I didn't know any better and honestly thought that was the way of the world. I was related to the founder of the cove and that in itself made me special. At least that's what I was led to believe. I wished I had at least one parent who hadn't bought into that idea, but they both did. Dad even went so far as wanting to keep the French blood flowing in his offspring's veins by marrying a woman of French descent."

Sierra's eyebrows shot up. "How can you say that?"

"Because it's true. Dad told me himself. I'm not sure if my parents even loved each other. I believe they had a mutual goal, which was to mold us into being proud of our heritage that was passed on to us by Lafitte and our great-great-great-great-grandmother—our Creole heritage came from her because of her African roots."

"The first Zara, right? Lafitte's wife?"

He shrugged. "Or his mistress, since it was never proved that she was his wife, although my parents and grandparents believed that she was. Regardless, they were proud of our family's heritage, which is why they named my sister after her. She's the third female named Zara in my family."

Vaughn told her again how great the bisque was. She told him that when he came to dinner, she would show him that she could cook up more than just soup. He laughed over that. They continued to talk and enjoy each other's company.

Twice, she excused herself to go upstairs to check on Teryn. Her goddaughter rarely woke during the night, not even to take a potty break. She would sleep through until morning.

When Sierra returned downstairs she saw Vaughn clearing off the table. "You didn't have to do that," she said.

"I don't mind. Besides, I wanted to. Where's your kitchen?"

"This way," she said, and he followed her into the kitchen.

He glanced around. "I've never been in a restaurant kitchen before. This is interesting."

She chuckled. "What's so interesting about it?" she asked, taking the bowls out of his hands to rinse and place in the dishwasher. The moment their hands touched she felt something, and wondered if he had felt it, too.

"Everything in here is big. I don't think I've seen a stove that big before and you have two of them."

"If business continues to grow, I might need a third." She leaned against the counter. "One of my customers mentioned something last week that got me to thinking."

"What about?"

"Mr. Sams and his wife are regulars who dine here at least three times a week. He suggested that I start serving desserts."

Vaughn looked surprised. "Do you make desserts?"

"No. But I know someone who does. Do you know Freda McEnroe?" She turned to lead them out of the kitchen.

"No, I don't," he said, following her.

"You probably wouldn't since she graduated the same year I did. Well, she moved back to town six months ago to start a small bakery. Ashley served some of Freda's pastries at the meeting tonight and they were delicious. I thought of teaming up with her to supply my restaurant with desserts."

He nodded. "That sounds like a great idea, and worth giving serious thought."

"Thanks, and I will."

They had reached the door and he said, "Thanks for tonight, Sierra. I always enjoy spending time with you."

She was tempted to ask if he would enjoy spending time with Laura Crawford as well, since the woman had him on her radar. She shouldn't let the woman's words bother her since she and Vaughn were not in a relationship. But then she had asked him over for a celebratory dinner...

She decided not to tell him what Laura Crawford had said. She figured Vaughn would find out soon enough, and it would be up to him how he handled his business. However, she would appease her curiosity and ask him something she should have asked weeks ago. "I know you told me that you're not seriously involved with anyone, but you can date someone without any serious involvement. So, are you presently dating anyone in the cove?"

Vaughn wondered where that question had come from. He held her gaze as he leaned back against the wall with his hands shoved into the pockets of his slacks. "No, I'm not presently dating anyone. In fact, I haven't dated anyone living in the cove since I've been back."

"So you haven't dated in all the years you returned?"

"I didn't say that."

There was no way he would not be completely honest with her. She'd told him enough about that asshole she had been married to and he knew she had trust issues. The man had cheated on her. He didn't know all the details, but knowing her ex had been unfaithful was enough. She hadn't deserved that. No man or woman did.

More than anything he wanted Sierra to feel comfortable with him, to know he would never hurt her, that she could trust him and that she already meant a lot to him. On top of that, he wanted her to believe that a relationship with him would be easy and not difficult, and that it wouldn't be one she'd come to regret.

Straightening, he took a step forward and reached out and took her hand in his. Immediately, he felt sensual energy pass between them. Not fast and furious like last night, but slow and composed, yet just as hot and raw. He squeezed her hand to keep her from pulling away.

"When I was released from prison and came here, I was still trying hard to get over what Camila had done. And like you, the last thing I was interested in was a serious involvement with anyone. The job Reid hired me for required a lot of travel and attending social events in his stead. I met women there. We didn't date, we shared affairs that led to nowhere. Most lasted that one night."

"Oh, I see." When she tried tugging her hand from his, this time he let her. She tilted her head and asked, "Is that all you want from me, a short affair that leads nowhere?"

Vaughn knew if he were to tell her what all he wanted from her, it would probably scare her out of her wits. He went to bed each night thinking of seeing her naked, touching her, burying his head between her legs and tasting her, easing his body over hers, sliding inside of her to connect his body while they made love in a…

"I guess your silence pretty much answered my question."

She reached out to open the door and he put his hand on hers to stop her. He was fully conscious of the sexual awareness between them and knew she was, too. "My silence was the result of me thinking about all the things I do want from you, Sierra. A short affair that leads nowhere isn't one of them."

He took a step closer, wishing there was some way he could tell her that, unlike with other women, he needed her for more than simple sexual gratification. "I deliberately avoided dating any woman in the cove for various reasons," he said softly, "but that day I came in here, and I saw you… For me that was a game changer on so many levels." He took a deep breath. "I felt a connection to you that I had never felt with anyone. What I told you, I meant, Sierra. I want to get to know you, I want you to get to know me. I don't intend to rush you because I understand your need to feel comfortable with me. To know you can trust me. I'm willing to do things on your terms and your timetable."

"Why me, Vaughn?" she whispered.

He knew he could tell her that, as crazy as it might sound, she was beginning to mean a lot to him. Sierra was the ray of sunshine he'd been missing in his life. He knew this after spending just a few weeks with her. He wanted and needed to spend more time with her. Talking to her was easy and around her he felt a sense of contentment he hadn't felt in a long time. In fact, it was only when he read Marie's letters that he would feel so at peace.

Taking a step closer, he reached out and tilted her chin up to look into her eyes. "Why not you, Sierra? There's no other woman I want more than you."

That admission caused a tightness in his chest. He had spoken the truth, but he wondered if she believed him. "I mean it," he said, seeing the uncertainty in her eyes. His gaze held hers, determined for her to see the truth in his.

"Vaughn," she breathed in a soft tone, and he leaned in and captured her mouth.

The kiss started off soft, gentle and, hopefully, convincing. Then, feeling possessive, he deepened it. He loved her taste and wanted more of it. Releasing her chin, he continued to kiss her while he moved his hands to her waist, pulling her closer to fit against him. He needed the taste of her for tonight, tomorrow night and all the other nights he went to bed thinking about her, dreaming about her and needing her. She tasted sexy, feminine and so damn delicious.

He tried to hold back a groan, but he couldn't. Nor could he stop the quiver that passed through him when she began hungrily mating her tongue with his. When her fingers gripped his shoulders, he eased her legs apart with his knee for a better fit between them, knowing doing so revealed how aroused he was. He wasn't sure how long the kiss lasted but knew he had to end it, or they would go beyond the point of no return. When he broke off the kiss, she slowly opened her eyes.

When he looked into her eyes and saw such potent desire, he felt intoxicated. He also saw a deep, intense sexual hunger that had her pushing his jacket off his shoulders to rub her hands over his chest. She went after the buttons of his shirt as if she needed to touch his bare skin.

He was determined to stay in control while allowing her to do whatever she wanted. When her hand touched his bare flesh and her fingers ran through the hair on his chest, he nearly lost it. He lowered his mouth to kiss her again, putting everything that he was feeling into it, ravishing her tongue greedily.

She snatched her mouth away and he saw the fiery look of intense need in her eyes. "Vaughn, I need…"

"Tell me, *cherie*. What do you need?" he whispered against her moist lips, although he had a pretty good idea.

She'd told him that she hadn't been involved with anyone since her divorce two years ago. It goes without saying that some women failed to understand and accept that they could have primitive longings just as strong as any man. Abstinence wasn't for everybody, and he'd heard from more than one woman that battery-operated toys didn't always cut the mustard.

Her answer was in her kiss. She pulled his head down to capture his mouth with a frantic hunger. He tightened his hold around her, knowing she was coming undone in his arms. She broke off the kiss and stared into his eyes and he saw the sexual agony…and the plea.

That's when he swept her in his arms and began walking, not sure where he was taking her. Then he recalled the office he'd passed when they were leaving the kitchen. Kicking the door shut behind him, he walked over to the love seat and sat down with her in his lap. Then he kissed her again.

When he released her lips, they were both panting for breath. He met her gaze when she said, "I need…"

When she didn't finish, he knew she was pushed beyond her limit, yet he asked again, "Tell me what you need, Sierra."

Instead of answering, she buried her face in his chest, as if she was trying to absorb his scent into her nostrils. She spread kisses all over his bare chest then leaned in to hungrily take his mouth again.

Shifting her in his lap, he lifted her skirt and eased his hands under, working their way up her legs, which seemed to automatically spread for him. He dragged his mouth from hers and whispered, "I'll take care of you."

Holding his gaze, she pleaded, "Please…" in a tortured whisper.

That's when he worked past her lace panties to slide his fingers inside of her.

"Vaughn…"

He captured the sound of her moaning his name with another kiss as he worked his fingers inside of her, stroking her. Her wetness and her feminine scent were proof of just how aroused she was. He had to fight back his own desirous need, determined to concentrate on hers.

She broke off the kiss to whisper his name in a deep, throaty sound just moments before throwing her head back, and he felt her explode in an orgasm. Tugging on her hair he brought her lips back to his, covering her mouth to silence her scream.

When he pulled his lips away, he watched as she forced her eyes open to stare at him for the longest time before whispering, "Thank you."

Then she closed them again.

CHAPTER TWELVE

"What do you mean you passed out?"

Rain had kept Sierra from walking Teryn to school and she'd driven her instead. Now, as Sierra drove back home, the rain was coming down harder and she had her sister on speakerphone.

"I really don't want to talk about it since it's so embarrassing, Dani."

"Yes, you want to talk about it. Otherwise, you wouldn't have mentioned it to me."

Sierra knew Dani was probably right. "I meant what I said, Dani. I passed out. I woke up during the night in my bed with my clothes on. I figure Vaughn carried me up the stairs and put me on the bed."

"I think you need to start from the beginning."

Sierra would rather not, but knowing her sister's penchant for details, she had no choice. When she returned home, instead of getting out in the pouring rain, she decided to sit in the car to tell Dani what she wanted to know.

"Vaughn was the last customer at the restaurant and he and I talked well beyond closing time. Probably until ten," she said. "I walked him to the door, and he kissed me good-night, like the last time. But this time something happened, something that's never happened to me before, and I still find it hard to believe that it did."

"What?"

"My body suddenly had a mind of its own and became feverish. I increased the kiss, needing more, but it wasn't enough. Some sort of an intense ache came over me. And then I needed... I needed..." She couldn't make herself say it.

"You needed what?" Dani asked, her interest definitely sparked.

Sierra closed her eyes and rested her head against the steering wheel, remembering. "I needed him. It was as if Vaughn was the only one who could take the ache away."

When she didn't say anything for a moment, Dani prompted, "And?"

Sierra whipped her eyes open. *And?* "For heaven's sake, Dani, isn't that enough?"

"No."

Her sister's simple reply had her groaning in frustration. Then she remembered this was Dani, the sister who had more passionate bones in her body than she knew what to do with.

"I kissed him, stuck my tongue as far into his mouth as I could, might have even tickled his throat. I was like a woman gone mad. My flesh felt sensitized. I was consumed with an agony I've never encountered before. The need was killing me, a sexual torment I couldn't control." She released a deep breath. "Has anything like that ever happened to you, Dani?"

"Of course not. I'm married and very much sexually active. In other words, I get it whenever and how many times I want. What happened to you was the result of years of neglect, Sierra. You denied your body what it needs. And please don't think your battery-operated boyfriend can work as well as the real thing, because it can't. I'm glad Vaughn Miller recognized the signs and gave you the release you needed."

Sierra covered her face with her hands. "And that's what's so embarrassing. How can I ever look into his eyes again?"

"You have nothing to be embarrassed about, Sierra. I'm glad he wasn't a man who took advantage of the situation. A lot of men would have. He's moved up a few notches in my book."

"I just don't understand it. Nothing like this has ever happened to me before. Why now and why with him?"

"Only you can answer that. Just be forewarned this is probably just the beginning. Things might happen this way every time the two of you kiss."

Sierra frowned, not liking the sound of that. "Then we won't kiss."

Dani laughed. "Kind of drastic don't you think? There's nothing wrong with kissing him. In fact, there's nothing wrong with sleeping with him either, if you decide you want to. Sounds like you need to get laid in a bad way, and he only scratched your itch."

"Then I'll become just another meaningless affair to him."

"What are you talking about?"

She'd rather not go into that part with her sister, but she would tell her this, "I was approached by a woman yesterday who evidently feels Vaughn and I are getting too friendly."

"And her point?"

Sierra could hear the anger in her sister's voice. During Dani's dating stage with Emory, she'd had to put more than one woman in her place. Those women discovered Dani was not one to mess with.

"Her point was to warn me that she had Vaughn on her radar."

"I hope you told her that she could stick that radar right up her ass. The nerve of her. Did you tell Vaughn about it?"

"No."

"Why not?"

"Because the last thing I want is drama, and I refuse to give her

a platform. Vaughn and I aren't dating, and this is a free country. I don't have dibs on him, and he doesn't have any on me."

"Umm, I don't know about that. After last night your body
knows him. He's going to be the man it hungers for."

"I don't believe that nonsense."

"Okay. Don't say I didn't warn you."

Just then, Sierra noticed another call coming in, and when
she saw who the caller was, she drew in a deep breath. It was
Vaughn. She could answer or ignore it. The one thing she wasn't,
was a coward. However, at the moment she was filled with
enough embarrassment to last a lifetime. "I got another call
coming in, Dani. We'll talk again later."

She clicked over to the other line. "Hello?"

"How do you feel this morning, *cherie*?"

Why did he have to sound so good this morning with his
deep voice? And why the term of endearment? *Cherie* was a
Louisiana-French term for *dear* or *darling*, and he made it sound
so sexy and intimate. She rested her forehead on the steering
wheel again, remembering he'd also called her that last night.
"I feel fine. Thanks for asking."

"I'm calling from the airport. I've been called away on business for a couple of days, but I'll be back by Sunday."

"Sunday?" she asked, lifting her head.

"Yes. I'm to dine with you and Teryn on Sunday, remember?"

Of course, she remembered. She was just about to come up
with an excuse to cancel when his next words stopped her.

"I'm looking forward to seeing Teryn again. She is such a
smart little girl."

She appreciated his interest in her goddaughter. He had met
her just once, but whenever Sierra was with Vaughn, he asked
about Teryn. Not once had Nathan inquired about Teryn, her
well-being or otherwise.

She grimaced. "Have a safe trip and I'll see you on Sunday
at four, Vaughn."

"You bet. See you then, Sierra."

It had stopped raining, and Sierra got out of the car and went inside. She had to come up with a strategy to deal with Vaughn by the time he returned.

Nathan Flowers pressed the intercom button on his desk. "What is it, Christine?"

"Mr. Charles would like to meet with you."

A frown settled on Nathan's face and he felt a bout of nervousness float around in his stomach. He had a feeling what this meeting was about and dreaded it. "Thanks, and I'm on my way."

Nathan stood and slid into his jacket. Six months ago, the firm had been bought out. For ten years, he'd busted his butt with the goal of being promoted to the executive team. One good thing was that he and a number of others had been able to keep their present positions and maintain their salaries.

The bad thing was that the CEO, Duncan Charles, was a staunch traditionalist, who'd been married close to fifty years. He wanted his executive team to reflect his high family values, meaning, he wanted them married as well. Presently, all the single men were scrambling to find wives. At first, Nathan had found the old-fashioned notion rather amusing, since he considered himself not in that category. After all, he was a divorced man who'd been married. Unfortunately, he soon discovered Charles had grouped the divorced men in a separate category.

The man actually believed the BS that marriage vows were to last forever and once you got married, it was a lifetime commitment—for better or worse. Charles believed whatever problems a couple encountered during their marriage could—and should—be worked out.

Basically, Nathan had been given six months to patch things up with his ex and renew his vows, or his name would be removed from the list of candidates for promotion to the executive team. A list he'd worked his ass off for ten years to get on.

He had sought legal counsel, thinking such a requirement was clearly illegal. However, he'd been told as the owner of the company, Charles could set whatever parameters for employment advancement he chose, and there was nothing that could be done. His attorney had suggested that if he truly wanted to move up in his career that he should try to work things out with his ex-wife.

Twice he had called Sierra and asked her to consider getting back together with him, and both times she had refused. He would admit that the tryst with Andy and Lillie Dennison had been a mistake and he'd told her that. Hell, he'd even let that little girl live with them, just as long as he could ignore her.

He walked down the hall to Mr. Charles's office. When he reached Christine's desk, the older woman looked up at him with her usual unreadable expression and said, "You may go on in."

Taking a deep breath, he slid open the door to find Duncan Charles sitting behind the desk like a king on a throne. "Come in, Nathan. I hope you have good news for me."

Playing dumb, Nathan said, "Good news?"

"Yes. Have you and your wife worked things out? Are you back together? You are an excellent employee, and I would hate to have to remove your name from consideration for the next senior executive position."

Nathan steeled himself. He had worked hard for that position and rightly deserved it. "I tried, Mr. Charles, but our situation is rather complicated."

"Why? Has she remarried?"

He swallowed, thinking he could lie and say that Sierra had. However, if Mr. Charles discovered he'd outright lied then he would definitely lose his job. He decided to come up with something he figured the man couldn't verify. "No. She was unfaithful. I caught her with another man."

He inwardly smiled about how easily he could place the blame on Sierra. Served her right for being so difficult. Besides, to tell the man that he was the one who was unfaithful would probably make Charles cut him from the list immediately.

The man shook his head sadly and, privately, Nathan was proud of himself. Now he was off the hook. However, Mr. Charles's next words threw cold water on that assumption. "That's where forgiveness comes into play, Nathan. I know it will be hard to do, but I believe a man can forgive his wife for any transgression."

The CEO leaned back in his chair. "With that said, I stand behind my earlier recommendation. You and your wife should work out your problems and get back together. You need to find it in your heart to forgive her. I expect you to meet with me with an update after the holidays, and I hope it's a good one."

A short while later Nathan was back in his office, pacing. The last time he had spoken to Sierra she was totally against the idea of them getting back together. There had to be something that could force the issue. He pulled his phone from his pocket and tried calling her, only to discover his call went straight to her voice mail after a half ring. That was a sure sign she had blocked his number.

He sat down at his desk angry as hell. Sierra was going to regret blocking him. Now he had no other choice but to visit her in Catalina Cove. But first, he had to come up with a plan to assure he got what he wanted from her, and he knew the one thing that meant the world to her now.

That little girl.

CHAPTER THIRTEEN

On Sunday evening Vaughn parked behind the Green Fig. The backside of the building was larger than he'd expected. She had a driveway with a few spots for parking. The rest of the outdoor space was fenced off and converted into a yard for her goddaughter. It was grassy, with flower beds and a play area that included a swing set, a tall slide and a seesaw.

He walked up the steps and there were two back doors. One had the name of the restaurant painted on it and a sign that said the entry was for employees and deliveries. The other was a regular exterior door that was solid and painted a light shade of blue with a transom window above it.

He rang the doorbell and waited with his arms full of gifts for the ladies, more than a little anxious to see Sierra again. He hadn't arrived back in Catalina Cove until late last night after having spent the last couple days in Baton Rouge to support the passage of an important bill needed to protect the waterways. The vote had been close but the bill had passed nonetheless.

Although this section of town was a couple of blocks from the gulf, a cool breeze permeated with the scent of the ocean ruffled his clothes. This was the type of day you would want to go out in your boat and enjoy the beauty of the waterways and gulf.

The door opened and he pulled in a deep breath when Sierra appeared. He had missed her and now seeing her made that realization more profound. "Hello, Sierra."

"Hello, Vaughn. Welcome back to the cove. Come in."

He stepped inside the cozy entryway. He saw Teryn, who was wearing a pretty yellow dress, peek out from behind Sierra with a huge smile on her face. "Hello, Mr. Vaughn."

Vaughn smiled, surprised the little girl had remembered him. "And hello to you, Teryn."

He turned his attention to Sierra. "These are for you." He handed her a large vase filled with fresh flowers. Then to Teryn, he leaned down to her level and handed her a smaller version of the flowers he'd given Sierra. Instead of a vase, her flowers were in a beautiful wicker basket.

"And these are for you, Teryn."

The little girl's eyes lit up and she grinned happily as she took the flowers. "They are so pretty. Thank you."

"Thanks for my flowers as well," Sierra said when Vaughn straightened back up to his full height. "Our apartment is this way." She turned to lead him toward the stairs.

He tried not to recall he'd been up these stairs before. That night last week when he had carried Sierra up to her apartment and placed her, fully clothed, on her bed before leaving.

"I can get up the stairs faster than you and Goddy, Mr. Vaughn."

Vaughn's attention was brought back to the present as Teryn laughingly raced up the stairs ahead of them.

"Be careful, Teryn, and remember what I've told you about running up the stairs."

The little girl slowed down immediately. Vaughn smiled when he saw that although she was no longer rushing up the stairs, she was taking them two at a time, which put her way ahead of them anyway.

Sierra smiled over her shoulder at him. "I don't know what I'm going to do with her."

Vaughn returned the smile and said, "You're going to do just what you're doing now. Love her and continue to take good care of her."

"Thanks." She quickly broke eye contact with him and continued up the stairs.

He walked behind her, trying not to notice the sway of her hips. She was wearing a pair of mauve-colored slacks and a pretty light pink blouse. He thought the color combination looked good on her and the perfume she was wearing smelled nice.

Although she had smiled when she opened the door, he had not missed the fact that she'd avoided eye contact with him as much as she could. She came across as a little unsure of how they should interact after the other night. It was important to him that she still feel comfortable with him and know that what happened was nothing for her to be self-conscious about.

"Welcome to our home, Vaughn," Sierra said when they reached the landing.

He hadn't really noticed how big the place was the night he'd come up here to put her in bed. He'd left right after he put her down. Now he was really getting a view, and the place was spacious.

The living room had a comfortable-looking sofa, a wingback chair, coffee table and several potted plants. There was a huge bay window that would have given her a glimpse of the gulf, if the view wasn't blocked by other buildings.

He was certain if you stood in a particular spot and looked between two of the buildings, you could see a bit of the water. He liked the decor. She had selected a seaside theme with ocean colors and a misty gray. On one of the tables sat a ceramic bowl filled with seashells.

He looked over at Sierra, with Teryn standing by her side.
It was as if both were curious about what he thought of their
home. "This place is amazing."

"It's beautiful," Teryn said, as if her words could describe it
better.

"Yes, it is beautiful," he agreed.

"Thanks," Sierra said, grinning. "The prior owner used the
upstairs as a place for storage. I decided it would be perfect for me
and Teryn. I had it remodeled into a three-bedroom, two-and-a-
half-bath apartment. It has this living room and a spacious eat-in
kitchen with a window that looks down into Teryn's play yard.
My sister is an interior designer and pulled everything together
for me. I told her the theme I wanted and she went from there."

"She did an outstanding job. I love the colors and it's beautiful how everything flows together."

"Come see my room, Mr. Vaughn," Teryn said and tugged
his hand to pull him toward a room off the living room. Her
bedroom was clearly a little girl's room and reminded him of
how Zara's bedroom once looked.

"I'm going to put my flowers right here," Teryn said, placing the basket of flowers on her dresser next to a huge stuffed
animal. "Where are you going to put your flowers, Goddy?"

Vaughn turned to Sierra, who was standing in the doorway
still holding her vase of flowers. "I'm not sure, Teryn. Where
do you think I should put them?"

"Right in here," the little girl said, racing past Sierra and out
of the room. Sierra followed and so did Vaughn. They entered
Sierra's bedroom. Vaughn's attention was immediately drawn to
the king-size bed he'd put her on that night. It had looked so
warm and inviting—and still did. He liked the colors of chocolate and lime green in here. Walking over to the window he
noted there was a better view of the sea, one that wasn't ob-
structed by buildings.

"You're right, Teryn. This is the perfect place," she said,

quickly setting the vase on her dresser and turning to leave. It was as if the two of them in her bedroom made her nervous.

She showed him the guest bedroom, which had a beachy theme of ocean blue and white. The bedspread had a print of seashells with matching curtains. Then, they returned to the living room.

"How was your trip, Vaughn?" Sierra asked, as she and Teryn settled on the sofa.

Vaughn sat across from them in the wingback chair. "It was productive. An important bill shippers needed to get passed seemed in limbo last week. It was imperative we reminded a few politicians why it was important, not only to the cove but other waterways in Louisiana, to get that bill passed."

"We're eating chicken today," Teryn said, as if to make certain she was included in the conversation.

"We are?" he asked her, smiling.

"Yes, and I helped Goddy make it. We also made a cake."

"What kind of cake did you make?" he asked.

"Chocolate. That's my favorite."

He grinned. "That's my favorite, too." Then he asked, "Whose idea was it for the blue front door?"

Teryn excitedly raised her hand. "Mine! It's blue for my mommy and daddy. They're in heaven, way beyond the blue sky," she said, spreading out her arms. "So I asked Goddy if we could have a blue door the color of the sky."

Sierra stood. "I'm sure you have a lot to do today, so we can go ahead and eat now," she said.

Vaughn figured Teryn's words probably left Sierra a little emotional. "Where can I wash up?" he asked, standing as well.

"There's a bathroom down that hall," she said, pointing.

"Thanks."

Sierra hoped by the time Vaughn returned she would have regained her composure. When he appeared in the doorway to

the kitchen, she hadn't. He stood there with his shoulder leaning against the doorjamb. He had removed his leather jacket and
the entire package he presented was too good to ignore. It was
hard to take her eyes off him. Everything fit. Almost too well.
His button-up shirt and the pair of jeans he wore… She'd never
admired the fit of jeans on a man more than on Vaughn. The
denim stretched perfectly across a pair of taut thighs.

"Need my help with anything?"

She blinked, realizing he'd spoken to her. She nervously licked
her lips. "Anything like what?"

"Anything," he said in a deep, husky voice. "I even know
how to set the table."

"I'm doing that."

They both turned to look across the room at Teryn. For a
moment, Sierra had forgotten she was in the kitchen with them,
busily setting the table and having fun doing it. "Teryn's got that
covered, but if you'd like, you can open that bottle of wine."

"Sure."

He crossed the kitchen to the counter and she watched every
step he took, unable to pry her eyes away. She quickly pushed a
strand of hair out of her face and blew out a deep breath. This
kitchen had grown hotter in just a few seconds, and she knew
why.

Other than an occasional repairman, Vaughn was the first
man who'd taken up space in her kitchen since she'd moved in
here. And she had to remember why he was here. He had gotten a huge promotion at work and she had invited him here to
celebrate…as an alternative to them going out.

Inviting him here was just a simple way of showing him how
happy she was for him. That's what friends do for each other,
and she considered him a friend. She pushed aside the thought
that suddenly flared through her mind, that what had happened
between them the other night in her office was not something
"friends" would do.

As if he felt her staring at him, he glanced up from opening the wine and met her gaze. Immediately, a surge of sexual energy passed between them and caught her; she had to fight back a groan. She was aware of him in every part of her body. She didn't want this. She didn't need this, but at the moment, she couldn't fight it.

"How does it look, Goddy and Mr. Vaughn?"

Sierra snatched her attention from him to Teryn, who was excited with how she had set the table. Swallowing, Sierra said, "I think it looks beautiful."

"And I think it looks beautiful, too," Vaughn said.

Sierra watched as Teryn's smile widened, and she felt good knowing what a happy child her goddaughter was. The flowers Vaughn had brought for her and Teryn were a nice gesture and had made Teryn even happier. She appreciated his kindness in that regard.

Drawing in a deep breath, she said, "I'm ready to serve dinner, if everyone will be seated."

CHAPTER FOURTEEN

Vaughn was convinced he had not eaten a tastier meal. The Cajun fried chicken had been delicious, the macaroni and cheese was cooked to perfection, the broccoli was the best he'd ever had and the yeast rolls had practically melted in his mouth. And he also enjoyed their company.

Teryn was a chatterbox and told him all about school, her gymnastics classes and how she was doing with the Christmas songs she was learning. He thought she conversed well for a child her age and found the conversation interesting and enjoyable.

Vaughn didn't make it a habit of having dinner with most people because he never wanted to impose. However, dinner with Sierra and Teryn was different.

"I really appreciate you inviting me to dinner, Sierra," he said.

She smiled at him. "As your *friend*, I wanted to show how proud I am of your accomplishment."

Vaughn noticed her emphasis on the word *friend*. He was okay with that for now. He would take his time to make their relationship into more than that. "Thanks."

"Do you have a Christmas wish, Mr. Vaughn?"

He looked across the table at Teryn. "A Christmas wish?"

"Yes. You must have a Christmas wish that you want Santa to give you."

"I do?" he asked.

"Yes. But you just get one."

Vaughn nodded. "What if I want more than that?"

She shook her head. "You're a grown-up, so you only get one."

"Oh, I see." He really didn't and looked over at Sierra, hoping she would explain.

Her eyes twinkled and she said, "It's a tradition that started with Teryn and her parents. Everyone has to make a Christmas wish. However, although Teryn gets to make as many as she wants, adults only get one."

"One Christmas wish?" he asked.

"Yes," Teryn said. "Just one, so you need to make it a good one. My list of wishes is all ready to go, but Goddy hasn't made one yet."

Vaughn recalled that last week when he'd asked Sierra about Teryn she'd mentioned her goddaughter was upset that Sierra didn't have one Christmas wish ready to give Santa. Now he understood what Sierra had meant.

"Well, you know how it is with grown-ups. We tend to get busy and forget to do things," he said.

"Then I'll just have to remind you and Goddy about it. We need to mail our letters to Santa on time. My mommy said if we wait and mail them too late, he might not get a chance to read it before Christmas."

He could hear the anxiety in the little girl's voice. In a soothing tone, he said, "Well, I'm sure your Goddy will get hers done."

"And what about yours?" Teryn insisted.

"I will start working on it."

"Good," Teryn said, smiling. "Please give it to Goddy so she can mail yours to Santa when she mails ours."

"Teryn. He might want to mail his Christmas wish to Santa himself."

When Vaughn saw the little girl's crestfallen look, he said, "I'll be glad to give you mine to mail with the two of yours."

Teryn happily clapped her hands. "Good."

Vaughn studied Sierra's face and figured she wasn't too keen on that idea, although Teryn clearly liked including him in whatever plans she and her godmother made. Now he had to make sure her godmother didn't mind either.

For Vaughn, dinner ended way too soon, but it was close to six o'clock. The chocolate cake had been delicious, and he'd eaten two slices. He offered to stay and help with the dishes, but Sierra assured him that wouldn't be necessary. All she would be doing is rinsing them off and placing them in the dishwasher.

He was impressed that Teryn had daily chores. Sundays were her day to sort her dirty clothes since tomorrow was laundry day.

When Sierra walked him to the door, he noted that she made sure Teryn was with them. That meant there would be no good-bye kiss for him tonight. He thanked her for dinner.

In a low tone, she said, "And remember this wasn't a date."

"I'll remember," he said, giving her a smile. Whether she knew it or not, to him it had been more than a date and had meant even more.

"Goodbye, Teryn," he said, hunkering down to the little girl's level to take hold of her hand. "I enjoyed eating dinner with you."

"And I enjoyed eating dinner with you, too. I like you, Mr. Vaughn."

That made him smile. It definitely made his day. "And I like you."

"So, how did dinner with Vaughn Miller go?"

Sierra should have known her sister would call the minute she'd gotten Teryn into bed.

"Everything went fine. Teryn and I enjoyed his company."

Dani laughed. "Oh, so you kept Teryn around as a buffer? You know that's going to backfire on you. You won't have Teryn with you all the time."

"I'll worry about that when the time comes," she said, easing down in the same chair Vaughn had sat in earlier.

"Stop being so afraid of connecting with a man, Sierra. That's not healthy."

"So you say."

"What did Teryn think of him?"

"He made her day."

"How so?"

"Vaughn is a real charmer, but I'll have to say that today he went above and beyond."

"In what way?"

"He brought us flowers. He brought me a vase of beautiful mixed flowers and brought her a smaller version in a cute little basket. You should have seen her face when he handed them to her. He made her feel special."

"Ohh…that is so wonderful. Sounds like he's accepted Teryn's place in your life in a way Nathan never did."

Dani was right and Sierra had thought about that a lot during dinner. Especially when he'd included Teryn in conversations. Teryn even mentioned Vaughn in her prayers that night, asking God to keep him safe every day.

After her call with Dani ended, Sierra had showered and was in her pajamas when she got a text message from Vaughn. May I call you?

Sierra raised a brow, wondering what Vaughn could possibly want to talk to her about. She hesitated before texting him her answer. Yes.

Within seconds her phone was ringing. "Hello."

"I didn't get my kiss and I want it."

Sierra was glad she wasn't drinking a glass of wine or she

would have choked on it. "You think you're entitled to one?" she asked, not certain how to take what he'd said.

"Entitled? No. No man is entitled to anything when it pertains to a woman, Sierra. But he can want, desire, need. The final decision is always hers."

Sierra closed her eyes for a second as she drew in a deep breath. How could she fight this? How could she fight a man who was so charming, so charismatic, so full of sex appeal and who had more magnetism than any man she knew?

"Will you want a kiss whenever you see me?"

"Umm, that would be nice," was his response.

She couldn't help but smile. "My sister, Dani, likes you and hasn't even met you." Too late, she wished she hadn't said that. Now he knew she'd been discussing him with Dani.

"That's good to hear. What I really want to know is if you like me."

"Of course. I invited you to dinner, didn't I? I told you we're friends."

"I want more. And before you ask, the answer is no. I don't think I'm entitled to more, Sierra. I'm merely stating what I want. Again, the final decision is yours."

She thought about what he'd said. "And if I told you I didn't want to give you more than friendship, would you respect my wishes?"

"Yes, I'll respect them, but I would try my best to change your mind. I can be very persuasive."

She fought a smile as she shook her head. "Can you?"

She heard the teasing glint in his voice when he said, "Yes, I can."

Deciding to change the subject, she said, "Thanks for the flowers. They are beautiful."

"So are you."

She chuckled. "Boy, you're laying it on thick."

"Not as thick as I'd like, trust me." He paused a moment and then said, "I'll be leaving town again in the morning. Flying to Boston to meet with our suppliers there. I'll be gone for a week and hope to see my sister while I'm there."

To Sierra that seemed so far away...and for so long. But then she needed the time and the space. Today she'd felt herself being drawn to him, something she shouldn't let happen again. "Have a safe trip, Vaughn."

"Thanks. Good night, Sierra."

A part of her was actually regretting the call was ending. She was missing him already, although she didn't want to. "Good night, Vaughn."

CHAPTER FIFTEEN

Sierra was convinced this had to have been the longest week of her life. Although she'd tried telling herself it had nothing to do with Vaughn, deep down she knew it did. He'd told her he would be gone for a week, yet every day during the late afternoon she would look up each time the door chimed to see if it was him walking in.

She hadn't expected to miss him. He hadn't called or texted, but he hadn't said he would. Why should he? Hadn't she pretty much given him the impression that she wished he wouldn't? She had told him she wasn't ready for a serious relationship and all she could offer was friendship. There was really no reason for him to stay in contact.

It was Friday and the restaurant was full. Her new white chicken chili had been a hit and by popular demand, she had made it twice this week. Everybody loved it and she was glad of that. Teryn had been invited to a sleepover for a classmate's birthday. The little girl's parents were members of their church and a couple Sierra had grown up with here in the cove.

Teryn had made her promise to water the flowers Vaughn had given her. She was still happy about them, and more than once this week Sierra had to caution her goddaughter about overwatering the flowers. The roses in the bouquet had opened and Teryn had been delighted. Sierra would admit she'd been just as happy to see her roses bloom. Both flower arrangements were as fresh and beautiful as the day Vaughn had brought them, and still smelled divine, too.

Since Teryn would be gone until late tomorrow evening, Sierra made plans to drive into New Orleans and spend the day there. It had been a while since she'd visited the French Quarter, and eating a beignet or two sure sounded good. She might even drop by Madam Josey and have her tarot cards read.

On second thought, maybe not. The last time she'd done that while in college, Madam Josey had predicted she would live a long and happy life with the man she loved. So much for that forecast, now that she was divorced and the man she'd thought she loved had cheated on her. As far as she was concerned, Madam Josey didn't have a great track record.

She decided to stop being a door watcher since it was obvious Vaughn would not be dropping by. He'd said he would be gone a week, but that didn't necessarily mean he would return today. Since he mentioned he would also be visiting with his sister, she figured he'd probably stay through the weekend.

Turning to one of her waitresses, Sierra told her that she would be in her office if she was needed. It didn't take her long to get caught up tallying the week's receipts and planning next week's menu. She looked up when there was a knock on the office door. "Come in."

"Everything is closed up and I'm about to leave."

She smiled at Levi, her assistant manager. "I hadn't realized it had gotten so late," she said, closing the books. "How did things go tonight?"

"It was busy until the end, but the last thirty minutes were only take-out orders. We sold out all of the soups."

"That's good to hear," she said, standing. "By the way, Levi,

I plan to drive to New Orleans tomorrow since Teryn is spending the night away."

"That's great. I hope you enjoy yourself. You've been working hard, nonstop since this place opened. Between this restaurant and taking care of Teryn, you need to slow down once in a while and take care of yourself."

"I will."

A short while later she decided to call it a night and was headed upstairs when her phone rang. When she saw the call was from Vaughn, her heart started pounding. "Hello, Vaughn."

"Hello, Sierra. I just got in. Bad weather caused my flight to be delayed."

She wondered why he was telling her this when he hadn't contacted her all week. "Sorry to hear that. Glad you made it home safely."

"So am I. How did the new soup turn out?"

She was about to ask how he knew she would be trying out a new soup recipe this week when she remembered mentioning it over dinner on Sunday. "It was a huge success. My customers loved it. I had to make it twice."

"I had intended to come by tonight."

"Unfortunately, we don't have soup left of any kind."

"Soup isn't what I would have wanted, Sierra."

She swallowed, knowing she shouldn't ask, especially upon hearing the deep, throaty tone of his voice. However, she asked anyway. "And what would you have wanted?"

"That kiss I didn't get on Sunday. Could you please open your door so I can get it now?"

Through the transom window above her front door she saw the porch motion light was on. Just knowing Vaughn was outside sent an immediate surge of yearning through her. Desire, the one she had managed to contain until she was in her bed at night, clawed at her, sending a throb to the area between her legs.

"Sierra?"

The sound of his voice made her realize she was standing there, frozen in place, and still holding her cell phone to her ear. "Yes?"

"Would you like to open the door?" he asked. "Please."

Would she? Should she? If she opened the door then he would assume she wanted the kiss as much as he did. If she didn't open the door, he'd assume she didn't want the kiss and go away.

She would *not* open the door. "Vaughn?"

"Yes?"

She paused a moment and then said, "I am opening the door."

CHAPTER SIXTEEN

Vaughn had braced his hands on either side of the doorjamb and the moment Sierra opened the door, he wanted to pull her into his arms. He had only been gone five days, but he'd missed her like crazy. It never mattered how exhausted he was after long days of meetings and conference calls, and visiting with Zara, he'd always gone to sleep thinking of Sierra.

Damn, if she wasn't beautiful, standing there bathed in the glow from the foyer's lamp. His eyes took a leisurely sweep of her. She was wearing a pair of dark slacks and a plaid print blouse. She always wore stylish blouses and they fitted perfectly against the shape of her full breasts. She was wearing light makeup, if she was wearing any at all, and her hair flowed around her shoulders.

He exhaled a deep breath before his emotions got the better of him. "Hello, Sierra."

"Vaughn."

With greetings out of the way, they both stood there, staring at each other. He wanted to kiss her. Bad.

"Please come in," she said at last, stepping back and breaking the intense silence between them.

He entered her home, closed the door behind him and turned to face her. The main reason he didn't pull her into his arms right then was because he wasn't sure if Teryn would pop up at any moment. He recalled over dinner the little girl saying she got to stay up late on Friday nights.

"Is Teryn asleep?" he asked, talking in a low voice, just in case she wasn't still up.

"No. She's not here. One of her classmates had a sleepover birthday party. I'll pick her up tomorrow evening."

That meant they were alone. That knowledge sent sexual excitement and anticipation curling low in his stomach and down, throbbing heavily in his groin. Not able to contain himself, he reached out and tugged her close, wrapping his arms around her waist.

He'd told her what he wanted and why he was there…and she *had* opened the door. But first he needed to tell her something. Looking deeply into her eyes, he said, "I missed you this week."

"Really? Is that why you didn't call?"

He could tell from the way she broke eye contact with him that she hadn't meant to say that.

"I wasn't sure if you wanted to hear from me or not. I thought maybe I'd worn out my welcome on Sunday."

She looked back at him and he saw vulnerability in her eyes. "If you honestly thought that then why are you here now?"

The answer to that was easy. "I couldn't stay away." Unable to help himself, he lowered his mouth to hers in a deep, seductive and thorough kiss. Moments later he pulled back, wanting her to get prepared before he went in full force. She stared up at him. They both took several breaths, and he lowered his head to kiss her again.

This time he kissed her with all the passion, need and desire he'd held back the first time. His tongue immediately went inside her mouth to reclaim her.

While she said she wasn't ready to get seriously involved with anyone, her body told a different story. The bottom line was that they were already involved and she would eventually realize that. Desire clutched hard at his insides and when she leaned into him, he was certain she could feel his erection pressing against her.

Sliding his hands up from her waist, he cupped the back of her head to deepen the kiss. He loved kissing her and could tell by her response that she liked being kissed by him. Her lips were perfect. Where his were firm and strong, hers felt soft and gentle.

He might be devouring her, but returning his kiss, she was just as greedy. That made him wonder about all the passion she'd been holding back. From their last encounter in her office, he knew that she was a passionate individual. He couldn't help but wonder if she really knew the extent of her sexual hunger. He had a feeling he was just scratching the surface and there was a lot to be discovered.

Vaughn broke off the kiss and was breathing hard, trying to catch his breath, and he saw she was doing the same. He also noted the deep, dark glaze in her eyes.

"You're good at this, you know," she whispered.

He leaned in and nibbled around her lips. "Good at what?"

"Kissing."

"I'm glad you think so." The way he saw it she was just as good. He loved her taste and the way her tongue would mate with his.

When her arms slid around his neck, he knew she was ready for another kiss. This time he intended to give her a kiss she'd never forget. Lowering his head, he took her mouth again and his hands were on the move. He wanted to touch her, feel her all over as their mouths mated vigorously.

He heard her tiny whimpers but he didn't let up. He could kiss her for days, hours. Hell, he could kiss her until every single ship docked at the pier went out to sea and returned home again.

When he felt his control slipping, Vaughn pulled back. He wanted her so bad he was tempted to strip off their clothes, lower her to the floor and take her right here and now. But he couldn't do that. Fighting for the little control he had left, he whispered against her moist lips, "Your office or upstairs?"

Vaughn waited for her response and knew whatever she decided would be a turning point in their relationship. He figured she knew it as well and that was the reason for her pause.

Finally, when he thought he couldn't handle the silence any longer, she whispered, "Upstairs, but..."

His brows rose. "But what?"

"Tonight, I don't want more than just the moment, Vaughn."

Reaching out, he caressed her cheek with his finger. "Are you sure that's all you want, Sierra? You deserve so much more."

"The moment is all I can handle."

He didn't say anything, searching her face, then said, "What if I said that I hope to persuade you otherwise?"

She leaned in and rested her forehead against his. "You'll probably be wasting your time, Vaughn."

"I won't be wasting it, Sierra."

He then swept her up into his arms.

Vaughn placed Sierra on the bed and stepped back to look at her. He'd pictured this very scene so many times in his mind and now that it was happening, he felt fire blazing inside of him, he was that overheated, that aroused. From the way her eyes gave him a slow, sweeping perusal, he knew she hadn't missed a thing. Especially his solid, hard erection.

He was determined to show her—with time and patience— that this single moment was not all she could handle. She could handle him. He couldn't think of any other woman who could— or who he would want to—handle him. Sierra Crane had, without even trying, done something no other woman had been able to do, make him want more. He was practically burning for it, and he intended to make her want more as well.

Retracing his steps to the bed, he drew Sierra into his arms and captured her mouth in another scorching hot kiss. With their mouths connected, he felt a flood of sensations invade his entire being, taking over his senses and making him feel crazy with need.

Her hands had a tight grip on his hair, keeping him in place as she held his lips to hers. With her possessiveness spurring him on, he kissed the hell out of her.

When he ended the kiss and stared into her eyes, he felt how his heart rate...as well as the size of his erection...had increased. He moved away from the bed, glad to see her flowers were still blooming as he took his wallet and phone from his pants pocket and put them on her dresser beside the vase.

Glancing over at her he saw the way she was looking at him, and actually felt the intense heat they were generating. Feeling overheated, he began stripping off his clothes. Vaughn saw her eyes widen when he eased off both his pants and his briefs.

He got a condom packet from his wallet and strolled, naked, back to the bed. "Have you ever put a condom on a man before, Sierra?"

She gave a negative shake of her head. He offered the condom to her. "Do you want to try it, *cherie*?"

She looked at the packet and then back up at him. He released his breath when a slow smile spread across her lips. "You trust me to do this?" she asked.

"Yes, I trust you to do that."

He knew he was taking a risk, knowing her touch might drive him right over the edge, but he was willing to take the chance. He'd never allowed any woman to sheath him before, but he wanted her to be his first.

She carefully opened the packet and pulled out the condom. She studied it, and then she stared at his penis as if trying to figure out how it would work.

"Hold the tip of the condom between your forefinger and

thumb and then roll it over the full length of me," he instructed huskily.

She nodded and followed his instructions. He drew in a sharp breath the moment she touched him, and she glanced up at him. "You okay?" she asked.

He clenched his jaw, fighting for control. "Yes, I'm okay," he said, when he really wasn't. She had him in her hand and took her time to put the condom on him, making sure she was doing it correctly.

Sweat broke out on his forehead because even though she had put the condom on, she still held him in her hands.

"I didn't think it would fit," she said, as if in awe.

"I knew it would."

And then she began running her fingers along his shaft, drawing circles around the condom tip and then dipping a finger lower to caress his balls...while staring up at him, holding his gaze.

Jesus, did she have any idea what she was doing to him? He noticed her breathing had changed. It was coming out harder and her cheeks were even flushed.

When he couldn't stand it anymore, he reached out for Sierra and pulled her up against his torso and covered her mouth with his. At that moment the only thing he could think of was stripping her naked and joining their bodies...but not before he tasted her all over.

He released her and asked, "May I undress you?"

She nodded silently.

He started with her shoes, noticing she had such small, pretty feet. He loved the red nail polish on her toes, which matched the red on her fingernails. Sexy. Fiery hot. Too tempted to stop, he lifted her leg and pressed the sole of her foot against his groin, loving the feel of it there.

Vaughn felt the moment his actions made her shudder. Leaning in he kissed her again, loving the way she tasted and the way she was clinging to him, her mouth reciprocating his kiss.

He pulled back and quickly removed her blouse and bra, seeing the twin globes for the first time. He felt a tingling sensation in his lips with the need to devour her breasts, taste them, suck them, lick them all over.

Unable to help himself, he leaned in and captured a nipple between his lips and began sucking on her breast.

"Vaughn…"

He loved the way she said his name, the breathless wonder of it all. He eased her on her back and removed her pants and panties. She wore pretty lacy panties that matched her bra, but her panties weren't the main thing on his mind at the moment. What they'd been shielding was.

When he saw her, totally naked before his eyes, he let out a possessive growl. Her feminine scent encompassed him, took over his senses, drove him to reach out and cup her hips, tilt her upward toward his mouth as he leaned in to bury his face between her legs.

Sierra's hands gripped the bedcovers. Just like she hadn't expected Vaughn to ask her to sheath him, she hadn't expected this either.

He'd spread her legs wide and rested them on his shoulders. Seeing what he was doing while feeling the impact of his tongue inside of her was driving her crazy. He held her thighs steady, although she couldn't help but thrash about. And when she felt him tonguing her clit, licking it and sucking it, she couldn't stop her hips from lifting, wanting more.

She didn't know a man's tongue could go that far inside a woman. As he pushed her to release, she moaned feverishly while grinding herself against his mouth.

Sierra screamed his name when her body exploded into an orgasm that was even more powerful than the one she'd had that night in her office. Before the spasms ceased, he lowered her legs from his shoulders to straddle her.

She gazed up at him, and with what sounded like a roar, he entered her, burying himself deep. He began pumping his hips, thrusting hard inside of her. Instinctively her hips arched up and her inner muscles clamped down, trying to hold him inside, and pull everything out of him.

"Sierra…you are killing me."

He was killing her as well. She doubted he knew how good he felt inside of her, how hot she was for him and how he was making her hotter still. It was as if that orgasm didn't happen just moments ago, and her body was already paving the way for another.

For a minute she thought he was about to pull out of her when he thrust back inside and began pounding harder. The pleasure was almost too much to bear, she felt it everywhere.

Thrashing her head against the sheets and pillows, she wanted him to take even more. All they had was this moment and if this moment couldn't last, she intended to get everything that she could out of it.

On and on, he kept a vigorous pace, an even rhythm that sent intense need throbbing all through her body. The sinfully erotic movement of his hips as he thrust nonstop inside of her made her feel as if a live wire was sending stimulating currents all through her.

His pace increased and just when she thought he couldn't possibly go any deeper inside of her, he did. He managed to strengthen and lengthen his thrusts, feeding a sexual hunger she had never experienced before. Now she felt like she was drowning in the very essence of Vaughn Miller. His masculine scent and his ability to pleasure her were almost more than she could handle.

Suddenly, she felt it. Convulsion after intense convulsion wracked her body and the full impact of pleasure with an orgasm that was so strong made her feel light-headed. She felt like a lit powder keg, headed for ignition with no way to put out the spark.

When she looked up, she saw Vaughn staring down at her. Throwing his head back, he roared and it felt like his body detonated on top of hers.

She felt every single tremor that passed through him. The intensity of his release made her come again. Even when their bodies should have been winding down, aftershocks consumed them. Holding her tight, he remained planted inside of her until their spasms subsided.

Sierra had never experienced anything like that before, where although satiated, her body had wanted and needed more. The orgasms had been the most intense and profound she'd ever known.

She met Vaughn's gaze and she wondered if the degree of pleasure had been the same for him. When he whispered her name and then leaned in to kiss her, the intensity of it made her want him again.

This was just supposed to be for the moment, but Sierra had a feeling sharing this one time with him was not going to be enough.

CHAPTER SEVENTEEN

Vaughn slowly opened his eyes to daylight and to find a sleeping Sierra spread on top of him. He closed his eyes again and drew in a deep breath. In all his thirty-five years he had never experienced the level of intimacy he had shared with her all through the night and early morning. He felt so sexually satisfied, and it was all because of the woman whose warm and soft body was covering his. He could imagine waking up this way every day for the rest of his life.

Vaughn studied her features while she slept. She looked like an angel and nothing like the spitfire whose bed he'd shared. The woman who had surprised him when she pushed him on his back and began riding him like a woman who craved him as much as he craved her. She had released all that pent-up desire, but he had a feeling there was even more she still needed to let loose.

Although she'd been all in with their lovemaking last night, it wouldn't surprise him if she woke up this morning filled with regrets. If Sierra still thought what they'd shared last night was one of those "just in the moment" things, he would take every opportunity to convince her that their time together would always mean more than that.

His plans for Sierra hadn't changed. He intended to build on every good thing that was between them. Especially this, a night of earth-shattering and powerful lovemaking.

She didn't love her ex-husband anymore, she'd said as much; however, she couldn't get beyond the pain the man's betrayal had caused her. But he had time and plenty of patience. And as one of the letters his pen pal Marie had written to him said, he had to believe that brighter days were coming, and if anyone deserved brighter days, he truly believed they both did.

Sierra stirred and he watched as she slowly lifted her eyes as she became awake. Then, as if she realized just where she was and whose body she was on top of, she jerked her head up and looked directly into his eyes. He saw panic followed by remorse in their dark depths and he said, "Good morning, *cherie*." He cupped the back of her head and brought her mouth down to his for a kiss as a way of calming the storm that wanted to rage within her.

Vaughn moaned when Sierra began kissing him back. Never had he enjoyed kissing a woman as much. When she finally pulled back, he tightened his arms around her, not ready to release her just yet.

"We need to talk, Vaughn."

And quite honestly, he wasn't ready to talk either. Especially when he had an idea where the conversation was probably headed. "Alright, we'll talk, but let's do it over breakfast, okay? I have a taste for blueberry muffins."

She frowned. "You want us to go out? To the Witherspoon Café?"

He smiled. "Sure. Unless you have blueberries in your kitchen and can make muffins as good as Debbie Witherspoon."

When she rolled her eyes, he thought she looked kind of

cute. "Nobody can make those muffins like Ms. Debbie, so don't even go there."

"I was just wondering. Are you ready to get dressed? I need to go home, shower and shave."

Vaughn watched her nibble on her bottom lip and knew she was thinking. Probably too much. "Do you have a problem being seen with me?" he asked.

Her eyes widened a fraction. "Of course not. We've dined together at the Witherspoon Café before."

He shook his head. "No, you were dining there, and I joined you. I have an idea. How about you come home with me while I shower and get changed. Then we can go to the café together."

She rolled off Vaughn to lie beside him. "I don't think that's a good idea."

Shifting in bed on his elbow, he looked at her. "Why not, *cherie*?"

She hesitated a moment and then said, "I don't want to flaunt our 'just in the moment' thing all over town."

He didn't say anything for a minute, then said softly, "I don't consider what we had as a 'just in the moment' thing."

"Okay, then a one-night stand. It means the same thing."

"We didn't have one of those either, Sierra."

Sierra released a frustrated breath. "Okay, then what would you call it?"

Vaughn leaned over and cupped her face and said, "I would call it one hell of an amazing night. The best one of my life."

He kissed her, needing to taste her again, and doubted he would ever stop wanting to.

She returned the kiss with as much passion as he was putting into it. And whether she knew it or not, he was putting everything he had into it. Every ounce of his being, his heart, body and soul. This kiss was like none other…but then he'd thought the same of the last one, and the one before that. He was convinced that every kiss they shared went up a notch or two on the passion scale.

When he finally released her lips, they were panting like they'd run a marathon. Before she could catch her breath to say anything, he quickly asked, "What were your plans for today?" She had mentioned last night that she wouldn't be picking Teryn up until late evening.

She unconsciously licked her already moist lips. "I plan to drive into New Orleans to spend the day. Why?"

"Mind if I tag along?"

"You might not want to after our talk."

He smiled. "I doubt there will ever be a time I wouldn't want to spend with you."

Sierra paused a moment and then said, "It would save time if we shower and dressed at the same time. You at your house and me at mine and I'll be ready when you return."

He nodded. "Alright."

Sliding out of the bed, he didn't miss the way her gaze raked over his naked body. "I'll be back in less than an hour."

She sat up, making sure to keep the sheet almost up to her chin. He sat on the edge of the bed to put on his socks and shoes and thinking the gesture was unnecessary, granted just how much he'd seen of her last night, how much of her body his tongue had tasted.

"Vaughn?"

"Yes?"

"Part of the reason I want to talk to you is to reiterate that last night was—"

"Fantastic. Simply amazing." He leaned in and captured her mouth in another kiss.

Sierra eased out of bed and on her feet the minute she heard the door close behind Vaughn. Last night had been *fantastic* and *simply amazing* like he'd said, but over breakfast she needed to make him understand why she still had to think of it as a moment thing for them.

She relived everything Vaughn had done to her, what she had done to him, what they had done to each other—and she had enjoyed every single minute of it. He possessed all the qualities a woman would want in a man…if she were free to pursue and indulge. No matter what Vaughn thought, she wasn't ready to do either. If he thought he could change her position on that, he was mistaken.

Sierra headed for the bathroom and once there she gazed at herself in the vanity mirror. The reflection looking back at her was that of a woman who looked like she'd been made love to most of the night. Her hair was all disheveled, her eyes were brighter than normal and her lips looked like they had been thoroughly kissed more than a few times. And then there was that mark on her neck. Yikes!

She stood back and looked down at herself. Similar marks were on her stomach, thighs, and there was no doubt there were even some between her legs. Especially there. She blushed when she recalled how they got there.

Like she'd told Vaughn, she had no problem being seen in public with him. However, there was no reason for people to assume they were an item when she wasn't ready to start dating again and wasn't sure she ever would be. Last night was all about last night. It was about the moment and the fulfilling of needs.

Sierra looked at the clock. She would shower, get dressed and head over to the café. When she got there, she'd text Vaughn to let him know she decided not to wait for him and was there already. Might as well let him see her stubborn streak. Besides, regardless of what he'd said to the contrary, she was convinced after her talk with him, he wouldn't want to spend the day with her in New Orleans.

A short while later she had changed clothes too often to suit her but wanted to look her best, and then wondered why she was making so much of an effort.

She straightened and looked at herself in the mirror again after finally deciding on a pair of jeans, one of her high-low blouses and her favorite boots.

To hide the mark on her neck she grabbed one of her favorite scarves from the closet. No one would think anything strange about her wearing one since they were stylish and were commonly worn this time of year.

Glancing out the window she saw that although it might be a little cool outside, a short jacket instead of a light coat would work. It was a nice day to walk the two blocks to the café. Doing so would clear her head, and she needed all her wits to deal with Vaughn.

The moment she stepped outside and locked the door behind her, she could smell the scent of the sea.

She paused before crossing the road and noticed a number of people had their boats out today and were passing the pier and heading out to the gulf.

It didn't take her long to reach the Witherspoon Café. Once she got a table she would text Vaughn. She smiled, thinking he would see that instead of him being one step ahead of her, she was one step ahead of him, and that's the way it would always be.

Adjusting the scarf around her neck she walked in and smiled at the waitress who approached her. "Good morning."

The young woman smiled back. "Good morning. Your table is ready."

Sierra's eyebrows drew together in confusion. "My table?"

"Yes. This way please."

She followed the waitress and nearly stumbled when she was led to a table occupied by none other than Vaughn. *What the hell?*

He stood when she reached the table, and with a smile he leaned in close and whispered, "Checkmate."

CHAPTER EIGHTEEN

Vaughn took his seat after Sierra sat down. He was certain the glare she was giving him would bring a lesser man to his knees. However, seeing her only stirred his desire, and it didn't help matters that she was wearing jeans—the first time he'd ever seen her in a pair—and a pretty light blue blouse.

The moment she'd walked in, his gaze had found her and flowed over those curvaceous hips in denim. And then to recall just how hard he'd ridden those hips last night made his body throb something mercilessly.

"That's a nice scarf, Sierra." No need to mention that he knew the reason she was wearing it.

The waitress came and took Sierra's drink order. When she walked off, Sierra asked, "How did you know?"

Vaughn took a leisurely sip of his coffee before saying, "How did I know what? That you were going to reveal your stubborn streak?"

He saw the smile she was fighting hard not to show. "Something like that, yes."

"Strategic thinking from my Wall Street days."

The waitress returned with Sierra's tea and a basket of hot

blueberry muffins. Vaughn thought they looked and smelled good. "Before you get started on whatever you feel we need to talk about, I want to ask you something," he said.

"What?"

"Did you talk to the woman at that bakery about working with you to sell desserts?"

He could tell his question was not what she'd expected; it knocked her off balance and deflated her irritation some. It was another ploy from his Wall Street experience.

"Yes, I met with Freda and she was excited at the prospect of us doing business together. She gave me a list of possible treats and I'll be meeting with her for a tasting. I'm hoping to introduce the desserts the week of Thanksgiving."

"You plan to be open that week?"

"Yes, but I won't be spending a lot of time in the restaurant because that will be a short school week for Teryn."

He nodded. "Will you be going to Atlanta to visit your sister?"

"No. My parents are coming home the week of Thanksgiving and we're looking forward to that. Once they got me and Dani out of college, they sold their home here and bought an RV and love traveling in it. They've seen a lot of the country."

"Will everyone be staying with you?"

"Heck no. My parents own my grandmother's lake house. They stay there whenever they come back home. Plus, since it's on three acres, it gives them a place to park the RV." She took a sip of tea and said, "Dani and I are happy they are living their dream."

Vaughn knew in a way his parents had lived theirs, too. His father had always promised his mother that once he retired, they would move to her hometown of Paris, and Catalina Cove would become their second home. His father had kept his promise. They had only been in Paris for a couple of years when the boating accident happened.

"Now that you've tried distracting me, can we finally discuss why I'm having breakfast with you?"

Sierra's question broke into his thoughts. He smiled and asked, "Do you want me to believe you didn't wake up as famished as I was this morning?"

There was no need to tell her what he'd really awakened with was a boner and he'd wanted desperately to slide his body into hers again.

"I could have prepared something at home."

"Yes, but I have a feeling you would not have invited me to stay. Besides, I needed to get as far away from your bedroom as I could," he added. "No need to wear out my welcome."

She sipped her tea and said, "You were right, Vaughn. Last night was fantastic and amazing. I will even admit it was something I needed. However, nothing has changed, it was just for the moment."

He didn't say that he thought that last night was just getting started. "May I ask you why?"

"I told you. I'm not ready for any serious involvement with a man. Right now, Teryn is my sole responsibility."

"Taking care of a child doesn't mean you have to put your life on hold, does it?"

"No, and you're also aware of the other reason I prefer not dating."

"The scars from your divorce?"

"Yes."

"Will you allow me a chance to heal them?"

"Not sure that you can."

"Will you let me at least try?" Whatever it took, he would show her how to love again, the same way Marie had shown him how to believe in better days. That made him probe deeper by asking, "Is there something you are afraid of, Sierra?"

Sierra didn't respond because the truth was that a part of her was afraid. Maybe she shouldn't be but she was. She was afraid of falling for another man who'd only break her heart. She had promised Rhonda she would provide Teryn with a loving home, and she intended to do that. She refused to place her and her goddaughter's happiness with someone else.

Last night was a prime example of what could happen if she let her guard down. Especially with Vaughn. So, yes, there was a fear factor, but that was something she would never confess to him. "No, there's not anything I'm afraid of."

"Then please give me a chance. I think once you get to know me you'll see I'm harmless."

Harmless? Could a man who looked like him truly be harmless to a woman? But she knew he was harmless in the ways that mattered to her; he treated women with dignity and respect. And she truly believed he wouldn't betray someone he loved.

"I know you're harmless, Vaughn. Had I thought otherwise you would never have shared my bed."

He leaned back. "Now I am asking to share more of your time, Sierra."

She nibbled her bottom lip, a nervous gesture she wished she could get rid of. Over the years, more than one man had told her for them it was a total turn-on. From the way Vaughn was looking at her mouth she wondered if that was true for him as well. "Like I said, my time is taken up with Teryn."

"Then my time will be as well."

Her brows arched. "Excuse me?"

"If your time is spent with Teryn then I have no problem doing the same. In fact, I would enjoy it. There will be times when I'd want you all to myself, but I can think of a number of activities the three of us can do together. Why would I want to exclude her? She is a part of you."

He must have noticed the funny look on her face. "What?" he asked.

"A lot of men don't like kids."

Sierra's statement made Vaughn suspect her ex-husband was

one of those men. "Let me assure you that I'm not one of them. I had planned to marry and have kids. If those plans hadn't gotten ruined, chances are I would have been a father by now."

For him it was about wanting to be a better father to his children than his father had been to him and Zara. It wasn't that Eugene Miller had been a lousy father, it was just that during Vaughn's growing years when he would have enjoyed a closer relationship with his father, he was busy building his wealth and rarely had time for his children.

Needing to shift his thoughts from his family and back to the topic of Teryn, he smiled and said, "I like Teryn and enjoyed her company Sunday. And Teryn did say she enjoyed mine."

Sierra returned his smile. "She did."

"And I hope you did as well."

"You know I did, Vaughn."

"Then may I make a suggestion?" he asked.

"And what is your suggestion?"

"How about if we take things one day at a time to see how it goes, Sierra."

Sierra concluded what he was proposing couldn't be too bad since she'd had him over for dinner, he'd met Teryn, and Sierra and Vaughn had shared a bed. Something Dani had said was also true, that although being afraid of getting attached and burned made sense, at some point Sierra needed to get past Nathan and understand that not all men were like him. Teryn was getting older and needed to see that a healthy relationship between a man and a woman was a positive. She had come from a loving home and probably would expect that. All Sierra had to do was recall her goddaughter's excitement after being told Vaughn was coming to dinner to accept that was true.

"What does taking things one day at a time entail?" she asked.

"Things would be no different than they are now, and I'll let you set the pace. However, I do have another suggestion."

"What?"

"If you agree for us to continue to see each other, next weekend I'd like to invite you and Teryn to join me for a picnic on my boat. At dinner last week Teryn mentioned she'd never been out on a boat before."

Sierra could recall her goddaughter saying that. "Teryn and her mom had a cruise planned for a few days in Cancún, but Rhonda died a week before they were to set sail."

"I'm sorry to hear that."

She could tell by the look in his eyes that he really was. "I think she would enjoy a picnic on your boat. Thanks for inviting us, Vaughn."

"Don't mention it." He looked at his watch. "Are you still planning to spend the day in New Orleans?"

"Yes."

"I would still love to join you."

If nothing else, he didn't believe in giving up on going after something he wanted. In a way she admired his tenacity. "What if I said I would prefer spending the day by myself?"

He gave her that hot, sexy smile that put her entire body on throb alert. "Then, Sierra Crane, I would have to convince you that you'll enjoy the day a lot better if you shared it with me."

She knew he wouldn't have to do much convincing. Even now all kinds of sensations were curling around in her stomach.

Would she enjoy the day better if she spent it with him? As much as she didn't want to believe that was true, a part of her knew it was.

"Yes, Vaughn, you may join me on my trip to New Orleans."

His smile told her everything. It wasn't cocky, but appreciative. "You won't regret it, Sierra."

She hoped not. A short while later they were heading out of the café just when Laura Crawford and another woman were coming in.

"Well, hi, Vaughn. It's good seeing you out and about." Then she glanced at Sierra, gave a fake smile and said, "Hello, Sierra. This is my friend from college, Belva. She's thinking about moving to the cove."

After Sierra and Vaughn greeted Belva, Laura said, "I'm glad I ran into you, Vaughn. Belva and I would love to talk to you if you have some time to spare."

"I don't have any at the moment," he said. "As you can see Sierra and I were on our way out."

"Then perhaps Belva and I can stop by your house later," Laura suggested.

"What's it about?" Vaughn asked.

Sierra could hear annoyance in Vaughn's voice. Laura was choosing to ignore it or she hadn't yet recognized it. "Belva wants to open a clothing boutique here and was interested in getting one of Reid Lacroix's low-interest loans."

Vaughn turned to Belva. "Sorry. Unless you grew up in Catalina Cove and are moving back to town, you won't qualify for the loan. Being a Catalina Cove native is a prerequisite."

"That's nonsense, Vaughn. Belva would often come home with me from college most summers, so you can say she has connections here. Besides, you'll be the top man at Lacroix Industries pretty soon, so you can bend the rules a little, can't you?"

Sierra had to fight from rolling her eyes at the way Laura was batting her lashes at Vaughn. "No, I can't," Vaughn was saying. "Reid made the rules, and I won't change them. Now if you don't mind, Sierra and I are leaving. Enjoy your breakfast."

He took hold of Sierra's hand and led her to where his SUV was parked.

CHAPTER NINETEEN

Vaughn always enjoyed this stretch of open highway between Catalina Cove and New Orleans. The beautiful scenery made the drive one of the most pleasant he knew of.

Giant oak trees, whose leaves were now the fall colors of yellow, orange and brown, lined both sides of the highway. Through the low-hanging branches you could clearly see the sea marshes. Above, they were so tall and huge their limbs stretched across the roadway to join and formed a colorful autumn canopy for miles. It was like driving through a picturesque tunnel.

He tried putting his encounter with Laura Crawford out of his mind. That wasn't the first time she had approached him, trying to garner his attention, since his name had been cleared.

Vaughn remembered her from their high school days and recalled how in their senior year she'd shown interest in him, and when he didn't return that interest, she'd then set her sights on Julius. Julius had been secretly in love with Vashti Alcindor, so Laura had wasted her time there.

He wasn't sure who was worse, Laura or her cousin Alicia. Both were in his graduating class and both had a tendency to put themselves on pedestals and weren't very nice women. Vaughn recalled how at the school's holiday class reunion Alicia shamelessly went after Isaac Elloran when it was obvious that he and his divorced wife, Donna, had been trying to get back together.

Vaughn did a side-glance at Sierra. "I picked up on Laura's less-than-nice attitude toward you. She's that way with everybody."

Sierra chuckled. "Not with you, though."

"Well, she was only friendly with me because she wanted something. Namely, to make her friend an exception to the rule."

"I don't think she liked your answer, Vaughn."

Now he was the one to chuckle. "She'll get over it."

And speaking of getting over it… He decided to ask her something he needed to know. "Tell me what I'm up against, Sierra. What did your ex-husband do to make you so set against developing a serious relationship with a man?"

"I told you that he cheated on me."

Yes, she had told him that, but for some reason he thought there was more to it than that. "Did you know the woman?" he asked.

"Yes. I also knew her husband. They were our neighbors."

Her husband had had an affair with one of their neighbors? "Did the man suspect that his wife and your husband were having an affair or was he caught unawares like you?"

She chuckled and the sound was filled with so much derisiveness that Vaughn gazed over at her. "Oh, he knew alright. In fact, he was in on it. I caught my husband engaging in a threesome, Vaughn."

"What the hell! Are you kidding me?"

"Nope. Although I wish I was. I went to Houston to visit Rhonda, who wasn't doing well. I returned home early and that's what I walked in on. Three people having sex in our bed."

"What did you do?"

"When I finally recovered from shock, I left and went to a

hotel. The next day I went back to get my things and then filed for a divorce."

Damn. No wonder she had trust issues. "And you hadn't suspected anything?"

"No. The three of them were into sports so I didn't think twice about him hanging out at their place or when the three of them would take fishing trips over the weekend or go hunting together. Some women are into stuff like that, but I'm not, and it didn't bother him when I didn't go. Now I know why." She paused and continued, "I later found out that his threesome was just the tip of the iceberg. He was into swinging. It seemed a number of times I thought he was on camping trips they were sharing cabins in mountains having group orgies."

"How did you find out?"

"He told me. It was one of those 'come to Jesus' moments and he figured confessing all and promising to change would stop me from going through with the divorce. It did just the opposite. I was more determined to see it through."

Vaughn shook his head. "He honestly expected you to take him back after that?"

"Yes. We were at a point in our lives where we'd become a power couple. We both had good jobs and had accumulated a lot of wealth and assets. He figured I wasn't willing to lose it all, no matter what. I proved him wrong."

"How long were the two of you married?"

"Seven years. We met my first year out of college."

Vaughn didn't say anything as he tried to wrap his head around what she'd shared with him. "At least the two of you didn't have any kids. I understand divorces can be hard on them."

"Nathan never wanted kids. He'd had a voluntary vasectomy years before we'd even met. I knew if I married him, I would never become a mom."

His brows shot up. "And you were okay with that?"

"At the time, yes. He'd told me what a rough childhood he'd

had as a foster child, and that he never wanted to bring a child into this world under any circumstances. I loved him enough to accept those conditions although my family and Rhonda tried talking me out of it. They knew how much I loved kids. Nathan convinced me that we should put our energy into building our wealth instead of building a family." She paused, then added, "I bought into his vision for our future."

Vaughn let that sink in. She had given up something she'd wanted for her ex-husband and in the end, he had betrayed her. What an asshole. "How would he have adapted to Teryn coming to live with the two of you?"

"Luckily, I didn't have to find out. Nathan and I weren't together when I adopted Teryn."

Vaughn pulled into a parking space in front of a shop in the French Quarter and brought the car to a stop. A part of him wanted to pull her into his arms and hold her. No woman deserved to have gone through what she had. Reaching out he gently caressed the side of her face with his fingertip.

"Just so you know, Sierra. I'm a one-woman man. I'm not into sharing or swinging, and like I told you, I love kids. I'm nothing like that bastard you were married to."

Dropping his hand, he gave her a smile and said, "Now, get ready, because we'll have fun today."

Sierra looked at Vaughn and couldn't help smiling. He'd said they would have fun and so far he'd stayed true to his word.

As soon as they'd arrived in New Orleans, they had grabbed beignets and coffees at a sidewalk café. Afterward, they were just in time to take in a matinee at the movie theater. It was a movie both of them had wanted to see.

While walking around the French Quarter, he'd held her hand. They had enjoyed lunch at Snappers, one of her favorite seafood restaurants. What she liked most was the live jazz band that always played. She had eaten her fill of shrimp and oysters while thumping her feet to the music.

It had been Vaughn's idea to have their tarot cards read by Madam Josey. Even after she'd told him how wrong the woman had been the last time she'd visited her, Vaughn had still wanted to do it.

"Next time you'll listen to me," Sierra said. They had just left Madam Josey, who'd given them tarot readings that were so inaccurate it was laughable. "I told you a few years ago she claimed I would live a long and happy life with the man I loved, and look how that turned out. And today, she actually looked us both dead in the eyes and said our destinies have been entwined since we first connected six years ago." She laughed. "Boy, was she off base."

"I know," Vaughn said, grinning. "I was tempted to tell her that couldn't be true since I didn't even know you seven years ago."

Sierra shook her head. "Madam Josey definitely needs to retire."

Vaughn checked his watch. "What time do you have to pick up Teryn?"

"By five."

"Then it's time for us to head back to the cove."

"Okay." She walked beside him as they headed for the SUV.

Sierra tried not to side-eye him but he looked good in jeans, a sweatshirt and sneakers. She had truly enjoyed herself. He had been so accommodating with everything they'd done. He hadn't taken anything for granted and always asked for her preference on things and had never decided for her. At the movies he had held her hand. She couldn't recall the last time she and Nathan had gone to a movie, let alone held hands. Today they had shared popcorn but he had drawn the line when it came to his gummy bears. He liked them as much as she did and had bought Sierra her own box.

When they reached the vehicle, he opened the door for her to get in, and then walked around to the other side. Before starting the engine he turned to her and said, "I enjoyed our day together, Sierra. Our first official date."

Had it been a date? Did she want to think of it as one? At that moment, it really didn't matter what it was called. The bottom line was that she had enjoyed their day together, too. "And so did I, Vaughn."

He gave her that smile that was droolworthy and said, "We're going to have to do this again."

"What?" she asked, although she had an idea what he meant.

"Spend another day together. That's why I'm looking forward to next Saturday when you and Teryn go boating with me."

"I'm looking forward to it as well."

He still didn't make a move to start the car. Instead he kept looking at her. She wanted him to kiss her and wasn't sure what gave her away. Maybe it was the way she was staring at his mouth, or maybe he'd detected it by the way she was breathing. All she knew was that when he began leaning his head toward hers, she was ready for a Vaughn Miller kiss.

She was operating on a primal need she hadn't known she was capable of feeling until last night. Now, his mouth fit perfectly with hers and his tongue…that tongue that knew how to pleasure her so much…was taking things up a notch. She was getting aroused and she greedily returned his kiss. He always managed to do that…drive her to match his passion.

It felt as if they were alone, and she was enjoying the moment. The kiss. The feel of being kissed by him. Everything.

When someone hit the window and hollered, "Get a hotel room," they broke off the kiss. Before he pulled away, he traced his tongue around her lips. They stared at each other for a moment and then she instinctively licked the path on her mouth that his had traced.

"You're killing me, *cherie*. I hope you know that." Reaching out, he took her hand and brought it to his lips to place a kiss on her knuckles.

She didn't know that. But the one thing she did know was that their relationship had changed. At some point during this fun-filled, whimsical day, they had reached a silent agreement and Sierra had a feeling her life wouldn't be the same.

Later that night after taking a shower, Vaughn sat outside on the screened veranda that overlooked the gulf and sipped a beer. He reached for his cell phone, recognizing the ringtone. He answered, "It's Saturday night. Why are you calling me and not on a date?"

He heard his sister chuckle. "I could be asking you the same thing."

"My date was earlier today."

There was silence and he understood. Zara was taking it all in. He hadn't ever mentioned anything to her about dating anybody. For one, the kind of dates he'd gone on while on his business trips weren't ones she needed to know about. And there hadn't been any others.

"You went on a date?" she asked, with disbelief in her voice. "A real date?"

"I thought of it as a real date but not sure if she did. We spent the day in New Orleans."

"Wow! Who is she?"

He started to say it wasn't anyone she knew, but then she just might. Sierra mentioned they had graduated the same year. "Sierra Crane."

"Sierra Crane? I remember her. We came out of school the same year. Her father was Preston Crane, that nice man who ran Dad's gas station. In school, she was best friends with Rhonda Fleming. I recall seeing her at the school's holiday reunion two years ago. She's moved back?"

He shook his head, amazed his sister could remember all of that. "Yes, she moved back. She's divorced and is raising her six-year-old goddaughter, Teryn. Teryn is Rhonda's daughter."

"Where is Rhonda?"

"She passed away. Her husband had been killed two years earlier in Afghanistan. Sierra's deathbed promise to Rhonda was that she would raise Teryn as her own."

"I'm sorry to hear about Rhonda. She was nice. Both she and Sierra were."

"Sierra said the same thing about you."

"Vaughn, I want details. How did the two of you begin talking and how serious is it?"

His sister asked too many questions. He would only tell her what he wanted her to know for now. "Sierra owns a soup café in the cove and I drop by on occasion to get takeout. I'd never seen her up close before, but one evening I did. I liked what I saw."

"So, it's just lust for you?" she asked, and he could hear the disappointment in her tone.

He could let her continue to think that way, but he wouldn't sully what was—and could be—between him and Sierra. "No, Zara, it's more than that. And that's all I plan to tell you."

"Well, you've told me more than I expected you to. I hope things work out."

"I hope so, too. She had a bad first marriage and is in no hurry to enter a serious relationship. That means I have my work cut out for me." Deciding to change the subject, he asked, "Anything I need to contribute toward our Thanksgiving dinner?"

"No. This year is my treat, Vaughn, and since I won't be spending Christmas with you this year, I want to make Thanksgiving special."

After ending the call, he thought about what he'd told Zara. Although he loved making love to Sierra and got turned on whenever he saw her, it was more than lust for him. Much more.

CHAPTER TWENTY

"Goddy! Look how big Mr. Vaughn's boat is."

Sierra *was* looking. She hadn't known that what Vaughn had referred to as a boat was really a yacht, and it was a beauty.

"Good morning, ladies," Vaughn said, climbing down off the yacht and heading to meet them.

It was hard to believe a week had passed since their day in New Orleans. He'd only come into the restaurant twice this week due to working late at the office, usually past ten. On those nights that he hadn't seen her, he would call her. This had been a good week for them. "Hello, Vaughn," Sierra greeted when he reached them.

"Hello, Mr. Vaughn," Teryn chimed happily. Then, glancing around the pier, "There are a lot of boats but yours is the biggest."

Vaughn laughed and Sierra loved hearing the sound. It was deep, rich and raspy and always sent sensations sparking through her. Although he hadn't shared any details, she knew he had a special day planned for her and Teryn. She was just as excited about today as her goddaughter.

"You and I have been invited to a party."

Sierra tilted her head back to look up at him. "We have?"

"Yes. Arnett Staples is giving Nina a birthday party, and Isaac and Donna Elloran are hosting it at their place."

Donna Elloran, the mother of a one-year-old son, was on the Christmas committee with her and a very likable person. The Ellorans also owned an ice cream shop a few doors down from her restaurant. She'd gotten to know Nina through Donna—they were best friends. Nina and Arnett, who had gotten married last year, had grown up in the cove but currently lived in California.

"Sounds nice. When is it?" If she attended the party with Vaughn, it would be the first time they'd be seen together in public...if you didn't count the two times they'd met for breakfast at the Witherspoon Café. Or today. There was no doubt in her mind that even now people were noticing that she and Teryn were standing by his yacht.

"The party is next Saturday night."

"I need to make sure arrangements can be made with my sitter for Teryn and will let you know."

A huge smile stretched his lips. "Okay."

There were times Sierra couldn't get over just how down-to-earth Vaughn was. He acted as if he was just a normal guy when he was anything but that. His family had been wealthy and from what she understood, Vaughn and his sister had inherited their parents' millions. Yet both he and Zara had decided not to live on their riches and had jobs.

"Will we go on the boat now?" Teryn asked excitedly, making it obvious she was ready to board.

"Yes, we can." Taking both of their hands, Vaughn helped them on the yacht. "Welcome aboard."

"I'm glad that you and Teryn enjoyed yourselves today, Sierra," Vaughn said as he walked them to their car.

"Thank you for inviting us," Sierra said. "And thanks for dinner as well."

"You are welcome. I couldn't let you ladies go home hungry."

After returning to the dock, he had treated them to dinner at the Bounty, a seafood restaurant on the pier. He had ordered a pirate's platter, which had been plenty for the three of them.

Teryn was skipping ahead, and Vaughn couldn't help but smile. "She certainly has a lot of energy."

Sierra chuckled. "Yes, she does. But trust me, as soon as she gets home and takes a bath she'll be out like a light and sleep through the night. You kept her busy today."

"I wanted to make sure she had fun."

"Trust me, she did. We both did, and having pizza delivered out to sea for lunch was a great idea."

"Thanks. Mr. Johnson said as long as we weren't too far out that he could deliver it for us. I'm glad the weather cooperated. It was a nice day to be out on the water."

Although there had been a breeze, it was still a fairly sunny day. He had rented a kiddie fishing pole to teach Teryn how to fish. She was so happy when she caught her first one, although she'd had to throw it back. She had been fine with that. She'd also been excited when they came across a pod of dolphins.

Because his yacht provided all the comforts of home, Teryn still was able to watch her favorite cartoon shows on television. She had been eager to practice her Christmas carols with them and that had been fun. Sierra thought Vaughn had a nice sounding voice when he was singing.

There were a number of boaters out on the water. Ray, Ashley and their twins cruised by, as well as Kaegan, Bryce and the baby.

"It was good seeing so many taking advantage of the nice weather today," Sierra said.

"Yes, it was. I'm hoping the work on my home dock will be finished by the time I take my boat out again. I like having it parked at my place instead of here." He'd told her earlier how he'd had the old dock torn down and was having a new one built.

"How often do you take it out?" she asked him.

He tried keeping his gaze trained on her and not let it slide down to her shoulders, a part of her body he'd kept looking at today. She was wearing jeans and an off-the-shoulders blouse. Those shoulders had begged to be kissed all day.

"It depends," he finally said. "I like going fishing, so I try to take it out most weekends. Not so much now as we head into winter. Today was an exception. It's hard to believe that Thanksgiving is in a few weeks."

"I know. Then it's the holiday season and I can't wait. The one thing I missed when I moved away was Catalina Cove during the holidays."

Vaughn leaned in and asked in a low voice, so Teryn wouldn't hear, "Have you come up with your one Christmas wish yet?"

"No, not yet. I'm surprised she didn't ask us about it today. Count our blessings," she said, grinning.

When they reached Sierra's car, Teryn turned and asked, "Mr. Vaughn, will you be decorating your boat for the Christmas parade?"

He smiled down at Teryn. "Umm, I hadn't really thought about it. What do you think I should do?"

"Decorate it for the parade," she replied, hopping up and down.

His eyebrows lifted. "Will you help me?"

"Yes! I'll help," she said excitedly.

He turned to Sierra. "What about you? Will you help us decorate my boat?"

She smiled. "I'd love to help."

"I'm glad you've decided to give Vaughn a chance, Sierra."

Sierra sat curled up on the sofa, enjoying a glass of wine. She'd had no intention of calling Dani, but her sister couldn't resist calling her to see how things had gone today.

"Let's not get carried away, Dani. Vaughn and I agreed to take things slow."

"Umm, a date two weekends straight. That's taking things slow?"

Sierra took a sip of wine, deciding for the time being not to mention Vaughn had asked her to attend a party with him next Saturday. "I don't consider today a date. It was a fun day for Teryn. She really enjoyed herself."

"I think it was nice to include her. Some men wouldn't."

She knew that was true. "Vaughn was the one to suggest we do things with her, so she could feel included."

"Again, some men wouldn't be so thoughtful. I'm going to admit I had misgivings about Vaughn Miller at first, because I didn't want you to get caught up with the first guy you dated after your divorce, but from what I'm hearing, he sounds like a keeper."

"Not sure I want a keeper, Dani. I like his company, but I don't want to get wrapped up in any man again. I've learned when the going gets tough, they get going."

"Not all men."

"Enough of them do," she said bitterly as memories flooded her mind. "Knowing I was about to lose my very best friend in all the world was hard on me. Instead of Nathan understanding what I was going through, he would get mad saying Rhonda was taking up too much of my time, and that surely she had other friends she could turn to. He couldn't understand that it didn't matter that Rhonda might have had other friends, I was her *best* friend and there was a difference. It's sad he couldn't see that."

That was why she'd never told Nathan about being a pen pal to a prisoner either. He would not have understood her need to reach out and give words of encouragement and motivation to anyone who needed to hear it. She often wondered about the person who received her letters and hoped they had helped him or her in some way.

After the call with Dani, Sierra decided to see if there was anything interesting on television. When she picked up the remote, her phone rang. Thinking it was Dani calling her back she clicked on without checking ID and said, "Okay, what did you forget to tell me, Dani?"

There was a pause and then a deep, throaty voice said, "It's not that I forgot to tell you something. I didn't get a chance to get something from you today, Sierra."

She swallowed, recognizing the male voice. "And what didn't you get from me, Vaughn?"

"Open your door and I will tell you."

Open her door? Sierra stood and went to the stairs. Looking down, she saw through the transom window above her door that the motion light was on. Lifting the hem of her caftan she walked down the stairs. She checked the peephole to make sure it was Vaughn before opening the door.

When she saw him standing there, she felt a gush of pleasure inside of her. "Haven't you seen me enough today, Vaughn?" she teased, stepping aside for him to enter.

"Not nearly enough," he answered, giving her a too-sinful smile as he entered her home and closed the door behind him.

"So, what do you need from me?" she asked, tilting her head back to look at him. She wished he wasn't looking at her like he could eat her alive, and more than anything she wished she wasn't remembering the night when he practically had.

His hair was slightly damp and touched the collar of his shirt. That, and the fact that he was wearing a different outfit, indicated he'd showered and changed before coming here. He smelled good, too.

When he didn't say anything but kept looking at her, she figured she needed to repeat her question. "So, what do you need from me?"

He took a step closer to her. "I'd rather show you, Sierra."

He cradled her jaw in his hand, leaned down and captured her mouth with his.

CHAPTER TWENTY-ONE

When Vaughn slid his tongue inside Sierra's mouth, a low growl erupted deep in his chest and he felt hot. Truth be told, he was feeling hot before he got here. Just knowing he was going to see Sierra alone had nearly burned him up. He couldn't remember ever being filled with so much need.

He had seen her only hours earlier. Hell, he'd spent six hours with her out on the gulf. But at no time had he been able to do this, and after he'd taken a shower, a primal force had taken over his senses and demanded that he come get this, the taste of Sierra that he needed.

And he couldn't get enough.

With his hand still holding her jaw, he slanted his mouth over hers while his greedy tongue swept her mouth. Her taste was like an addictive drug he couldn't do without. It was making every single part of his body sizzle. His heart skipped, then started to race when he deepened the kiss.

Her scent enveloped him in the most erotic way, and he felt it all the way to his toes. He felt his erection swelling and figured she had to feel it through the material of her caftan.

Just when that thought entered his mind, she pressed her

body against him, making his erection even harder. The throb of desire in his veins made sexual need curl in his stomach and when he felt the tripping of his pulse, he knew he had to pause or else he would take her on the stairs.

He eased his mouth from hers but didn't step back. Instead, he traced a path along the curve of her neck with his lips while trying to bring his ragged breath under control. When he began licking a certain spot on her neck, he heard her whisper, "Don't you dare suck on me there and leave a mark."

His mark. Vaughn leaned back and smiled at her. She licked her lips and his gut tightened. "You don't like my marks?" he teased, still trying to slow his breathing.

"Not there. Too visible."

"If you need another scarf, I will buy you one." Her soft chuckle made him shiver. It sounded so damn sexy. "But that just means I'll have to leave my marks where they aren't too visible."

He leaned in and captured her mouth again, loving the sound of her moans. Moments later he pulled back from the kiss. "Teryn's asleep?"

She tilted her head and grinned. "Now you ask?"

He grinned back. "The reason I didn't ask earlier is because you mentioned when I was walking the two of you to the car that chances were after such a busy day Teryn would be knocked out. I took you for your word."

"And you aren't wrong. After her bath, she chattered about how much fun she had. Her exact words were to tell Mr. Vaughn that she had such a fun-fun time."

"A fun-fun time?"

"That's what she said. And by the time she made it to her bed she fell right asleep—with a huge smile on her face. Thank you for that."

"You don't have to thank me. But I am concerned about something, though."

Sierra lifted a questioning brow. "About what?"

"What about Teryn's godmother? Will she have a huge smile on her face when she falls asleep tonight?"

Why did just being around Sierra bring on such profound awareness, such intense need? He had battled it all day, being in her presence and breathing in her scent. He wanted her. There was more than something sexual at play when it came to her, but right now that sexual thing was about to eat him alive if he didn't do something about it.

He watched as she nibbled her bottom lip. From past experiences, he knew the gesture meant she was thinking. He thought there were times she probably thought too much, but then he had no problem with her doing so. He wanted her to be as sure about them as he was.

Then, as if she'd made up her mind about something, she said, "If Teryn's godmother will have a huge smile on her face when she falls asleep tonight, it depends."

"On what?"

"If you're going to leave me with one."

Sexual excitement curled in his stomach and he felt a sweet, intense pull of desire. She'd issued an invitation he had every intention of fulfilling. Leaning down, he took her mouth once again and the kiss was as raw as it was seductive. He wanted her to know what she did to him, and at the same time give her an idea of what he would be doing to her.

Only Sierra had the ability to do this to him, make him crave things he used to think he could do without. Sierra Crane had ignited a flame within him that he doubted could ever be extinguished.

When he could tell that she was getting weak in the knees, he swept her into his arms and began moving.

Sierra knew Vaughn was taking her somewhere, but it wasn't up the stairs. Instead, it was to her office. When he laid her on the love seat she opened her eyes. She watched as he locked the door. He hadn't just kissed her tonight. Vaughn had made love to her mouth. That was becoming a habit every time their mouths connected.

Now he was stripping out of his clothes and she suddenly wanted to do something she'd never done before, not even with Nathan.

She watched Vaughn remove every stitch of clothing, then he grabbed for a condom packet he'd taken from his wallet. She still couldn't believe she'd put it on him the last time, and from the look of things, he was about to give her the opportunity to do so again.

He offered it to her. "Here you are, *cherie.*"

Easing off the love seat she crossed the room to him. She took the condom but put it on her desk. "Not yet."

She began touching him everywhere, running her hands over his shoulders, his hairy chest and then to the lower part of him, feeling his shaft and those glorious balls. Her fingers were tingling and she felt herself getting wet and overheated.

Sierra met Vaughn's gaze to decipher his reaction to her touch. What she saw in his eyes was red-hot fire. "You like this?"

"Sierra…" His husky voice trailed off when her hand dipped low to cup him and his breathing grew ragged. Leaning in close she began spreading openmouthed kisses over his shoulder, loving the taste of his skin. Then she lowered to his chest, determined that her mouth would follow the path her hands had taken, down to that part of his anatomy she was now holding in her hands. She ached for something she'd never experienced before and that was the taste of a man. But not any man. This man.

"Are you trying to kill me before I make you smile?" he forced out.

"No. I just want you to feel the same bone-melting fire you've ignited within me."

He gritted his teeth as her lips continued wandering over him, sucking, licking and nibbling, leaving her own marks along the way.

"I feel it, baby." He practically moaned the words.

She eased down to her knees and looked up at him. "No, Vaughn, you haven't felt anything yet."

Hungry for the taste of him, she drew his shaft into her mouth. She sucked him in deep. Then she began sliding her tongue up and down his hard length, while simultaneously massaging his balls.

Glancing up she saw he was staring down with a wild look in his eyes as her mouth, tongue and hands continued to work him the way she'd read of in the romance novels she and Rhonda would share in college.

Suddenly, Vaughn arched his back, and she continued to work his entire shaft, licking and lightly skimming the skin with her teeth.

He threw his head back and began growling words in French. The only one she recognized was *très bien*, which meant very good.

She sucked harder, determined to get the taste she desired from him. He was so big that she had to work her mouth to make sure he stayed inside, right where she wanted him. He must have felt himself ready to come and grabbed her hair to pull her to her feet, but she resisted and gripped his hips tighter. She wasn't going anywhere.

Giving in to his desire, he pumped his hips seconds before he began shuddering. He let go, exploding, and she accepted everything he gave.

The feel of his hand pulling her hair only added to the excitement. At that moment she felt like a woman in total control, secure in the knowledge that her touch, her mouth and her hands had totally pleasured him. For her that was a powerful feeling, a mind-blowing revelation, and one very significant moment.

And for a little while tonight, he was hers. All hers.

* ★ ★

Panting and feeling as if a surge of electrical force was taking over his body, Vaughn pulled Sierra from her knees and they moved to the love seat.

He had not expected her to take him in her mouth. It had been the most spectacular experience he'd ever shared. Now he felt even more possessive of her. If he hadn't claimed her before, he was definitely claiming her now.

He quickly removed her clothes and when she was totally naked, he *had* to taste her. He started with her lips and after thoroughly kissing them, he licked a path down her neck. He then leaned in and traced the tip of his tongue all over her shoulder blades and began sucking her skin. These were the beautiful shoulders he'd been tempted to taste all day, and was having a grand time doing so now.

He continued working his way on down to bury his head between her legs. After making her come with his mouth, he tossed the pillows and cushions from the sofa in front of the fireplace. Then he carried her there. It didn't matter that it was unlit. Tonight, the fire was raging within the both of them.

He grabbed the condom packet off her desk and sheathed himself. There was no way he could let her touch him there right now.

Joining her on the floor he eased her back on the pillows and spread her legs wide. "You're so wet, *cherie*."

Straddling her, he leaned in and kissed her as he slid inside her body, feeling her wetness surround him, and then her inner muscles clench him.

Unable to hold back, he began pumping in and out with a greed that no longer astounded him. He set a pace and then increased it to a fast and furious tempo.

He ignored the slight pain of her fingernails digging into his shoulders. What he couldn't ignore were the sensations caused by his slick skin sliding over hers.

"Vaughn!"

Hearing her scream his name as her inner muscles clenched him hard triggered his orgasm and he exploded.

She tugged on his hair to bring his lips down to hers and he took her mouth with a hunger that had him trembling. Moments later he eased off her and gathered her into his arms as their spasms subsided.

It was near daybreak when he lifted Sierra and carried her upstairs to place her in her bed. She opened her eyes and looked at him. He thought she was magnificent and looked totally gorgeous.

Before walking out of her bedroom, he paused to look back and saw she had fallen asleep with the most beautiful smile on her face.

CHAPTER TWENTY-TWO

Sierra slid a forkful of cake between her lips and closed her eyes in heavenly delight. This was so delicious. She'd tried five different baked goods—four cakes and one double chocolate brownie—and knew all five would be an excellent addition to her menu.

She noticed Freda McEnroe was watching her closely, waiting for a reaction. Freda and Sierra had graduated from high school together and, like her, Freda had returned to the cove to open a business.

Before his death Freda's father had operated a bakery on the pier for years. Now she was doing the same but on a smaller scale. Sierra was glad Freda had agreed to work out an arrangement with her to supply desserts for the Green Fig.

"Well, what do you think?" Freda asked.

Sierra smiled. "I think you are in the right business, and I'm so glad you decided to return to the cove." She might have been mistaken but Sierra could have sworn she'd seen a flash of pain in Freda's eyes.

"I'm glad I came back, too," Freda said softly.

"Well, these are the five desserts I'd like to add to my menu." Sierra then gave her the order needed each day for the café.

A huge smile spread across Freda's face. "That's great!"

"Will the week of Thanksgiving be too soon to start?"

"No, that's fine. I'm making a lot of sweet potato pies that week. I have a list of fifty already."

"Can you add one more for me? My parents are in town that week and I'm in charge of bringing dessert."

"I'll be glad to add you to the list."

When Sierra left Freda's bakeshop, she was glad the weather was still nice. It was Tuesday, so she had walked Teryn to school. She appreciated Freda agreeing to meet with her so early. She'd told Sierra that although she didn't open her shop until eleven, she would be there baking as early as seven. Just like Sierra made her soup fresh daily, Freda did the same with her baked goods.

As Sierra walked along the pier, she couldn't help but think about Saturday night with Vaughn. He wasn't supposed to leave a passion mark on her neck, but he'd done so anyway, which was why she was wearing another scarf today. She hadn't needed a photograph to know he'd left her with a smile on her face, and that smile had remained all through the night. And in a way that's what worried her.

After Nathan, she had told herself time and time again that she would never depend on a man for her happiness. She had resolved to focus her love solely on Teryn and her family. She had welcomed not having a man in her life. But now...

Even when she tried rationalizing that what she and Vaughn were sharing was purely sex, a part of her knew that wasn't really the case. She'd known weeks ago that Vaughn could disrupt the life she had planned for herself and had tried to resist him. But there was only so much of Vaughn Miller's charm she could resist.

She hadn't seen him since Sunday. He'd called that night to tell her that chances were he wouldn't be coming by the café this week since he would be tied up with numerous interviews for key positions he needed to fill at Lacroix Industries.

Sierra was actually looking forward to the party they would be attending together Saturday night. She'd told Vaughn that she would attend with him and he seemed pleased.

A block from her restaurant her phone rang. Pulling it out of her jacket pocket she saw it was Velvet. She clicked on immediately. "Hello, are you back?" She knew Velvet and her best friend, Ruthie, had gotten together for a girls' weekend in New York. One of the goals was to find Ruthie a wedding dress.

"Yes, I got back Sunday afternoon. I had fun, and we did find a wedding dress. It's perfect and Ruthie will look beautiful in it."

"I bet she will."

"So how did your weekend with Vaughn go?"

Sierra had told Velvet that Vaughn had invited her and Teryn to go out on his boat. There was no way she would mention their extracurricular activities later that night. "We had fun on his yacht. Teryn really enjoyed herself. I did, too."

"I'm glad, and what I like more than anything is the way he is including Teryn. That says a lot."

She thought so, too. "Will you be stopping by this week for soup? Your favorite is the soup for the day tomorrow." As of last week the gymnastics lessons had ended until the first of the year. That meant she wouldn't see Velvet as often as she used to.

"Then I guess I'll see you tomorrow, Sierra. Take care."

"You do the same, Velvet."

Vaughn looked across his desk at the man he'd just made a job offer to. If his expression was anything to go by, Evans Toussaint was happy about it. Standing, Vaughn extended his hand to him. "Welcome aboard and welcome back to Catalina Cove."

A broad smile spread across Evans's face. "It feels good to be coming back home."

Vaughn grinned. "Trust me, I know the feeling."

"Do you know of a Realtor in town I can contact about housing?"

"Yes, I don't know if you remember Bryce Witherspoon. She's the town's Realtor and one of the best around if you're looking to buy or rent."

Evans nodded. "I remember Bryce. She's related to the Witherspoons who own the café."

"Yes, their daughter. In fact, she's married to Kaegan Chambray."

"I remember him as well," Evans said. "Kaegan graduated from high school the year before I did. I also remember Bryce's brothers. Now I regret not making it back to the school's holiday reunion a couple of years ago. I was out of the country at the time. I'm looking forward to moving back and getting reacquainted with everyone."

A short while later, Vaughn was alone in his office. He felt good and, based on the man's credentials, he was bringing skills to the table that Lacroix Industries could definitely use.

Evans had aced the four rounds of interviews, including the one with Reid, who had drilled the man on various topics. It was clear that he had a strong work ethic, and his present employer spoke highly of him. Vaughn would put Evans in charge of handling the low-interest loans, as well as the new housing development Reid would be announcing soon.

He smiled when his thoughts shifted to Sierra. He was still trying to take things slow with her and not crowd her space, while at the same time letting her see what a good team they made, both in and out of the bedroom. However, he would admit what went on in the bedroom, including her office, was pretty spectacular.

She would be his date to the party Isaac and Donna were hosting for Nina. If things went well on Saturday night, and he had no reason not to think they would, he planned to invite her for dinner at his home after Thanksgiving.

He closed his eyes and recalled the last time they'd made love, in her office, and how he'd left her in her bedroom with a smile on her face. Hell, he'd had one on his own face—and was still smiling almost a week later. Even Reid had commented on his good mood—not that he wasn't always in a good mood, Reid had explained, just usually a more serious one.

Vaughn had been tempted to tell Reid that he'd found someone, certain the older man would understand since he'd found someone as well when he thought he would never fall in love again. But he had.

When the buzzer on his desk sounded, Vaughn opened his eyes. He pressed the button. "Yes, Kate?"

"I have a Camila Elderberry on the line for you."

Vaughn went still. What in the hell could Camila want with him after all this time? How did she know how to find him? Upon his release, he'd bought a new phone and his number had changed. He'd lost all of his contacts in his old phone, which didn't really matter because he'd stayed in touch with the people he really cared about. And according to Zara, Camila had pretty much severed their relationship when she'd gotten married.

He had every right to refuse the call, but curiosity got the best of him and he wondered what Camila could possibly want. "Put the call through, Kate. Thanks."

He heard the click and then said, "This is Vaughn Miller."

"Vaughn? Hi, this is Camila."

He didn't say anything for a moment. There had been a time when just the sound of her voice would send his heart, as well as his entire body, into overdrive. Now it did nothing for him. "And what can I do for you, Camila?" he asked in a brusque voice.

"I'm in New Orleans with a few friends and ran into someone from Catalina Cove last night. I asked him if he knew you and he said he did, and said you'd moved back there. I'd heard that all the charges against you had been dropped and was surprised when you hadn't moved back to New York."

"Why would I move back to New York?" he asked. "There was nothing there for me anymore." Definitely not her, he thought, recalling how she hadn't wasted time marrying someone else.

"Well, just so you know, I'm divorced now and have been for almost a year. I called Zara a few months ago so you and I could reconnect, and she wouldn't give me your contact information."

Zara hadn't mentioned anything about Camila reaching out to her, which was fine since she knew Camila was the last person he wanted to hear from. He was close to telling Camila just that, but instead he asked, "Why would we want to reconnect, Camila?"

"For old times' sake. I'm sure you'd admit those had been some good times."

Yeah, they had been good, but he was discovering the time he spent with Sierra was so much better. She was good all the way around and not just in the bedroom. "You've moved on, Camila, and so have I."

"I understand you're not married."

Whoever she'd run into from the cove had told her a lot. But then, he could see her pumping the person for information. "Why would my marital status concern you?"

"Because I'd love to see you while I'm in New Orleans. I understand Catalina Cove is just an hour away. I could rent a car and drive there."

He frowned. "Don't waste your time. I'm extremely busy right now. Besides, like I said, you've moved on and so have I."

There was a pause, then Camila asked, "And what if I said that for me moving on was a mistake?"

"Then I would have to tell you how sorry I am to hear that. I am not interested in rekindling a relationship with you. I am seeing someone and it's serious."

"Oh. I didn't know." She paused and then said, "I'm sure your lady friend wouldn't mind you meeting up with an old friend, Vaughn."

"She might not but honestly, I would. We have nothing to talk about."

"What about how much we had meant to each other at one time?"

Her statement pissed him off. "How much we meant to each other didn't mean a damn thing to you when I was arrested or when you decided to marry Titus Wheeler."

Although Zara hadn't told him the name of the man Camila had married, Vaughn had used the prison computer to find the wedding announcement. Titus had not only been a coworker but also a friend…or so Vaughn had thought.

There was a pause and Vaughn was curious to know what Camila had to say to that. He wondered what happened to Titus's girlfriend Melissa. The four of them used to double date on occasion.

"It was our love and concern for you that brought me and Titus together, Vaughn. We were so worried about you and—"

He chuckled, interrupting her spiel. "That's the best you can do when neither of you corresponded with me while I was locked up—and innocent? Spare me, Camila. Like I said, I'm seeing someone and it's serious. Please don't ever reach out to me again. You're in my past and I want you to stay there. Goodbye."

After hanging up, he checked the time. He had a few more interviews before he called it a day and then he would have to meet with Reid. It would be close to nine before he left work tonight. He missed Sierra, and while he was looking forward to seeing her on Saturday, after that phone call with Camila, he wanted to see her. *Now.*

His next interview was in an hour. He had time…

He texted her. Need a kiss.

She texted back. When?

I could be there in ten minutes.

Come to front door.

On my way.

Sierra paced in the foyer by her front door wondering about Vaughn's text messages. Granted, they hadn't seen each other for a few days, but they had talked every night before they'd gone to sleep.

She stopped pacing when she heard the sound of a car and figured it was him. It was a little before dinnertime and it appeared to be a busy day, but nothing her staff couldn't handle. Glancing through the peephole, she saw Vaughn dressed in a business suit, taking her steps two at a time.

Sierra didn't give him time to knock and quickly opened the door, stepping back for him to enter. He closed the door behind him and pulled her into his arms. She wasn't sure what had driven him to come here for this kiss, but she was glad he had.

She'd discovered there was nothing like a Vaughn Miller kiss and, at the moment, he was kissing the hell out of her. She returned the kiss with equal hunger.

He pulled back and looked into her eyes. "I needed that, Sierra," he said, his voice husky.

"I needed that as well," she replied, deciding to be truthful.

He kissed her again.

CHAPTER TWENTY-THREE

Sierra looked at her reflection in the full-length mirror. Tonight was Nina Staples's birthday party. It would officially put her and Vaughn out there as a couple that were dating.

She knew tongues had been wagging. He'd always said they would take things slow. She, on the other hand, hadn't wanted to become involved with anyone at all. But they *were* involved.

Vaughn had said to dress casual, so she was wearing a pair of black slacks with a printed tunic-style blouse with ruffles at the hem, one of her favorite tops.

Jacquelyn had already arrived to babysit and, since this was a Saturday night, bedtime had been extended for Teryn. They would be eating popcorn and watching a Disney movie. Since Sierra wasn't sure when the party would end, Jacquelyn would be staying the night.

Sierra checked her watch. Vaughn would be arriving shortly. Leaving her bedroom, she headed for the kitchen where Teryn and Jacquelyn were busy coloring. Both girls looked up when she entered the kitchen.

"Wow! Goddy, you look so pretty."

Sierra smiled. "Thank you, sweetheart."

"She's right, Ms. Crane. That's a nice outfit and I love your hair."

Sierra knew that when a teenager gave you compliments, you took it to heart. "Thanks."

Taking Dani's advice, she had gone to the salon and let an expert style her hair instead of running the curling iron through it herself. Sierra would admit she liked the results.

When the doorbell sounded, Teryn rushed past and down the stairs. "Don't you dare open that door before I get there, Teryn Marie," she called after her goddaughter. "And what have I told you about racing down the stairs."

Sierra couldn't help smiling at the thought that thanks to Rhonda, Sierra and Teryn shared the middle name of Marie. By the time Sierra made it to the foyer, Teryn was dancing excitedly. She hadn't seen Vaughn since their boating trip a week ago.

Taking a deep breath, Sierra glanced down at herself. Then she opened the door. She immediately saw a sign of male appreciation in Vaughn's hazel eyes and was convinced if Teryn had not been present, he would have pulled her into his arms and kissed her. "Hello, Vaughn."

"Hello, Sierra." His gaze roamed up and down her, and he smiled.

Before he could say anything else, Teryn spoke up and asked, "Doesn't Goddy look beautiful, Mr. Vaughn?"

Looking down at Teryn, he chuckled and said, "She most certainly does. I am convinced she will be the most beautiful woman at the party."

"Thanks," Sierra said, smiling self-consciously. "I just need to grab my shawl and the bottle of wine."

"Bottle of wine?" he asked, following her inside.

"Yes. It's a birthday party, remember?" she said. "And I just happen to know Nina loves Chardonnay."

"And how do you know that?" he asked, as they climbed the stairs with Teryn between them.

"Whenever she dines in the restaurant, that's what she orders to drink."

"I appreciate you taking care of that. This week I've been—"

"Extremely busy," she finished for him. "I understand and didn't mind doing it. I'll be right back," she said, walking off to her bedroom to grab her shawl and purse.

Moments later, she returned and saw Teryn was still with him, chattering away and again reminding him of his one Christmas wish.

"I'm back," Sierra said, and showed him the bottle of wine that was nestled in a cute birthday wine-purse and told him she'd signed both their names on the card.

Jacquelyn appeared and introductions were made. After giving Jacquelyn last-minute instructions, Vaughn escorted her out the door.

When Vaughn pulled into the huge horseshoe-shaped driveway of what used to be the Landrum Estates, Sierra said, "I didn't know Isaac and Donna lived so close to you. They're your neighbors."

He gazed over at her. "We're not that close since we're separated by acres of land," he said. "Like Zara's Haven, the Landrum Estates sits on five acres."

"And both are oceanfront."

He grinned. "Yes, both are oceanfront. When I moved back here, it was still vacant since old man Landrum died without any heirs. I was glad Isaac decided to buy it."

Bringing his SUV to a stop, he cut the ignition and turned to her. "I can't say enough just how beautiful you look tonight, Sierra."

"Thanks."

He'd told her several times already, and hoped she believed him because she truly looked good. He loved her outfit and the way she'd styled her hair. "You'll never know how much

I wanted to kiss you when I saw you. The only reason I'm not kissing you now is because when I finished, it would be pretty darn obvious what we've been doing."

"There's always later, Vaughn."

Vaughn smiled at her comeback and said, "And I will hold you to that, Sierra." He opened the driver's door and walked around to the other side to open her door. Taking her hand he led her to the front door.

He pressed the doorbell, and a few moments later Donna Elloran opened the door with a huge smile on her face. As far as Vaughn was concerned, the woman who'd been voted the most popular girl at his high school basically looked the same. Pretty as ever. "Vaughn and Sierra, come on in. Thanks for coming, and the party is just getting started."

"Where's your little one?" he asked.

"Ike is upstairs with the sitter," Donna said, smiling. "He's probably asleep by now."

Vaughn scanned the room and was glad there were less than twenty people there, and most he knew from high school. He figured Sierra didn't know many from her school days, since she was younger, but she knew most from living in the cove and as patrons of her restaurant.

The gift Sierra gave Nina was a huge hit.

After they'd gone around and spoken to everyone they headed for the buffet table to fill their plates. Vaughn asked, "What do you want to drink? I think they have every beverage imaginable here."

"A wine cooler will work."

"A wine cooler it is. I'll be right back," he said, walking off. "You and Vaughn look good together," Vashti Grisham said, sidling up to Sierra with a warm smile.

Sierra returned her smile. Vashti and Bryce had been the first two women to welcome her back to the cove. They'd even given her decorating ideas when she'd decided to turn the upstairs storage area of the restaurant into a home for her and Teryn. "We're just friends."

Vashti rolled her eyes. "Whatever. That's what Sawyer and I claimed in the beginning, too."

Vashti had moved back to town to open a bed-and-breakfast her aunt had left to her, and ended up falling in love with the town's sheriff. The B&B, Shelby by the Sea, was a beautiful inn that sat on the gulf, and was normally booked to capacity year-round.

Deciding to change the subject, she asked, "How are the kids?" Vashti and Sawyer had four. College-aged twin daughters and a three-year-old son and a daughter who was one.

"Everyone is doing fine. Shelby and Cutter are keeping us busy, and Jade and Kia are coming home for Thanksgiving and we're looking forward to that. How is Teryn?"

"Teryn is doing well. I don't recall getting as much homework when I was in the first grade. She's enjoying school and has made a lot of friends."

"I'm glad to hear that. She reminds me so much of Rhonda. I remember when Aunt Shelby used to babysit you and Rhonda after school."

Sierra laughed. "Yes, those were the days. Everyone loved your aunt Shelby."

"Here you are," Vaughn said, returning with her wine cooler. "Thanks."

Vaughn smiled at Vashti. "I understand you're taking a step back from the running of Shelby by the Sea."

"Just from the day-to-day operations," Vashti explained. "I want to concentrate more on the marketing side of things since that's my specialty. I have a very capable staff who're doing great. I understand congratulations are in order for you, Vaughn. I am so proud of you."

"Thanks, and I will say it was a surprise. I figured Reid would be running that place forever."

"And he probably would be if Gloria hadn't come into his life. They are so good together."

At that moment Donna and others joined them. Some Sierra had met before and some she hadn't. All had been friends of Nina and Arnett in school. Sierra sipped her wine cooler and tried to remember the names of everyone. She was glad to see Freda and gave her a hug. Sierra had forgotten that Arnett and Freda were cousins.

"Is it true that Lacroix Industries has hired Evans Toussaint?" Donna asked Vaughn.

He nodded. "That's true. He's going to be an awesome fit for the company. His parents are getting up in age and he wanted to come back to be close to them."

"If I recall, Saint, as we all called him, was quite a hottie back in the day," Nina said, grinning.

"I take it you know these two," Isaac interrupted to say to everyone as he joined the group with Bryce and Kaegan.

"Of course we do," Sierra said, and gave Bryce and Kaegan each a hug.

"Sorry we're late. It's the first time we'd left the baby with anyone other than my parents," Bryce was saying.

Vaughn mentioned that he was going to grab another plate of shrimp stuffed with crab meat, and others drifted off as well, leaving Sierra alone with Brody Dorsett. Although he was a little older than her, while growing up most of the people in the cove knew Brody because his father had been chief fire inspector, a job Brody came back to town to fill when his father had passed away.

"How's your mom, Ms. Kate?" she asked him.

"Mom is good. She's hinting at retiring now that Reid Lacroix has announced his retirement in a few months. She's been working there for thirty-five years and it's time she retires as well."

"And how are you and Bethany? The two of you haven't dropped by the Green Fig in a while."

She saw a flash of something cross his face. "There's a reason for that. Bethany and I aren't together anymore. In fact, she moved back to Pennsylvania."

"Oh, I didn't know that." Bethany had grown up in the cove and when she lost her job in Philly due to downsizing, she'd moved back and taken a job at the bank. Brody and Bethany began dating and everyone assumed things were serious between them. Obviously not. She regretted asking about Bethany. It wasn't her intent to create an awkward moment for Brody.

"I'm sorry, Brody. I should not have asked."

He smiled at her. "No reason why you wouldn't have. We'd certainly given the Green Fig a lot of business over the past months," he said in jest. "Bethany just wasn't ready for all the things I wanted, and she certainly wasn't ready to make the cove her permanent home. When she got a call with a job offer to return to Philly, she grabbed it."

Sierra changed the subject and she and Brody chatted about the cove's big Christmas plans when Vaughn returned. Moments later, Brody left to help Isaac bring in even more food. Turning to Vaughn, Sierra said, "I love this house."

Donna had given her a tour and told her how as teens in love she and Isaac would walk by this place on their way to school and dream of growing up, getting married and living here. Sierra was glad their dream had come true.

"It is nice. Sort of reminds me of Zara's Haven. Growing up I never thought about how humongous it was but now, since I'm living there alone, it's something else."

She nodded. "I bet it's beautiful, too."

He held her gaze for a minute and then said, "Why don't you see it for yourself when we leave here?"

In his eyes, she saw such intense desire that she took a sip of her wine cooler. She knew if she agreed, he would be showing her more than his home.

Lowering her wine cooler, she said, "I'd like that, Vaughn."

CHAPTER TWENTY-FOUR

"Welcome to Zara's Haven." Vaughn opened the door to his home for Sierra.

"Thank you," she said, crossing over the threshold and glancing around. "Wow! This place is larger than the Landrum Estates and everything is so immaculate."

He smiled as he led her into the huge foyer. They were both fully aware why he'd invited her here, yet he wanted her to feel relaxed, even though he would like nothing better than to sweep her into his arms and carry her to his bedroom.

"If you recall, Jean Lafitte built this house as a gift for my great-great-great-great-grandmother, Zara Musa," he said as she walked beside him to the grand foyer.

"The kidnapped African princess."

Vaughn nodded. The tale of Princess Zara's kidnapping by Jean Lafitte was widely known…at least by most living in Catalina Cove. According to the cove's history, Zara had been a beautiful African princess who was on a ship sailing to the Caribbean. Lafitte captured the ship, decided he wanted the princess, kidnapped her and brought her to his home on Catalina Cove. Then he did something he'd never done—at least not with his other mistresses—and that was to court the woman. He also built her one of the most beautiful houses in the cove, and together they had six children, of which Vaughn was a descendant.

"At the time, it was a common practice for men to provide their mistresses with an extravagant gift such as a house," he added.

"Yes, but there are some who believe Zara was his wife and not his mistress," Sierra stated as she continued to look around. "As a teen I loved reading the love story between Lafitte and Princess Zara. The romantic in me believes they were married."

"My parents would have loved you for believing that, but as I've mentioned, there's no proof. However, I will say he obviously thought highly enough of her to give her this," he said, waving his hand around.

"All the furniture is antique and has been owned by my family for generations. I'm told the carvings on the staircase banister were originally meant for a castle in Ireland. Fortunately for Zara—and unfortunately for the Irish castle owner—Lafitte and his gang of pirates pillaged the ship meant to deliver it to Ireland. In fact," he said, grinning, "a number of pieces in this house he smuggled in from other countries. That's why you don't get a Southern feel of this place like you'd get with other ancestral homes in town. Come on, let me give you a tour of the place."

First, Vaughn showed Sierra the living room, dining room and kitchen. His mother had modernized it by adding the double ovens, stainless steel appliances and granite countertops. "At some point Mom enlarged the butler pantry and then wished she hadn't when it became my sister's favorite hiding place."

He stood back and watched Sierra move around the kitchen, running her hands over the smooth countertops, and he imagined her running those same hands over him in much the same way.

Vaughn could feel his breath coming out shaky and his erection pressing against the zipper of his slacks. He presented his profile to her so his arousal wouldn't be so obvious when he asked, "Ready to take a tour of the upstairs?"

She smiled at him. "Yes."

As they walked toward the stairs, she commented on how she loved the dark oak floors and how beautifully polished they were. He led her up the stairs and told her that there were twelve bedrooms in addition to the master suite, which was on a wing of its own on the side of the house that faced the gulf. The third floor was the attic, but it was big enough to be converted into more rooms if needed.

"This house is huge for just one person or even for two. Do you and your sister ever plan to sell it or will you keep it?"

He shrugged as they walked down the long hall that led to the twelve bedrooms. "We haven't decided. I doubt she will ever move back to the cove. I'm here for good but this is too much house for me. I could have moved into one of the guest houses or cottages on the property, but either would have called for re-modeling and I wasn't into doing any of that. Besides, I didn't have time to oversee a project like that after I went to work for Reid. I needed to hit the ground running."

They walked side by side as they moved through the rooms and returned to the hall. He was trying to be patient, waiting for a sign from her, but the wait was almost killing him. He led her to the wing where the master suite was located and heard her gasp the moment he opened the double doors. This room alone was as large as her apartment. The four-poster bed was humongous and the curtains and canopy surrounding it matched those on the windows. The other antique furniture in the room added to the grandeur and spoke of opulence and wealth. There was a love seat across from the massive fireplace and several floor lamps were arranged around the room. Although it was dark outside, she could see the moon reflecting off the surface of the gulf. She knew the view had to be breathtaking.

The adjoining bathroom was larger than her and Teryn's bedrooms combined. A huge claw-foot tub sat in the center of the room with wraparound vanities and mirrors. There were his-and-hers dressing rooms and closets. There was even a fireplace in the bathroom.

"My word," she said, looking around. "How do you manage sleeping in here every night? I didn't know they made beds so big."

He chuckled. "The bed is custom-made. But to answer your question, I don't sleep in here. My living quarters are down-stairs," he said. "There's a second master suite. I understand my great-grandfather's ability to climb the stairs was challenging later in life, which prompted them to make one of the rooms downstairs into a mini master suite. It's half this size."

"Everything looks immaculate."

"Thanks," he said, leading her back toward the stairs. "My housekeeper comes in weekly to do laundry, dusting and other general housecleaning chores." When there was a lag in the conversation, he continued, "My cook only comes when I call her, which is seldom. To me that's a lot to ask when it's only me. She has prepared a few Thanksgiving and Christmas meals for me and Zara whenever she visited."

He paused at the top of the stairs. "My parents retained the housekeeper, as well as the gardener and cook, on the payroll until they reach the retirement age of sixty-five," he told her.

"What happens after that?"

"My parents' will stipulated after they retire, they are to receive a very generous monthly amount for the remainder of their lives."

"That was very thoughtful of your parents."

Vaughn shook his head. "After dealing with my parents for years, they deserve it, trust me. However, I'm sure it was my mother's idea more so than my father's."

He gestured for her to go down the stairs ahead of him and

then wished he hadn't. Just watching her ass sway had him heating up again.

"One day I'd like to invite you back in the daylight and you can see how beautiful it is out that bedroom window. The ocean view is gorgeous no matter what day of the year, and in the morning when the sun rises, it is breathtaking."

When she reached the bottom, she turned and waited for him to join her. She held his gaze and with every step he took, he felt his heart rate increase. In her eyes, he saw a look of primal sexual hunger he could no longer fight. Nor did he want to.

When he reached the floor, he gently pulled her to him. He was certain she'd seen just how aroused he was. Now he wanted her to feel it. He stared down at her, knowing what they both needed and wanted. When she shifted her body and pressed closer, he gritted his teeth and moaned.

She wrapped her arms around his neck, pressed her body flush against his and leaned up on tiptoe to connect his mouth to hers.

Sierra knew Vaughn was holding nothing back in this kiss. Having seen him only once this week, neither was she. More than anything, she wanted Vaughn to make love to her. She needed it.

She was mating with his mouth, the way she'd learned from him. Little did he know that as he was giving her a tour of his home, she envisioned them making love in every single room they passed through. For a woman who for years thought she didn't have a single passionate bone in her body, that was unprecedented. Desires she hadn't ever experienced were taking control of her body, making her feel hot and wanton, and sending her senses reeling.

He suddenly broke off the kiss and stared down at her. He moved his hands from her waist to cup her backside and bring her even closer to him. She felt him. But then she'd been feeling him from the moment he had picked her up tonight, even when their bodies hadn't been touching. He had a way of looking at her, training his scorching hazel gaze on her, arousing her as no man ever had.

"I want you, Sierra, but I doubt if I can make it to the bedroom," he whispered close to her ear.

She doubted that she could make it there, too. "Then don't."

Vaughn whipped her tunic-style blouse over her head and tossed it to the sofa.

"Good throw," she said.

His lips widened into a masculine smile. "I plan to show you a number of things I'm good at tonight."

"I'm all for it, just as long as you have me home by two."

He chuckled as he hooked his fingers into the waistband of her slacks and began easing them down her legs. "At least you didn't say midnight."

"Umm, do I look like Cinderella?"

He squatted to remove her shoes so she could step out of her pants. He glanced back up at her. "You're more beautiful than Cinderella. Plus, the prince never got to see this much of her. All he ended up with was a shoe."

Now she was down to her last stitch of clothing—a royal blue bra and matching panties.

"You always color coordinate your undies?" he asked playfully.

"Yes, it's something I like doing."

No need to tell him it had been Rhonda's idea, during their college days when they bought what they could afford, no matter the color, brand or style. Most of the time it was mix and match. Cotton. Cheap. Rhonda had convinced her that once they left college and got good paying jobs, they owed it to themselves to look just as sexy under their clothes as they looked wearing their clothes.

"And it's something I appreciate and like seeing," he said. He stood and then reached out to trace his fingers around the cups of her bra. His feathery touch ignited a hungry throb at the juncture of her legs.

"Now to relieve you of this." Reaching behind her, he aptly released the catch and eased her bra straps from her shoulders before removing it from her.

He stood there holding her bra while getting an eyeful of her breasts. He'd seen them before, had tasted them a number of times, yet he was standing there looking at them as if this was the first reveal.

"Do you know how I feel whenever I suck your nipples?" he asked.

She swallowed, not sure he expected an answer. Since she had no idea, she shook her head.

"I feel like I'm burning with pleasure from the inside out." He took a nipple into his mouth.

A short while later after feasting on both breasts, he eased his hands down the sides of her body, tracing his fingers over her stomach then down to the waistband of her panties.

"I like these," he said, running his fingers along the lacy edge of her panties. "Do you know what I like better?"

"No." The feel of his fingertips on her skin was sending intense sexual cravings through her.

"Taking them off of you."

He nudged her legs slightly apart and squatted again to ease her panties down. Neatly rolling her panties and bra into her slacks, he tossed them to join her blouse. When he began gliding his hands up the insides of her legs, her breathing hitched.

He leaned back on his haunches and looked up at her. "Did I tell you how much I love your scent?"

Yes, he had told her. During the times they'd made love Vaughn had told her a number of things.

"Yes, you've told me, but I don't mind hearing it again," she murmured.

"In that case, Sierra Crane, I love your scent. It makes me

want to fill my nostrils with it and feed my taste buds by devouring you."

As if to show her, he leaned in and began softly nibbling around her womanly core. Leaning closer still, he brushed his nose against her, making her shudder. She heard the deep sound of him inhaling, then felt the tip of his tongue tracing all over.

"Vaughn…"

She placed her hands on his shoulders and he gripped her hips as he continued to lavish the area between her legs with nibbles, nose rubs and licks. He said some phrases in French and she had no idea what he was saying but intended to ask him later. Right now, she could barely remain standing. The one thing she'd realized about Vaughn was he brought sexual potency to a whole other level, and since discovering her erogenous zones, he had no shame in exploiting that fact.

Her panties had gotten wet at the party when he'd done something as simple as placing his hand in the small of her back, or when he'd offered her a taste of one of the appetizers. She'd taken a bite and he'd finished it off. Anyone looking on would assume, and rightly so, that their relationship was more intimate than she was letting on.

"Why are you so edible, *cherie*?" he murmured, just seconds before sliding his tongue through her wet folds.

Her fingers dug into the flesh of his shoulders when he began showing just how edible he thought she was. Then she felt herself being gently lowered to the stairs. He quickly joined her and, lifting her legs to rest on his shoulders, he resumed the task of devouring her. Unable to hold back any longer, she cried out when pleasure consumed her. She pushed her hips up to grind against his mouth. As if that's what he wanted and needed, his tongue effortlessly penetrated her deeper as her body was jerked into still another orgasm.

When the last of her quaking subsided, he pulled his mouth away and lowered her legs from his shoulders. Through glazed eyes she watched him strip out of his clothes and sheath himself in a condom before easing between her open legs.

Lifting her hips in his hands, he thrust hard into her. She cried out, not from pain but from a pleasure so intense, she couldn't catch her breath. She felt him not just at her center, but throughout her entire body.

He moved in and out with an intensity that made her hips lift to meet his every stroke.

When another orgasm broke, she screamed his name. Her cry seemed to trigger Vaughn to thrust faster and harder until he reached an orgasm as well.

"Oh, my *cherie!*" he hollered and thrust hard, nearly balls-deep inside of her. She screamed in pleasure again and he threw his head back as his body jerked and bucked so hard she felt it in the depths of her core.

It took a while for the spasms to subside, and he held her while kissing her with hard, strong lips. When he released her mouth, he reached out and pushed a curl from her face. "How do you feel?" he asked with concern etched in his features. "I took you on the stairs, for heaven's sake. Are you hurt? Bruised?"

Sierra could tell he was worried that perhaps their lovemaking had been too wild and out of control. She didn't think that way at all. Reaching up, she traced the fretted lines on his forehead with her fingers. "I'm fine, Vaughn. I'm not hurt and I feel amazing."

A relieved smile spread across his face. "I feel amazing, too."

He gathered her into his arms. "Let's continue all this amazement in my bedroom, and I promise to have you home by two. Until then, I intend to show you just how much I desire you."

And Sierra intended to show him the depth of her desire as well.

Vaughn returned Sierra to her home with ten minutes to spare. He knew their relationship was about more than great sex, but tonight the sex had been powerful and the best he'd ever had. Even now, as he walked her to her door, he felt like he was floating on a cloud of sensual sensations, making it hard to keep his feet on the ground. They'd practically made love nonstop over the past three hours, yet more desire was throbbing through him, making him rock-hard. He'd never considered himself a greedy-ass when it came to sex but if given the chance, he would make love to Sierra every minute of the hour. Every single day, week and month.

Forever.

When they reached her door, the porch light came on. One advantage she had with living above the restaurant was that there weren't any residences nearby. So she didn't have to worry about nosy neighbors knowing when she got home late or whenever she had an overnight guest. In fact, she'd gotten a special zoning permit to live above her business. Once the shops and restaurants closed, typically no later than eleven on the weekends, everyone headed home, and the historical downtown district was almost deserted. He would worry about her living in this section of town alone except he knew the sheriff's office was at the end of the street with the fire station at the other end.

"Thanks for a wonderful evening, Vaughn."

Vaughn pulled her into his arms. "I should be the one thanking you. I meant to ask earlier if you'd made a decision about being my date at the New Year's Eve Ball."

She hesitated, then she said, "Yes, I'll be your date as long as you agree to something."

Vaughn leaned back and lifted a brow. "Agree to what?"

She nibbled her lip. "That although something is developing between us, I still want us to continue to take things slow. I don't want things to start speeding up just because of tonight."

"How slow are we talking, Sierra? I don't want to start feeling like all I am to you is a good time in bed and nothing else."

"How can you think that?"

"How can I not when you haven't even gone out to dinner with me?" he countered. Frustrated, he stepped back and rubbed a hand down his face. Tonight had been too wonderful for them to part angry and upset with each other. But there were times when he wanted to just shake her. The woman was just too stubborn sometimes.

He exhaled, deciding to drop the subject, for now. "Listen, I'll be flying out later today to join my sister for Thanksgiving. I hope you enjoy the time with your family this week."

"Thanks, and I hope you enjoy time with your sister." She paused. "When will you be back?"

For a moment he wondered why she cared. Still, he answered, "Next Sunday night around nine. I'll call when I get back."

"Alright."

He reached for her and kissed her in a way he hoped she would remember. When a ball of need burst to life in the pit of his stomach, he broke off the kiss and took a step back. "Good night, Sierra."

"Good night, Vaughn."

He waited until she opened the door and was safely inside before turning to leave.

CHAPTER TWENTY-FIVE

"You never did say how your date with Vaughn went last Saturday, Sierra." Dani slid into the chair across from her at the kitchen table.

Sierra's parents had arrived in town Sunday, and her sister and her family on Tuesday. Levi and her staff were running the restaurant most of the week, while she spent Thanksgiving with her family at their lake home on the outskirts of town.

"The party was nice and there was plenty of food. Isaac and Donna have a beautiful home. They bought the Landrum Estates and had it restored, so it still has that old Southern feel. Donna said she had fun redecorating. Most of the furniture she had to get restored to look like the original."

There was no way she would tell Dani about the after-party activities at Vaughn's home, or the vivid memories that kept repeating in her mind.

"So where is Vaughn? Why didn't you invite him to Thanksgiving dinner?"

"He left Sunday to spend Thanksgiving with his sister in Boston."

"When will he be back?"

Sierra wondered why all the questions. "He's returning Sunday night."

"And we're leaving Sunday evening," she groused. "It's too bad we won't get to officially meet him." Dani looked around and leaned closer to Sierra. "Just to give you a heads-up, Mom wasn't in town but a few hours when she heard that you've been seeing Vaughn Miller."

Sierra didn't have to wonder how their mother had come across that information. On her parents' first day back in the cove, they'd hooked up with old friends. Although the population in the cove was growing, there were still people who thought it was their God-given right to pry into other people's business. "And?"

"And she's worried."

Sierra lifted a brow. "Worried about what?"

Dani looked around again. Through the window, they could hear their father and the kids outside laughing as they washed the RV with Emory. Their mother was with them, but could come through the back door at any time.

"Mom's glad you're finally dating again after Nathan, but she's concerned you've fallen for the first man to show interest in you. She thinks you should be dating others."

Sierra rolled her eyes. "First of all, like I told you when you had that same concern, Vaughn is not the first man to show interest in me since my divorce. There have been others, but Vaughn is the only one I was attracted to." *Very much attracted to,* she thought to herself. "But even Vaughn knows our relationship comes with limitations."

"Do you?"

"Do I what?"

"Know your limitations with him, Sierra?"

"Yes."

Dani sighed deeply. "I think Vaughn is the best thing for you, and I even told Mom that when she expressed her concerns with me. I can hear how happy you are after spending time with him. Teryn likes him a lot, too. She told Mom about the flowers that he gave her and how he took her out on his boat."

"He's good with her," Sierra said, thinking of how he'd called from the airport Sunday while waiting on his flight. He had told Sierra to let Teryn know he would be bringing her a special gift back from Boston. Of course, Teryn was excited about that and was anxious for Vaughn's return.

"I am enjoying my time with him."

"And sleeping with him?" Dani asked in a low voice, smiling. When Sierra didn't say anything, a smirk appeared on Dani's face when she said, "You don't have to admit or deny anything, Sierra. I'm just happy you're finally getting some. And from what I can tell, with the improvement of your attitude, it's the real deal. I just hope…"

When Dani didn't finish what she was about to say, Sierra prompted, "You just hope what?"

"That you don't let your *I-am-an-independent-woman* soapbox mess up a good thing with Vaughn."

Sierra rolled her eyes again. "Since you've never had to flex your independence, Dani, I don't expect you to understand. Emory is what dreams are made of. You were lucky. I had a hard lesson to learn. It's just me and Teryn now and I have to be strong for her. I can't depend on anyone else for her or my happiness and I won't."

She figured her sister still didn't get it, but that didn't matter to Sierra. She knew what she had to do and knew the sort of woman she'd become and why. No man would change that.

Later that evening as Sierra lay in bed in one of the guest rooms, she thought about the conversation she'd had with Dani…as well as the one she'd had with her mother a few hours later. She was glad Dani had warned her about what their mother was thinking.

She'd had to first remind her mother she was a thirty-year-old adult, and whatever decisions she made about dating Vaughn and others—if she decided there would be others—was hers to make. She knew her mother didn't want her to be hurt again, but this was her life.

The one thing Sierra would admit to herself was that since seeing Vaughn, it was nice to have someone to share her time with…when she had time to spare. More than anything she enjoyed their phone conversations at bedtime, when they shared how their day had gone. He was an easy person to talk to and she'd learned a lot from him about the running of a business, and more than once she'd run ideas by him.

She hadn't heard from him since he'd left and she was a little disappointed with that. But then she shouldn't be. A voice in the back of her head was mocking her and saying, *Since you're such an independent woman you can just as easily contact him.* She knew that was true, but he had said he would call when he returned Sunday. He hadn't promised to call while he was away. Spending time with his sister was just as important as her spending time with her family, so she wouldn't bother him. She let out a frustrated sigh. Was she being logical or less independent?

Her thoughts were interrupted by the ding of her cell phone, indicating a text. Sitting up in bed she grabbed for her phone and read the message. I miss you.

Drawing in a deep breath, she ignored the flutters that went off inside of her when she texted back, I miss you, too.

Vaughn then texted, I am still thinking about Saturday night. Amazing.

Just the mention of that Saturday night sent sensuous shivers through her. Nibbling on her bottom lip, she decided to be honest with him. She texted, All the intimate times I spend with you are amazing.

So he wouldn't assume she was only thinking of the times they'd slept together, she quickly added, The non-intimate times as well.

He texted, No need to explain. I knew what you meant.

Yes, she figured he did. She recalled their last conversation and more than anything she wanted him to believe he meant more to her than just a good time in bed. She texted her response. Thanks.

You are welcome. Good night, Sierra. Pleasant dreams.

Pleasant dreams to you, too. Good night, Vaughn.

After clicking off the phone Sierra settled in bed. Knowing he had missed her like she had missed him meant so much. A warmth spread through her body and she knew it had nothing to do with all the bedcovers she lay beneath. It had everything to do with knowing Vaughn was charming his way deep into her heart, and she wasn't sure she was ready for it. However, whether she was ready or not, it was happening.

Vaughn stared at the text messages he and Sierra had exchanged moments ago. He wanted to call her, talk to her, hear her voice, but he was spending time with Zara—she'd just stepped away to make some tea.

Something was bothering Sierra. He wasn't sure what, and figured when she was ready to tell him she would. He'd learned not to stick his nose into her business unless she wanted it there.

"Well, at least you know Sierra Crane isn't interested in you just for your money," Zara said, returning with her hands full. Neither of them was sleepy, so they'd decided to sit and relax with a cup of tea, at least it was tea for her and a beer for him.

"Not that I thought for one minute my wealth mattered to her, I'm curious as to why you'd say that," he said, accepting the bottle of beer she handed him.

She chuckled as she sat across from him. "The obvious. She

is reluctant about becoming involved with you. Trust me, if she was after your money, you wouldn't be able to get rid of her."

Vaughn didn't say anything as he took a slug of his beer. Because money was something he and his family had always had, he'd never thought about it. He'd been aware of the term *gold digger*. At an early age his father had schooled him and Zara to marry within their social class. In other words, to fall in wealth and not in love.

He was glad those lessons had gone over both their heads. If either ever married, it would be for love. He had loved Camila and he knew Zara had loved Maurice. Unfortunately, they'd both been hurt by betrayals. So that proved money couldn't save you from heartbreak.

"You're right. Sierra doesn't care about my wealth. What she cares about more than anything is her independence."

"Independent women can be fierce."

He chuckled. "Says one who knows."

Zara frowned. "I can't help the way I am, Vaughn."

"I didn't say you should."

His sister didn't say anything for a minute, then she finally asked, "Do you ever think about the woman who used to write to you in prison?"

He figured her question was a way to change the subject, but that particular question had come from way out of left field. "Why would you ask me about that?"

"Just curious. I know how much those letters meant to you. They gave you encouragement, kept you inspired, motivated and—"

"Sane," he finished for her. "Although I would have to say that since I was locked up for a white-collar crime, I didn't suffer some of the same hardships some other criminals have to deal with."

He took another swig of beer, then said, "What was hard for me to deal with was the fact that I was an innocent man and my freedom had been taken away." He paused again. "To answer your question, the answer is yes, I often think of her and wish there was some way I could contact her to let her know the positive impact her letters had on my mental state. I figured she was a woman in her sixties or older who was probably in the education system."

"Why do you think that?" Zara asked.

"Her penmanship. A younger person would probably have typed on a computer then printed it out. She used the same kind of stationary each time and wrote using a fountain pen."

Zara raised a brow. "A fountain pen? I didn't know they still make those."

"Exactly. A younger person wouldn't know what a fountain pen was. I probably won't ever know who she is. I've accepted she was someone who was supposed to be a part of my life at that time."

Then, as if a light bulb had gone off in his head, he exclaimed, "That's it!"

His sister looked at him quizzically. "What is 'it'?"

"My one Christmas wish."

"What are you talking about, Vaughn?"

He told her about Teryn and how she expected both him and Sierra to come up with one Christmas wish. Zara thought it was cute that Teryn could have an endless list of wishes while adults got just one.

"My desire to find my pen pal will be my one Christmas wish," he said.

Zara reached out and patted his hand, smiling. "That sounds good. Just don't start believing in Santa on me. Remember how I used to write those letters to Santa every year and would get everything on that list I asked for? It was a big disappointment to find out that it wasn't a reward for being such a good girl that I got so much stuff. It was because Mom and Dad made sure we got anything and everything we ever wanted. Things don't work like that in real life. There isn't a Santa and there aren't miracles."

She went quiet and then added in a low voice, "There isn't even a happy-ever-after."

Vaughn didn't say anything as he finished his beer but could feel his sister's pain. "As adults we know that now but think of how happy our lives were when we thought otherwise. I want to make a little girl happy for the holidays. And in making my desire to one day meet my pen pal my one Christmas wish, although I know it's one that won't come true, I have nothing to lose."

CHAPTER TWENTY-SIX

"I hate to say it, but I'm going to miss you when you leave tomorrow," Sierra said, giving her sister a hug.

Sierra would have to admit this had been one of the best Thanksgivings ever. Her parents had left earlier that day and she and Dani could tell that they were happily living the life they wanted. Their parents told them they wouldn't see them for Christmas but would probably travel back this way sometime after New Year's.

Now she had some time with Dani. Sierra had forgotten just how much fun the two of them could have together, and Dani's husband, Emory, was the brother Sierra never had, and the son her parents always wanted.

"Are you sure you don't want to spend Christmas with us again this year?" Dani asked, as she stood at the window watching Emory and the kids play kickball.

"I'm sure. I got Teryn involved in a lot of activities here. She's joined the youth Christmas choir and will be performing at church the Sunday before Christmas, and we're decorating the restaurant for Christmas on the Main. I'm a contestant this year, so Teryn and I will be busy decorating for that. I want her to experience a Catalina Cove Christmas."

A huge smile touched Dani's lips. "I remember Christmas on the Main and how much fun it was. I guess there's still the lighting of the Christmas tree, Christmas Wonderland and the boat parade?"

"Yes, and since I'm a part of the Christmas planning committee, I need to be involved in most of the events."

Dani came to sit beside Sierra on the sofa. "One thing I can say, it was fun growing up in Catalina Cove and the holidays were the best."

Sierra saw Dani had a whimsical look on her face. "If I didn't know better, Dani, I'd say you're homesick."

Dani chuckled. "I honestly believe I am. I love living in Atlanta, but there's nothing like Catalina Cove. All it took was a week here to make me see the contrast between the two places. They are as different as night and day."

Sierra nodded. "Do you think you'd ever move back here?"

"Maybe one day. Emory and I have talked about it a few times. He likes it here, too. We even talked about looking into buying a place here to use as a summer retreat. Then it will be a place we can retire to years from now."

"That would be awesome."

"Yes, I think so, too," Dani said. "I understand Reid Lacroix will be developing land for homes near the gulf. I heard there's a list of interested buyers already."

"I wouldn't doubt it," Sierra said, looking at her phone when a text message came in. It was from Vaughn. Returning home tonight instead of tomorrow night.

Her lips slid into a smile. "Vaughn just texted me that he's coming home tonight instead of tomorrow night."

"Umm, sounds like he missed you as much as you missed him."

Sierra frowned at her sister. "I didn't say I missed him."

Dani laughed. "You didn't have to. I recognized that pitiful look in your eyes. It's the same expression any woman gets when she misses her man. Trust me, I know. Then it's followed by urges to jump his bones when you see him."

Sierra rolled her eyes. "That's how you operate, not me, Dani. I'll see Vaughn tomorrow sometime after you guys leave."

"Why wait when he's coming home today? I bet the reason he's coming home early is because he misses you. And regardless of what you say, I know you missed him as well."

Sierra did miss him, and she had told him that when they had texted each other. "It doesn't matter. Have you forgotten I have Teryn with me?"

Now it was Dani who rolled her eyes. "Stop making excuses. You weren't going home tonight. You and Teryn were spending the last night here with us. Teryn and Crane are joined at the hips anyway. She can spend the night here like we planned, but you can spend the night with your guy. Then we can all meet up for breakfast in the morning at Witherspoon Café so I can have some of their blueberry muffins before we fly back to Atlanta. Besides, I want to meet him."

"You know him already."

"I told you I used to see him whenever he picked up his sister from cheerleading practice. He was a knockout then. For all I know, he might have gotten bald and have a gut. You claim he's hot, but I need to see him for myself."

Sierra nibbled her lip. "For all I know, he might be tired when he gets in. He might not want any company. He might be—"

"Stop it, Sierra. There was a reason he texted you to let you know he was arriving a day early."

"You think so?"

"Of course I do, and I think this calls for a surprise."

"A surprise?" Sierra echoed, knowing that she really shouldn't. Her sister's ideas could be totally outlandish at times.

"Yes. Text Vaughn back and let him think that tomorrow

would be the earliest he'll see you because you're spending time here with your family. Then go home, get sexy, pack an overnight bag, and when you know he's home, pay him a booty call surprise visit."

Sierra's body felt hot with the thought of what Dani suggested. "I can't do that."

"Sure, you can. I used to do it all the time before Emory and I got married. One time I showed up naked beneath a trench coat for makeup sex."

Sierra shook her head. "That was too much information, Dani."

Her sister laughed. "I know, but I enjoyed telling you about it anyway. So, will you do it or are you just claiming to be Miss Independent?"

Sierra tilted her head back and blew out a deep breath. She straightened her head and looked at her sister. "Yes, I will do it."

Vaughn's plane had landed, and since he'd left his SUV at the airport, it hadn't taken him long to get home. It wasn't until after the plane landed that he received Sierra's text letting him know she couldn't see him until tomorrow. It had been a disappointing drive from the airport in New Orleans to home. Once here, he immediately took a shower then grabbed a beer and came out on the patio to stare out at the gulf and relax.

It was dark, but he could see the flashing lights of boats cruising by. He had begun missing Sierra so much that he'd cut his time with Zara short by a day. She had understood. Hell, his sister had understood way too much. In fact, she'd been the one to put the idea in his head to come back early. Only problem was, he hadn't planned things well. Actually, he hadn't planned things at all. He'd just acted on emotions and hadn't taken time to recall that Sierra's family was in town, and she'd mentioned they wouldn't be leaving until late Sunday. That meant they were still here, and he couldn't expect her to leave them just because he'd decided to come back early.

So here he was, sitting in his favorite patio chair, staring out at the gulf and missing Sierra even more. At least he was only a few miles away from her instead of thousands of miles away. And even now he was getting turned on knowing they were breathing the same air. Catalina Cove air.

More than anything, he wanted Sierra to see how good things could be if their relationship went in a different direction, and she could love him as much as he loved her.

And he did love her. He had finally accepted just what Sierra meant to him.

He was about to take the final sip of his beer when he heard the doorbell. It was close to nine. Who in their right mind would be visiting at this hour? Most of his friends knew he was out of town. The only person who was aware of his early return was Sierra.

He quickly headed for the door, trying to downplay the excitement rushing up his spine in case he was wrong. Her text had said she couldn't see him until tomorrow. Had she changed her mind and come anyway? Now he was practically racing to the door as adrenaline flowed through his veins.

When he reached the door, he paused to glance through the peephole. When he saw it was Sierra, he snatched the door open. He wasn't sure why she was there—and frankly, he didn't care. He was too elated to see her. Without a word, he pulled her into his arms.

CHAPTER TWENTY-SEVEN

Not for the first time, Sierra thought Vaughn was the best kisser on this earth. This kiss was raw, unapologetically intense, and he took her mouth for all it was worth. With determination, he was making this toe-curling kiss spill right into her very soul.

She felt herself being swept into his arms and carried across the threshold and heard when he slammed the door shut. He had managed to do that all while kissing her. And from the way his tongue was tangling with hers, he wasn't finished yet. He hadn't taken time to ask why she was there. Evidently it didn't matter.

He finally broke off the kiss and eased her to her feet, leaning his forehead against hers as they both tried to slow down their ragged breathing. And then, he was ravishing her mouth again, deepening the pressure. Chances were her mouth would be swollen tomorrow but she honestly didn't care. She rather liked being taken by strong, hard lips.

Vaughn finally released her mouth again. "I missed you."

His words were a whispered caress across her lips. He'd gone on trips before. What had made this one so different for the both of them? "I missed you, too."

He smiled at that. "You came."

She nodded. "Yes, I came."

"What about your family?" he asked, burying his face in the hollow of her throat. She could hear him inhale deeply, as if he needed to soak up her scent.

"My parents left today, and my sister, her husband and the kids are leaving tomorrow. Dani understood that I wanted to see you tonight."

He lifted his head to look at her. "What about Teryn?"

It was thoughtful of him to ask. "Dani is keeping Teryn. I'll join them for breakfast in the morning at the Witherspoon Café. You are invited to join us."

"Thanks, and I'd love to." Then, as if he suddenly realized all she'd said, he asked, "So, you're free to spend the night?"

She eased closer to him. "Only if I'm asked, Vaughn."

He lifted her chin so their gazes could meet. "Will you spend the night with me?"

She wrapped her arms around his neck and smiled up at him. "Yes, I'd be happy to."

He swept her into his arms again and headed toward the bedroom. He gently set her on his bed.

His bed.

"Why are you looking around like that? It's not like this is your first time in here," Vaughn said, easing on the bed beside her.

"I know, but the last time I was too busy trying to get you back inside of me to pay any real attention."

That was an understatement. All she could think about was that she had to be home by two and she had wanted as much of him as she could get.

"I'm glad you're here and we don't have to beat the clock this time."

She sat up. "I'm glad as well. How was your trip?"

He slipped off the bed and began pulling his shirt over his

head. Sierra loved looking at his perfectly toned abs. "Good. It's always that way when Zara and I get together. But…"

She switched her gaze from his muscular bare chest to his face to the worried lines bunching his brow. "But what?"

"Something is bothering Zara, but I don't know what. I wish she would tell me so I can handle it for her."

Sierra crossed her arms over her chest. "Typical man who thinks a woman needs a man to handle anything for her. From what you've told me about Zara, she can very well handle things for herself. Whatever it is, I'm sure if she wants your help, she will ask for it."

"Your independent streak is showing, *cherie*," he said with a laugh.

"Then let it." She exhaled. "I didn't come here to argue with you, Vaughn."

Now he was sliding his pants down a pair of muscular thighs. "That's good because I don't intend to argue. All I want to do is make love to you. And you look beautiful by the way. That outfit looks stunning on you."

"Thank you." She wore one of her favorite blouses and a skirt Dani had gifted her last year. She had never worn it since it was a lot shorter than the skirts she usually wore.

"I like seeing your legs," he said with his eyes on her. "I hope to see more of them. But right now, I want to see more of you." He slowly walked back toward the bed. "You are sexy as hell, Sierra, all over."

He pulled her toward him and then reached out for her skirt and eased it off her body.

"Aren't you going to take off my shoes?"

Vaughn smiled at her. "Not yet. Seeing such a beautiful pair of legs in stilettos takes my breath away."

"You sound like a man who is not hard to please."

"I am a man who appreciates beauty, and I'm about to show you just how much."

When he had stripped her down to just her panties and bra, a huge grin tugged at his lips. "Oh, *cherie*," he whispered as he leaned in to trace a finger around the lacy edges of her panties before moving to the lacy cups of her bra. "Your underwear is going to be the death of me yet. They are always so damn sexy."

"I guess you can say it's a fetish of mine."

"One I definitely appreciate," he said. He took his time removing both.

When she was naked, she looked at her feet. "What about my shoes?"

"They stay on."

"Oh," she said, wondering how that would work since she'd never made love before with her shoes on.

"Tonight, I'm going to make you come more times than you can count, Sierra."

"Oh my," she said, when he leaned in close.

She believed him.

The moment Vaughn opened his eyes, he thought, *déjà vu*. Sierra was spread out on top of him. Same position, but a different bedroom. Last time he awoke to find her like this, they had been in her bed. Now they were in his.

They had made love all through the night and early morning. At times, he had been on top and then other times, he had let her have her way with him. He smiled while thinking he liked giving her that control because she made it most enjoyable. She'd told him that one summer she and Rhonda had worked on a farm in Texas and had learned how to ride horses. He could tell she'd been pretty damn good at it.

"Why are you smiling?"

He saw she'd awakened. "Memories of last night."

"Umm, in that case," her lips spread in a huge smile, "what does that tell you, Vaughn?"

That tells me that maybe you're softening. That you can find it in

*your heart to love me as much as I love you. To want to give marriage
a try again…with me. To give you my babies. To let me make you my
queen.*

Instead, he said, "It tells me memories of last night are making you smile, too."

"You're right about that."

She glanced around as if looking for a clock. When she didn't
see one, she asked, "What time is it?"

He picked up his cell phone off the nightstand. "A little past
seven."

"I need to grab my overnight bag from my car."

"I can do that. What time are we meeting your family for
breakfast?"

"At ten. They'll leave for the airport from the café."

"Then we have time to make more memories. What do you
say?"

She wrapped her arms around his neck. "I say bring it on."

After making love again, they showered together in the huge
claw-foot tub. As she finished dressing, Vaughn went to the
kitchen to grab a cup of coffee. When he came out of the
kitchen, she was standing in the living room and staring at the
staircase.

He gazed at her thinking how stunning she looked in a pair
of jeans and a pullover sweater.

"That's odd."

Her words got his attention. "What's odd?"

"These stairs."

Vaughn came to stand beside her and took a sip of coffee and
looked at the staircase. It was long and winding and he thought
one of the most striking features of the house. "What's so odd
about them?"

"The last time I was here, we made love on the stairs."

He smiled, remembering. "We sure as hell did."

"I felt something hard."

Vaughn chuckled. "*Cherie*, what you felt was me. I was hard."

She playfully jabbed an elbow into his side. "I'm talking about something hard on my butt."

"Then it was wood. These are the original stairs, and they were probably made from the finest wood."

"Yes, but I still find something odd."

He stared at the stairs he'd seen practically all his life and didn't see a single odd thing about them. "And just what do you find odd?"

She pointed. "The fourth stair. It's shaped a little differently. See?"

He studied the fourth stair, tilting his head left to right. At first, he didn't notice any difference, and then he did. Moving forward he rubbed around the area of the stair with the pad of his thumb. When he touched something that felt like a knot embedded in the wood, he pressed it and a side drawer opened.

"Well, I'll be damned," he said, feeling around inside the drawer and pulling out a velvet packet.

"What is it?" Sierra asked, coming to stand beside him.

"I'm not sure. Let's see."

Taking the packet over to the dining room table, he opened it up and pulled out a rolled-up sheet of paper. Unrolling it, he and Sierra stared at it, and then they looked at each other.

A wide smile touched her lips. "Well, it seems the mystery has been solved. Your great-great-great-great-grandmother Zara was Jean Lafitte's wife, and this marriage license proves it."

"The two of you found Jean Lafitte and Zara's actual marriage license?" Dani asked with an incredulous look on her face.

Sierra and Vaughn had joined her family for breakfast, and Sierra couldn't wait to tell everyone what they'd found.

"Yes! Can you believe it?"

"That's wonderful!"

Vaughn smiled. "Yes, I think so as well. It will be up to the historical society to verify its authenticity."

"Then what?" Sierra asked.

"I'm not sure, but we shall see. I tried calling my sister to tell her what we found but couldn't reach her. I believe she went to church, which is probably why her phone is off."

Breakfast was delicious. Vaughn, Emory and the kids had stacks of blueberry pancakes, eggs, bacon and sausage. Sierra and Dani settled for tea and blueberry muffins. More than once, Sierra glanced over at Vaughn, and he smiled and winked at her. Whenever he did so, she could actually feel a throb between her legs. Would there ever come a time when she would not desire him?

At least Dani was no longer ogling Vaughn like she'd never seen a good-looking man before when she had one sitting beside her. Emory might have trusted Dani enough to find her interest in Vaughn amusing but after a while Sierra was finding it annoying.

"My goddy and I are helping Mr. Vaughn decorate his boat for the Christmas light parade," Teryn exclaimed happily. That got all the kids talking about how much fun it would be and Dani's kids saying they wished they could be there to help.

Emory and Vaughn were getting along great, and Sierra was glad of that. Her niece and nephews had a lot of questions for Vaughn about his big boat that Teryn had told them about. Time slipped by and, before Sierra knew it, it was close to noon. Dani, Emory and the kids had to leave for the airport.

When Sierra hugged Dani, her sister whispered in her ear, "He's hot, sis. He's also a keeper. Don't mess things up."

Any other time, whenever her sister and family came to visit and they left, Sierra would always feel teary-eyed. As their car pulled away today, she felt differently. She still regretted them leaving, but when she looked down at Teryn, she saw her goddaughter was the one crying.

Sierra was about to say comforting words to Teryn when Vaughn surprised her and squatted in front of Teryn so they were eye level. "You recall what you told me the other day about the reason your front door is blue?"

Teryn nodded, wiping her eyes. "Yes."

"Well, will you do me a favor?"

"What, Mr. Vaughn?"

"My mom and dad are in heaven, too, and during Christmas they would hang this huge wreath on our front door. Do you think for this Christmas I can hang it on your door?"

A smile lit Teryn's face. She looked up at Sierra. "Can we, Goddy? Can we hang Mr. Vaughn's mommy and daddy's wreath on our door since they're in heaven, too?"

Sierra smiled and ran fingers through the curls on her god-daughter's head. "Yes. I think that would be special."

When Vaughn stood, she mouthed the words *thank you* to him.

He winked at her and then said, "We're close to the Ellorans' Ice Cream Shop. How about if we go get cones? And then I can give you the gift I bought for you while in Boston."

Teryn clapped to show her excitement and, squirming be-tween them, she gave one of her hands to Vaughn and the other to Sierra.

"Goddy! Goddy! Mr. Vaughn is here!"

Sierra wiped her hands on the kitchen cloth and looked down at Teryn. Smiling, she said, "It certainly sounds like it. Let's get the door and remember, no running down the stairs."

"And I love my necklace," Teryn said smiling.

Sierra doubted she would ever forget the happiness on Teryn's face when Vaughn presented her with a small gift-wrapped box. Inside was a gold chain necklace, custom designed and person-alized with the name Teryn. Receiving that gift had certainly made her goddaughter's day. After eating ice cream they had parted ways, with Vaughn going home to find the wreath he'd told Teryn about and Sierra and Teryn going home to unpack after the days spent at the family's lake house.

Sierra doubted Vaughn knew just how much his request to hang his parents' wreath on their door had meant to Teryn. She'd been talking about nothing else since. Her goddaughter now felt she had a kindred connection to Vaughn since they both had parents in heaven.

She had tried to get Teryn to hold off putting up the wreath for a couple of weeks—after all, they hadn't started decorating for Christmas yet. But Teryn pointed out that they would have to start decorating the café windows this week for the Christmas on the Main contest. Besides, Teryn reasoned, putting the wreath up now meant not having to put it up later.

Holding hands, they walked down the stairs together, and Sierra checked the peephole before opening the door. Vaughn stood there with a huge Christmas wreath in his hand, and the only way she could describe it was beautiful. She immediately thought the blueberry and sleigh-bell ornaments entwined in it would complement the blue door among all the greenery.

Teryn was clapping her hands and jumping up and down. "It looks lovely, Mr. Vaughn. It's going to make your mommy and daddy so happy, and mine, too."

Vaughn grinned. "You want to help me hang it?"

"Yes!"

Sierra watched Vaughn effortlessly place Teryn on his shoulder. It took Sierra's help in handing him the wreath to angle it perfectly in the center while adjusting the wreath hanger in place. He had to move it around a few times so it wasn't covering the peephole.

"What do you think?" he asked Sierra, smiling. Teryn was still perched on his shoulder, and it was obvious she was waiting for her godmother's response as well.

"I think it looks beautiful and both sets of parents are in heaven smiling because they are happy."

Teryn happily bobbed her head up and down. "They are! They are in the 'parents in heaven club' together and happy with what we did!"

"This calls for cookies and hot chocolate," Sierra said. "I just finished baking a batch. I hope you can stay and join us, Vaughn."

"There's nothing else I'd rather do than join my favorite ladies for cookies and hot chocolate," he said, easing Teryn off his shoulders.

The wide smile he gave Sierra touched her all over. He had made Teryn's day and in doing so, he had made hers as well.

CHAPTER TWENTY-EIGHT

Sierra surveyed her reflection in the full-length mirror. She and Vaughn would be going on their first official date. The plan was to have dinner at the Lighthouse Restaurant, stay to enjoy live music and dancing, and then walk along the pier to see all the decorated boats.

Tonight, the carolers started rehearsal and Velvet, who'd volunteered to help the group, was keeping Teryn. Sierra smiled when she heard the doorbell. Not surprisingly, Vaughn was right on time. Grabbing her purse and a shawl she headed downstairs. After checking through the peephole, she opened the door. "I'm ready."

She couldn't help but grin when Vaughn let out a whistle and raked his gaze over her from head to toe. He'd said that he liked seeing her legs and tonight he was seeing them. Her dress was one she hadn't worn in a while and was dressier than most.

"You look absolutely stunning," Vaughn said, smiling at her.

"Thanks, and you look stunning as well," she said. Although he wore business suits all the time, she still thought he looked dashing in anything he put on his body. She would also admit he looked good wearing nothing at all.

After thanking her for the compliment, he stepped back for her to close and lock the door, and then he escorted her to his car. Opening the door, he said, "I am a lucky man tonight to be dining with such a beautiful woman." He closed the door and walked around to get in on the other side.

He was full of compliments and Sierra appreciated every one of them. She'd been nervous about tonight, but now in his presence she felt good because going out on a date with him felt right.

When he got into the car and started the ignition, she said, "You'll be happy to know I informed Teryn this morning that I mailed off all three letters to Santa."

Vaughn had dropped by on Monday and handed Teryn his envelope with his one Christmas wish, after she had reminded him about it that Sunday over cookies and hot chocolate. That had pressured Sierra to do the same, and she'd decided to make it simple. Her one Christmas wish was for happiness for the new year.

Of course, they did not get mailed as she'd told Teryn. Sierra had read Teryn's letter to make sure everything on her Christmas wish list was purchased. Vaughn's letter was in her purse to give back to him tonight.

"I bet Teryn was overjoyed about it," Vaughn said grinning.

"She was, and I also want to thank you for helping to decorate the café's storefront."

It was hard to believe Christmas on the Main had started this week and the winner of the most decorated storefront would be chosen tomorrow, right after the lighting of the Christmas tree in the town's square. Since she was on the committee, it would be a busy Saturday for her. In fact, this week had been busy for both her and Vaughn, so she was looking forward to dinner and unwinding with dancing and a walk on the pier.

"How have things been going at work?" she asked.

Vaughn hadn't left town on any business trips this week, but he had worked long hours at the office. She would put soup aside for him to eat since he would always drop by the café after work.

"Great. I got word today that Evans Toussaint will start after the holidays. That was good news."

"It certainly is. He was well-liked in the cove."

"That's what everyone is telling me." When he came to a stop at the traffic light, he said, "I also have more good news."

"What?"

"The Louisiana Historical Society verified the marriage license for Lafitte and Zara as authentic."

"Oh, Vaughn, that is wonderful," she said, blinking back happy tears. "I always believed Lafitte married Princess Zara."

"Yes, I have you to thank for uncovering the truth." A teasing grin curved his lips. "Now I don't feel so bad for taking you on the stairs that night."

She laughed. "You should not have been feeling bad about it anyway. I hold that night as one of my most special memories."

"Thank you for saying that, *cherie*, because I hold it that way as well."

Sierra gazed out her window when he moved the car forward. She thought the days leading to Christmas in Catalina Cove were the best. Driving through town was like entering a Christmas wonderland. The streetlights around town had been transformed into candy canes and Christmas holly hung from most of the traffic lights.

When they pulled into the parking lot of the Lighthouse Restaurant, Vaughn brought the car to a stop and turned to her. "My ladies are still coming to my home for dinner on Sunday, right?"

Vaughn had invited her and Teryn to dinner. "Your ladies will be there with bells on," she said, smiling.

The Lighthouse Restaurant was the best place in Catalina Cove for elegant dining. Dinner had been wonderful and very few people gave them a second glance. Sierra figured news had spread around the cove they were seeing each other, so them sharing dinner was no big deal.

"Will you dance with me, Sierra?"

"I'd love to, just as long as you know it's been years since I've been out dancing."

He chuckled. "Same here."

The band was playing a good mix of music and when Vaughn pulled her into his arms for a slow dance, she thought they fit well together. For years she and Dani had taken dance lessons while growing up, but there was nothing like being held in the arms of a man you cared about.

And she did care about him, maybe a little too much. Funny how she'd begun shifting from wanting "just the moment" to wanting more. It could have started Saturday night when he'd returned from Boston early and she'd spent the night at his home. Or maybe it had been that Sunday when he had hung the wreath on the door with Teryn and later joined them for cookies and hot chocolate. It really didn't matter when she began shifting, what mattered was that she had.

They enjoyed three more dances together. It seemed the musicians had deliberately played slow tunes just for them.

When Vaughn took her hand and escorted her out of the restaurant for their walk on the pier, he glanced at his watch and then at her. "What time will Velvet be bringing Teryn home tonight?"

She smiled. "Since this is Friday night, Velvet suggested I let her spend the night. I'll pick her up in the morning."

Sierra could tell by the smile that reached all the way to that sexy dimple in his chin that Vaughn approved of that arrangement.

Three days later Sierra pushed away from the computer on her desk and looked at her watch. Velvet was dropping by the café for lunch and Sierra would be joining her. It had been a wonderful weekend. Dinner with Vaughn at the Lighthouse Restaurant Friday night had started things off.

Saturday, her committee had selected the winner of the

Christmas on the Main contest. All of the storefronts had been beautifully decorated, and it had been hard to choose just one. The winner had been the Ellorans' Ice Cream Shop.

Teryn had gotten so caught up in the holiday spirit that it was contagious. After church yesterday, she had convinced Sierra they needed a Christmas tree. Vaughn had joined them in picking one out and helping to decorate it. He had bought a tree for his home as well, and later, when they went to his house for dinner, they helped him decorate his.

Vaughn's cook had done an outstanding job and dinner had been delicious. Teryn kept telling him that his house was as big as a castle and that she had counted twenty-two rooms.

After dinner Vaughn showed them his new boat dock, and Teryn had suggested that it would be the perfect place for a huge, decorated Christmas tree. That way it could be seen by any boats passing by at night. He had agreed and suggested Teryn invite the kids in her first-grade class to help decorate. The event would be this coming weekend.

After news about it got around, Vaughn had called that morning with a great idea. Since a lot of the people living in the cove had never set foot on Zara's Haven, he thought now would be a good time for them to do so and he wanted to make Saturday a fun day for all. Sierra thought Vaughn's hospitality was more than generous and told him he didn't have to do everything Teryn suggested. However, it seemed he had liked the idea as much as Teryn.

When Sierra got up from her desk to join Velvet for lunch, all she could think about was that it would be another busy weekend.

"You look happy," Velvet told Sierra when she sat across from her in a booth a short while later.

Sierra couldn't help but smile. "I am. I think the holidays

bring out the happiness in people. Seeing Teryn happy makes me happy."

"And what about you and Vaughn?"

Yes, what about her and Vaughn? she thought, wondering how to define their relationship to Velvet. Hot and explosive quickly came to mind. However, it was more than just the physical. Now she could define their relationship as meaningful.

"I really like Vaughn and enjoy the time we spend together. He's very attentive when it comes to Teryn and goes out of his way to include her in many of our activities." She paused a moment and added, "Vaughn is someone I can talk to about anything."

Velvet nodded. "Do you see forever in your future with him?"

Sierra paused and then said, "Forever is a long time, but if I was honest, I would have to say yes. I thought I would never think that way again, but I do." To change the subject, Sierra asked, "Are you going to the town hall meeting Thursday night?"

"Yes, I plan to go," Velvet said. "I understand they'll unveil the new housing development on Lacroix land, update us on the water-taxi service and tell us who's taking over the bank now that Mr. Barrows is retiring."

"Sounds like a meeting none of us should miss," Sierra said. "I agree."

Suddenly, Sierra felt a presence by their table and the hairs on the back of her neck stood up.

She looked up and saw Nathan and she couldn't hold back a gasp of shock. Her ex-husband was the last person she expected to see here in Catalina Cove. The last person she'd expected to see ever. She frowned. "What are you doing here, Nathan?"

Not bothering to display manners by acknowledging Velvet, he said, "We need to talk, Sierra."

Her frown deepened. "We don't have anything to talk about."

A smirk appeared on his face. "I beg to differ."

Sierra glanced around and saw they were drawing attention. "Differ all you want. Please leave, Nathan."

"Trust me. You'll want to hear what I have to say. It's about your goddaughter."

Levi walked over to ask, "Sierra, is this man being a nuisance? Do you want me to call the sheriff?"

Nathan was tall but Levi was a lot taller and although he might be older, he carried himself like the ex-cop that he was.

She started to tell Levi to go ahead and call the sheriff, and then she thought better of it. What did Nathan mean that whatever he had to say concerned Teryn? Not for one minute did she think it did, but people were looking at them and she didn't want to cause a scene.

"No, I'll handle this," she said to Levi.

Sierra turned to Velvet and saw the concern in her friend's eyes. "It's okay. I'll call you later."

She narrowed her eyes at Nathan when she stood. "We can talk in my office. This way."

"You better have a good reason for coming here, Nathan," Sierra said, practically slamming her office door shut behind them. It had been two years since she'd last seen him, and little about him had changed. He still paid a lot for his clothes, and it was obvious he still spent time at the gym. Although she didn't want to admit it, he was a handsome man. However, as far as she was concerned, Vaughn was better-looking, more fit and a sharper dresser.

Nathan had the audacity to go to her desk and lean against it. He glanced around her office with an appraising eye. Then he smiled at her and said, "Nice setup you have here, although I think it's a waste of your skills. You were a darn good software development manager at Smithfield and Tyler. I ran into your former boss the other day and he still regrets losing you."

Sierra refused to get off topic with him. "I asked, why are you here, Nathan?" She crossed her arms over her chest. He would find out soon enough she wasn't the same woman he'd been married to. Now she had a backbone and could think for herself.

"I would have called instead of coming here if you hadn't blocked my number."

"Blocking your number was the only way I could assure that you stopped calling me with your foolishness."

"Getting back with you is not foolishness, Sierra. For me it means financial survival. The company I work for was taken over by a new group. The CEO, Mr. Charles, is a real asshole."

"It takes one to know one," she said snidely.

Nathan had the audacity to laugh. "Wow, my kitten has grown claws. Now back to what I was saying, this CEO is a traditionalist who doesn't believe in divorces. He has this thing about your first wife being your forever wife and all that bullshit."

Sierra rolled her eyes. "And this affects me how?"

"I've temporarily been removed from the promotability list. We need to remarry by January. I figured we won't need to stay together any more than three years. By then Mr. Charles will have retired, and I would have gotten that promotion I've been working my ass off to get."

Sierra stared at Nathan, not believing what she was hearing and getting royally pissed. She drew in a deep breath, trying to keep her temper under control. "I don't know what plan you've concocted in your mind to save some promotion status, but you're sadly mistaken if you think I'll have anything to do with you."

He gave her that smirky smile she'd always detested. "You have no choice…not if you want to keep full custody of your goddaughter."

That was the second time he'd mentioned Teryn, which gave her pause. "What does any of this have to do with Teryn?"

He straightened and sauntered over to stand in front of her.

She appreciated that it wasn't too close. He shoved his hands into his pockets. "It seems there is an old law on the books in Illinois that directly affects us. I didn't know about it until my attorney recently discovered it. Until the day our divorce was final, any legal dealings either you or I made separately, are still considered joint ventures. In other words, sweetheart, since your adoption of that little girl became final before our divorce, I am just as much her legal guardian as you are. Therefore, I had my attorney petition the state court for joint custody."

Sierra's head began spinning. What Nathan was saying couldn't be true. It just couldn't. "When I adopted Teryn, you and I were separated."

He shrugged. "That might have been the case, but it doesn't matter. In the eyes of Illinois law, we were still legally married."

He chuckled as he looked around her office again. "Cheer up, sweet-cakes. It could have been worse. Just think if you would have closed the deal on this place before our divorce. Then you and I would have been equal partners of your restaurant. Imagine that."

Sierra's entire body became consumed with anger. She took a step toward him, not caring that she was all in his face. "You bastard. You never wanted kids. Why would you want joint custody of Teryn?"

The eyes staring at her went cold and she felt anger radiating off of him. "Because I know how much that kid means to you. That's the only way to get what I want. So hear me and hear me well, Sierra. Unless you agree to remarry me for at least three, maybe four years, or until that bastard Charles decides to retire, I will take you to court to get that kid during the summer months."

She scoffed, thinking he had to be bluffing. "This will never stand in court, Nathan."

"Try me. My attorney has already filed a petition for joint custody, so you might want to contact your attorney. You'll be getting our court date soon, hopefully before Christmas, unless you agree to remarry me before New Year's Day. You have one week to give me your answer. You know how to reach me."

He moved around her, opened the door and walked out.

CHAPTER TWENTY-NINE

Vaughn stepped off the elevator and headed toward his office. This coming weekend he would be hosting a tree-decorating fun day for Teryn and her entire first-grade class.

He sat at his desk thinking about Sierra and their Friday night, especially when they'd made love after he returned her home after dinner. Just thinking about it filled him with an inner peace. He'd felt a love so strong for her, more than once he'd almost blurted it out during one of the most explosive orgasms that he'd ever shared with her.

He was deep in his musings about the time he'd made love to Sierra on her desk and imagining making love to her on his when the buzzer on his desk sounded. Slightly irritated at the intrusion, he pressed the button. "Yes, Kate?"

"There's a young lady here to see you."

"Who is it?" he asked.

"Sierra Crane."

His body jerked in his seat. Sierra was here? She'd never paid a visit to his office before. "Please send her in."

He was already out of his chair and heading for the door when it opened. The moment it did, his smile vanished abruptly. What the hell? She wasn't crying but he could tell from her expression that she was barely holding back her fury. He reached behind her and quickly closed the door then pulled her into his arms.

"What is it, Sierra?" he asked, holding her tight. He felt her body tremble in his arms. "*Cherie*, what's wrong?"

She drew back and looked up at him. The anger in her features was even more intense. "Nathan came to see me."

He frowned. "Nathan? Your ex-husband?"

"Yes."

Vaughn's body hardened with the rage he saw in her eyes. "What the hell did he want?" he asked through clenched teeth.

Sierra released a deep breath and said, "He wants us to remarry in order to get a promotion at work."

"What?" He tightened his arms around her and kissed her forehead. "I think you need to start from the beginning." He led her over to the love seat.

It took Sierra nearly twenty minutes to tell him everything from start to finish. Vaughn figured it might have taken her less time if he hadn't asked so many damn questions, but that couldn't be helped. He figured Nathan Flowers had to be out of his damn mind. When she'd finished, he said calmly, "Don't worry about anything, Sierra."

She pulled out of his arms and stared at him. "What do you mean?"

He wrapped his arms around her again. "I don't want you to worry because I got this. I'll handle Flowers."

Sierra pulled away from him with an angry glare. "No, you will not. I've already contacted my attorney, and he says old laws like that are getting eradicated off the books. He will file a motion to—"

"File a motion, my ass. All that takes time. According to Flowers, the two of you are scheduled to meet with a judge before Christmas."

"My attorney will ask for a postponement, Vaughn."

"And what if he doesn't get it?"

She released a frustrated breath. "Why are you being so pessimistic?"

"Sierra, I'm just being realistic here. You need to let me handle this. I know someone who—"

"I said no, Vaughn. I didn't come here for you to run roughshod over this. I don't need you to act like a knight in shining armor. I am not a woman who needs saving. I can handle my own business."

She exhaled. Then in a soft voice, she said, "The reason I came here was because I was so upset about it, and I needed you to hold me. I don't need you to solve my problems. Besides, you don't know Nathan like I do. He has a mean streak and if pushed, he will go for blood."

"I don't mind him going for blood. In fact, I would love to give him a taste of his own," Vaughn spat out, standing.

Sierra also stood. "You will do no such thing, Vaughn Miller." Her chin was tilted up a little and she was glaring at him fiercely. It was clear she was ready to go toe-to-toe with him if she had to.

"And you expect me to do nothing?" he snapped.

She put her hands on her hips. "What I expect you to do is to let me handle my business. Like I told you, I've contacted my attorney."

She turned to head for the door, but he reached out and pulled her into his arms again. She resisted at first and then her head fell against his chest. "I will handle this, Vaughn. Teryn is my goddaughter. I promised Rhonda I would take care of her and I mean to do that. I don't want her around Nathan. He'll use her to spite me."

Vaughn tightened his arms and simply held her, saying nothing. Moments later she lifted her head. "Tell me that you will let me handle my business."

He stared at her for a long while and then said, "I will let you handle your business."

★ ★ ★

Vaughn saw the relieved look that appeared in Sierra's eyes. Nathan Flowers would pay dearly for upsetting her this way. The man was a lunatic. Custody rights, his ass. The man could take those rights and shove them. There was no way Vaughn would ever let the man near Teryn.

"I feel better now," she said, trying to smile. "I knew all I needed from you was a hug."

A hug might be all she thought she needed from him, but he was about to give her a lot more. Leaning down he captured her mouth with his, and knew her concentration had shifted when she began purring. Or had it been when she began feasting on his tongue as greedily as he was feasting on hers. It didn't matter, he knew they both felt all that sexual energy rocking their bones.

Suddenly, he pulled back and released his hold on her. He went to the door and locked it. It made a loud clicking sound in the quiet room.

"What do you think you're doing?" she asked, watching him.

Vaughn smiled. "What does it look like I'm doing?" He removed his tie, then began unbuttoning his shirt.

Her eyes flew wide. "We can't do anything in here. This is your office."

He gave a smooth chuckle. "And? I recall us making out in your office plenty of times."

"You can't make love to me here, Vaughn," she said, backing away and looking around the room, as if searching for a place to run or hide.

"You want to bet, *cherie*? In fact, when Kate announced you, I'd been imagining you naked and spread out on my desk."

Her eyes widened even more. "You weren't."

"Trust me, I was," he said, sliding his slacks and briefs down his legs. "Lose the skirt, Sierra," he said, enjoying watching her watch him.

She'd seen him undress for her many times, but it was certainly a boost to his ego to see just how attentive she was as he stripped now. He wasn't just aroused, he was mega-aroused, and she was watching things develop right before her eyes.

"Your skirt, Sierra," he repeated when she just stood there staring at him below the waist and licking her lips.

Vaughn watched her slip her skirt down a pair of gorgeous legs and then remove her sweater. "Nice undies, yet again," he said, and felt himself get even more aroused, if such a thing was possible. Today her lace bra and panty set was red and sexy as hell.

When she was about to step out of her shoes, which weren't stilettos but a pair of ankle boots, he said, "Leave them on."

Her brows lifted. "What's with you and my shoes?"

He smiled. "The same thing with me and your panties and bras. They are a total turn-on. Right now, the panties and bra have to go, but not the shoes."

Vaughn walked toward her and she backed away, stopping when her legs hit his desk. He made short work of removing her bra. It took him a minute with the panties since he had to work them over her ankle boots. When they were both naked, he lifted her and placed her on his desk. Moving between her spread legs, he coaxed her to wrap them, shoes and all, around his waist.

He reached for her breasts and cupped them in his hands, loving the way his fingertips were making her nipples hard. "Maybe I should warn you that Kate has good ears so you might want to keep your voice low. In other words, Sierra. You can't scream."

"I don't scream."

He chuckled. "Yes, you do. I usually capture it with my mouth so you don't wake Teryn. I can't help you here."

She frowned. "Why not?"

Vaughn smiled. "Because I need to keep myself from hollering. Like I told you, making love with you on this desk has been a fantasy of mine for a while. So indulge me." He'd been teasing about Kate hearing them. It was after five and she'd left for the day, and so had anyone else with offices on this floor.

"Shouldn't we talk about this?" she asked, as he sheathed himself in a condom.

"What? My fantasy, your screaming or Kate hearing us?"

"All three."

"I'm letting this speak for me," he said, slowly easing his engorged penis inside of her. He pulled out, then quickly thrust back in, setting a slow rhythm. "Do you hear what it's saying?"

She didn't say anything, but the way she was looking at him—and her body was responding—said it all. "You're wet, *cherie*. So freaking wet," he said.

He felt her inner muscles tighten around him. When he couldn't take any more of her muscles clenching him, he began moving fast, then faster. Then he nearly went crazy and all but got on top of her on the desk.

Her moans were getting louder and when he leaned in and captured a nipple in his mouth and began sucking hard, he knew she was about to scream. He quickly left her breasts to cover her mouth. He wasn't ready for her to come yet.

After a frenzy of several hard thrusts, he threw his head back and let out a deep, possessive growl. Like the Energizer Bunny he kept going and going, thrusting harder, practically nonstop. Suddenly, simultaneously, they came. She screamed and he hollered as their bodies exploded in a powerful climax.

He leaned forward to take her mouth with a gentle kiss. This woman had become everything to him. Bottom line, he was madly in love.

A couple hours later, after making love a second time on his love seat, they dressed. He walked her to the elevator and out of the building so she wouldn't have any problems with evening security.

Back in his office he stood at the window, watching her drive away. Then he retrieved the cell phone from his desk drawer and punched in three numbers, 767, speed dial for SOS. The phone was answered on the first ring.

"What's the emergency, Vaughn?"

Vaughn exhaled. "I need to give you an assignment and, un-fortunately, you won't have a lot of time. I need it taken care of before Christmas."

"What is it?" Deke asked.

After Vaughn told him, Deke said, "Consider it done."

CHAPTER THIRTY

As Velvet and Sierra waited for the town hall meeting to start, Velvet leaned in to ask, "Have you heard anything from your attorney?"

Sierra smiled. "No. I'm hoping the saying that no news is good news turns out to be true."

"I hope so, too," Velvet said as she glanced around the hall. It was packed tonight. A lot of people had come out. Evidently, like her, they wanted to hear the news firsthand.

Velvet was especially interested in the housing development on Lacroix land. She'd fallen in love with the cove and could see herself living here permanently. Her lease at the rental where she lived would expire soon, and now was the time to think of buying her own place.

It was nearly seven. The meeting was about to begin. One thing she'd learned about the people living in the cove, they believed in starting a meeting on time and finishing on time as well.

She and Sierra had been lucky enough to find good seats in the middle of the room. There were still two vacant seats next to her and less than a minute before the meeting was to start,

Laura Crawford and her brother Webb arrived and claimed those seats. Velvet met Sierra's gaze and, without saying a word, they deciphered each other's thoughts. *Why us?*

At exactly seven o'clock the meeting was called to order. The mayor, who was presiding over the meeting, went over old business and pending business before they got into the new business. First up was the housing development. From the sound of it, it would be nice. A huge screen for all to see was erected that showed the diagram of where the housing development would be. All of it on Lacroix land and some would be oceanfront.

Velvet turned to Sierra and said, "I'm thinking about buying one of those lots."

Sierra smiled and before she could respond, Laura, who'd obviously overheard Velvet's statement, leaned close to them and said, "I doubt you could afford it on a teacher's salary, Velvet."

The woman didn't even try to whisper. In fact the couple sitting in front of them overheard and glanced back at Velvet. She was about to tell Laura that she had no idea what she could or could not afford when she decided not to even bother. Let her believe whatever she wanted.

Next on the agenda was the water-taxi service. Ray Sullivan did a great presentation. Afterward, a number of people raised their hands and were called on to stand and ask their questions. It was obvious everyone was excited that the service would launch in the spring.

Last on the agenda was the issue of the bank. Everyone paid attention as Reid Lacroix stood to speak. "As most of you know, Larson Barrows has decided to retire. We appreciate Larson and the Barrows family for taking care of all of our banking needs here in the cove for over fifty years."

Reid paused while the audience gave Larson a standing ovation. Then Reid continued, "It was important that whatever financial institution took things over understood the specific needs of our community. I must say the bank that has bought out Barrows truly impressed me."

"That's a good thing," Laura whispered to Webb, but not low enough where others close by couldn't hear. "Everybody knows that old coot has the most money in town."

Sierra and Velvet looked at each other again. Although Laura and Webb had thought her comment amusing, they had not.

"The bank we selected," Reid was saying, "is a national bank, so not only will they be able to take care of our financial needs but will give us access to a nationwide network, which is something I'm sure these young people moving back to the cove will appreciate."

There was a burst of loud clapping from the young people in the audience. When they finished, Reid said, "The name of the bank is Colfax National Bank and tonight you will hear from their CEO, Jaye Colfax."

Velvet gasped, and when Sierra looked at her, she shook her head, letting her know she was alright.

The truth was that Velvet was *not* alright. The one man she'd hoped she would never see again, the one man she'd relocated to Catalina Cove to get away from, to move on with her life, was here.

Jaye stood up from the front row and turned to face the audience. The moment Velvet saw him, her heart—which she'd hoped had recovered—let her know it still ached. All it took was to see him to know she still loved him.

"Damn, he's hot," she heard Laura say. When Velvet glanced over at Laura, she saw blatant feminine interest in her expression.

Velvet's mind began whirling. Did Jaye know she lived in Catalina Cove? Was he aware she was in the audience? So far, his eyes hadn't connected with hers, so chances were he didn't know either of those things. Of all the coincidences to happen, why her?

After Jaye introduced himself, he asked if anyone had questions. Several hands went up, including Laura's. Luckily he picked someone other than Laura. Velvet's heart was racing. If Jaye hadn't seen her before, when he called on Laura, there was no way he wouldn't see her. Velvet was sitting next to Laura, he wouldn't be able to miss her.

She knew the moment he looked in Laura's direction and saw her. Although he pointed to Laura and asked her to state her question, Velvet knew his gaze was directly on her. She immediately felt heat spike through her body and she squirmed in her seat. Jaye had always had that kind of an effect on her, and it seemed in two years nothing had changed.

"Yes, Mr. Colfax. Will you be making Catalina Cove your home?" Laura asked.

Jaye smiled and the heat inside Velvet intensified. Nobody had a smile like Jaye with dimples in both cheeks. "Yes, I'll be living here during the initial start-up period, which will be about six months."

"Are you married? Will there be a Mrs. Colfax joining you?"

Velvet couldn't believe Laura would ask such a thing and from the expressions on the faces of others, no one seemed surprised. Some even chuckled. Jaye continued to hold Velvet's gaze, although she was certain Laura assumed he was looking at her. "No, I'm not married. There isn't a Mrs. Jaye Colfax."

Nor will there ever be, Velvet thought. *You've made it clear so many times that you're not the marrying kind.*

"Thank you for answering my questions." The moment Laura sat back down she turned to her brother and stated, "I intend to change that."

Velvet was tempted to tell Laura not to hold her breath. But then, maybe Laura might turn out to be the kind of woman Jaye wanted, since he definitely hadn't wanted her.

Jaye took a few more questions before turning the meeting back over to the mayor. Jaye had taken a seat and Velvet was glad his back was to her. She would not have been able to handle it if he'd looked at her a minute longer.

"Thanks everyone for attending tonight's meeting," the mayor was saying. "The turnout was great and we want to encourage everyone to participate in the holiday activities planned for Catalina Cove. Good night."

Velvet stood, intending to leave as soon as possible, and noticed how Laura and a couple of other single women were rushing toward where Jaye stood. She couldn't blame their interest since he was a very handsome man and he'd stated he was single.

She turned to Sierra. "I'll see you Saturday at that fun-day event on Zara's Haven. Hopefully you'll have good news from your attorney by then."

Sierra smiled. "Let's hope." She studied Velvet. "Are you okay?"

Velvet nodded. "We'll talk when I see you again."

"Okay."

Velvet headed for the exit and, unable to help herself, when she reached the door, she glanced over her shoulder. Although Laura and the other women were all in Jaye's face, his gaze was locked on her. Velvet felt the heat of that gaze in every part of her body.

Inhaling deeply, she turned and walked out the door.

"You're such a softie," Sierra said, leaning up on tiptoe to place a kiss on Vaughn's cheek. She looked around and saw all the kids on the grounds of Zara's Haven, and they were having the time of their lives.

Vaughn wrapped his arms around her waist. "Hey, what can I say? When I discovered there were only two first-grade classes at Catalina Cove Elementary School, there was no way I could invite Teryn's class and not invite the other. Especially when school ended for the kids yesterday and the holiday break officially began."

"Yes, but the pony rides, bouncing house and a surprise visit from Santa were not part of the original plans," she said, laughing.

He grinned. "I know. Santa was Zara's idea when I told her about it. She asked how I could have a bunch of first graders and not invite Santa."

"Good question," Sierra said, pushing hair from her face. She wasn't sure who was enjoying themselves the most, the kids or the adults.

The kids had decorated the huge Christmas tree that was on the new dock and, later, right before dusk, Teryn would do the honors and flip the switch to light up the tree. Vaughn thought it was most appropriate since this whole thing had been her idea. And thanks to Reid's wife, Gloria, each child would leave with a Christmas stocking filled with treats with their names embroidered at the top. That would be another surprise for the kids.

The weather had turned out to be perfect. A number of people had passed by on their boats and tooted their horns. Sierra couldn't believe all the food Vaughn had had catered. There were hot dogs and hamburgers for the kids, and thanks to Kaegan and Bryce, who'd figured the adults might outnumber the kids, a tent was set up to serve blue crabs, shrimp, crawfish and lobster—as well as grilled spare ribs.

Sierra hadn't realized just how large the grounds of Zara's Haven were. There were six guest cottages on the property, a miniature golf course and a huge swimming pool. The pool, Vaughn had told her, had been added when he had been in junior high school.

Reid's twin granddaughters, who were home from college, were great with the kids, and Velvet had helped as well. It was a fun day and a busy day. Staying busy was what Sierra needed. It kept her mind off her problem with Nathan. Every time she thought about it, she grew angrier.

Not surprising, it had been Vaughn's lovemaking and frequent hugs that calmed her down. He'd stopped by every night since

Nathan's visit and she appreciated it. When she had talked to her attorney after Nathan's visit Monday, he felt pretty confident that she didn't have anything to worry about. She hoped he was right.

Later, when the sun went down, everyone gathered at the dock to watch Teryn flip the switch. Sierra doubted her goddaughter had been this happy since losing her parents.

When the lights on the huge Christmas tree came on, cheers went up and Teryn happily jumped up and down. It was a beautiful tree and next to the water it was even more so.

Teryn turned to Vaughn and he picked her up and she gave him a big hug. Looking at the two of them made Sierra's heart almost burst when she realized she was gazing at the two people she loved most in this world.

Love?

She drew in a sharp breath. She'd loved Teryn since the day she was born. But Vaughn? Did she love him, too? She knew the answer when he looked at her and smiled. At that moment she accepted what her heart had been trying to tell her for a while. She had fallen in love with Vaughn.

CHAPTER THIRTY-ONE

"You have good news for me, Marvin?" Sierra asked her attorney in a hopeful voice. Marvin was the husband of one of her good friends from college. It had been a week and she'd been trying to think positive although Nathan expected her decision today.

There was a pause, and she had a feeling whatever he had to tell her wasn't anything she wanted to hear. "Marvin?"

"I don't have good news for you, Sierra. Instead, it's pretty bad. Nathan Flowers was fired from his job today."

That came as a shocker, but she recovered quickly. "How is that bad? Losing his job is his problem, not mine."

"He doesn't think so. In fact, he's convinced you had something to do with it."

Sierra rolled her eyes. "Let him think what he wants because I had nothing to do with it."

"Are you sure, Sierra? Is anyone working behind the scenes on your behalf to ruin Nathan?"

She immediately thought of Vaughn, but then dismissed the idea. She had asked him not to get involved and he'd told her that he wouldn't. She believed him. "No. There's no one working behind the scenes to ruin Nathan on my behalf. Why would you think that?"

"Because according to Nathan's attorney, his employer received a packet detailing some of Nathan's extracurricular activities."

Sierra's eyebrows drew together. "What extracurricular activities?"

"Nathan's attorney wouldn't go into any details. Whatever the packet contained, it was enough to get him fired."

"Good. Then he can't continue with his custody suit," she said, feeling hope spring to life inside of her.

"No, that won't be the case. Whatever information his boss received was enough for his employer to fire him, but according to his attorney, it cannot be used to deny him custody of his child."

"Teryn is *not* his child, Marvin."

"Legally, she is."

Sierra began pacing. "Let me get this straight. Nathan was fired and he thinks I was behind it and is blaming me?"

"Yes. He'd worked for that company a long time and he was obsessed with getting that promotion. Now he believes you've taken that away and feels he has nothing to lose and wants to make you pay."

Sierra swallowed deeply. "Make me pay how?"

There was another pause. "Marvin?"

"Nathan's attorney has requested a special court hearing with the judge on Friday. He has changed his demands, Sierra. Now he wants Teryn six months out of the year instead of just for the summers. He's also requesting that he gets her this Christmas since you had her last Christmas."

"What!"

"Like I said, he's out for blood and will hurt you any way that he can."

"And he thinks nothing of using Teryn to do it," Sierra said angrily and continued pacing. "There has to be something we can do."

"I tried pushing back to get another court date, but my request was denied. I don't know how his employer got that information that got him fired, but it was really bad timing. I was close to working something out with his attorney by pressuring him to get Flowers to drop his petition or else I would advise Nathan's boss and explain to him why you got the divorce in the first place. Since the CEO is a traditionalist, that information was going to be our ace card, Sierra. Now that has been taken off the table. I have to think of a new strategy before Friday. The meeting will be with you, Nathan and the judge. Attorneys won't be allowed. The judge is hoping the two of you can work something out that will be in the best interests of Teryn."

"Nathan has no interest in what's best for her. You and I both know it, Marvin."

"Yes, and it will be up to you to convince the judge of that, Sierra."

Sierra blinked back tears. She wouldn't cry. She wouldn't. "Maybe I should call Nathan and—"

"No, Sierra. No matter what you do, do not contact Nathan Flowers. He will deliberately twist your words when you meet with the judge. He's already claiming that for the past two years he's been reaching out to you trying to determine the welfare of the child and you refused to tell him anything."

"That's a lie! At no time when Nathan called me has he asked about Teryn."

"It will be your word against his and trust me, Nathan is going to try to paint himself as the victim and you as the bad guy."

Sierra released a disgusted sigh. "I found my husband in bed with two other people and I'm the bad guy?"

"You had every right to divorce him for adultery and you did. On the other hand, what consenting adults do in the bedroom is not against the law. That's what we're dealing with, Sierra. Just because he's a swinger doesn't mean he can't be a good parent."

After ending the call with Marvin, Sierra looked at her watch.

Vaughn was on his way over. They had planned to take advantage of Teryn's sleepover with a classmate and take in dinner and a movie. Afterward, they would return to her place for a night of lovemaking.

She had been looking forward to it and had thought of it as Monday night delight. But now she was wondering if perhaps Vaughn had done the one thing she had asked him not to. If he had meddled, not only had he gone against her wishes, but he'd made a bigger mess of everything. What if that judge sided with Nathan and allowed him to have Teryn for Christmas? What if—

The ringing of the doorbell indicated that Vaughn had arrived. Moving quickly, she headed down the stairs to open the door.

"Hello, *cherie*," Vaughn said when he stepped inside. He paused when he saw her face. "What's wrong, Sierra," he asked closing the door behind him.

She took a step back and stared at him with eyes that appeared emotionless. Yet he could tell her entire body was tight and consumed with anger. "Sierra, what's wrong?"

"I need to know something, Vaughn." She sounded like she was struggling hard to hold herself together.

"What?"

"Did you have something sent to Nathan's employer. Information that could get him fired?"

"Yes."

She gasped and for a minute it appeared she was about to fall to her knees. When he moved toward her, she backed away quickly. "How could you do such a thing?" she asked, her words seething with fury.

Vaughn frowned, clearly not understanding what had her so upset. "I did it because the man needed to get fired."

Sierra set her hands on her hips. "You had no right to get involved. You told me that you wouldn't."

"What I told you was that I would let you handle your business."

"And what do you call sending Nathan's boss information to get him fired?"

"Handling *my* business," he said calmly.

"And just what business do you have regarding Nathan?" she lashed out.

"You, *cherie*. You are my business."

"No, I'm not!" she said, her voice rising.

"Yes, you are. You became my business the day I fell in love with you. So, any threats that bastard made against you, he made against me."

"And you think any feelings you might have for me give you the right to stick your nose where it doesn't belong?" she said in a loud angry voice.

"It gives me the right to handle any harm that might come to you. I refuse to let anyone hurt you or Teryn," Vaughn said through clenched teeth. "I told you I would handle it and I did. You won't have to worry about Nathan Flowers anymore."

"What you did, Vaughn, was make matters worse—much, much worse. Nathan's lifestyle was our ace to get him to back off. We planned to threaten to expose him to his boss unless he dropped his custody petition. Now that he's been fired, we can't do that. Now I have to fly to Chicago on Friday to meet with a judge to fight for custody rights. Not only is Nathan filing for joint custody of Teryn—for six months of the year—he's also trying to get her for the holidays."

"That won't be happening," he snarled.

"Because of you it very well might."

He ran a hand down his face in frustration. Then he reached for the packet he'd tucked under his arm and said, "You need to get this to your attorney right away, Sierra." He held out the dark gray packet to her. "He'll know what to do with it."

She looked at the packet and shook her head. "No! I refuse to give my attorney anything. I told you to let me handle things and you didn't. You went behind my back and messed things up, Vaughn. Now I might lose the one person I was supposed to protect with my life."

She paused, fighting back tears. "I don't want her with Nathan for the Christmas holidays or ever. She doesn't know him, and he doesn't want her. He's only doing this to hurt me and it's all your fault, Vaughn."

He took a step toward her. "Listen to me, *cherie*. I—"

"No! You lied to me, Vaughn. I trusted that you would let me handle things my way. And now because of you, I might lose Teryn. I failed her. I failed Rhonda. I allowed you to become a part of my and Teryn's life. Do you know how hard it was for me to do that after dealing with the likes of a man like Nathan? But I did, and the only thing I asked was for you to let me handle my own business. But you couldn't do that."

Vaughn tried to fight back his own anger. He knew she was upset, but if she would only give him the chance to explain things then she would see that everything he'd done had been in her and Teryn's best interest.

"Sierra, just give this to your attorney," he said, offering the packet again. "Please."

She met his gaze and the look in her eyes was so cold, he felt chilled to the bone. "You can take that packet and shove it, Vaughn Miller. Now please leave. I don't want to ever see you again, and you are not welcome to my home or the restaurant."

"Sierra—"

"Leave now and don't *ever* contact me again."

He stared at her, not wanting to believe what she'd said. "Seriously?" he asked, incredulous.

"Seriously."

Vaughn knew she meant it. Now he was angrier than hell. Turning, he opened the door and slammed it shut behind him.

CHAPTER THIRTY-TWO

Velvet sat in front of her TV with a glass of wine in one hand and the remote in the other. There had to be something worth watching other than romance movies, cop shows and sci-fi movies. She was in the mood for none of those. In her present frame of mind, she should just finish her wine and go on to bed. School had ended for the holidays and with nothing planned this week, she thought she might drive into New Orleans for some Christmas shopping. Shopping was always a girl's best friend.

Anything was better than sitting around and letting her thoughts dwell on that town hall meeting last Thursday, when she'd seen Jaye for the first time in two years. Just a few days later his presence was already the talk of the town. That next day at school, all the single teachers had been whispering about how good-looking he was and what it would take to capture such a man's eye. She had been tempted to tell them unless they were in for an affair that led nowhere, not to waste their time.

After that meeting, she couldn't get home quick enough to call Ruthie to tell her that Jaye was not only in town but would be here for a while since he now owned the only bank in town.

Her best friend was just as shocked as she was. Ruthie even

brought up the possibility that he had somehow found out her whereabouts and that was why he was in Catalina Cove. Velvet found that hard to believe. Jaye didn't run after women. Besides, why now, after she'd been gone two years?

She put the remote on the table and went into the kitchen. She was about to pour another glass of wine when her doorbell sounded. Who in the world could that be? Maybe it was her neighbor, Delisa.

When she reached the door, she asked, "Who is it?"

"Jaye Colfax."

Velvet's heart nearly jumped out of her chest. What was Jaye doing here? How did he know where she lived? Drawing in a deep breath, she tried to calm her erratic heartbeat. She glanced down at herself and was glad she was decent. She hadn't changed out of the slacks and top she'd worn to her dentist appointment that day. With slightly trembling hands she opened the door.

The porch light illuminated his features and she went still, taking in just how handsome he was. Simply gorgeous, from his head to his toes and every part in between.

"Jaye. What are you doing here?"

"May I come in, Vel, so we can talk?"

Hearing him say her nickname, which nobody in the cove used, gave her pause. Ruthie called her that all the time but hearing Jaye say it brought a lot of memories rushing through her mind…and her body.

"Vel?"

He'd said it again, making her realize she hadn't answered him. She could easily say no, he couldn't come in, and they had nothing to talk about. She had put distance between them two years ago for a reason. She had given up talking to him then, why should they talk now?

She could tell him just what she thought of him, but knew that wouldn't be a smart move. He was now the new banker in town and agitation between them could call for awkward moments she'd rather not deal with.

If nothing else, they needed to talk about the best way to handle things since nobody in Catalina Cove, except for Sierra, knew about her past.

"Yes, please come in," she said, stepping back to let him in.

When he crossed the threshold, her gaze roamed over him. He was six foot two, but he appeared taller than she remembered. Since he was in business mode, he was dressed in a tailor-made suit.

It was only when he spent time with her or hung out with his friends that he wore casual attire. Jeans never looked as good on any man and button-down shirts always emphasized his masculine build. Honestly, she preferred those times when he wore nothing at all. When he was as naked as the day he was born...

Regaining control of her senses, she closed the door behind him and repeated her question. "What are you doing here, Jaye?"

"I think we need to talk."

Yes, he'd said that, and they had, and it had gotten them nowhere. "I was about to have another glass of wine, would you like one?"

"Yes, thanks."

There was no need to make sure what she was drinking was what he'd want because she and Jaye always liked the same wine. In fact, they liked most of the same of everything—food, colors, places to visit, music, movies, political party. They'd been perfect together. Perfect for each other. Too bad he hadn't seen or accepted that.

"Please have a seat. I'll be right back." She hurried off to the kitchen, holding her breath. It was only when she leaned against the counter that she exhaled. When she'd rented this house nearly two years ago, she'd never given thought that Jaye would ever walk through the door, stand in her foyer, sit on her sofa or share a glass of wine with her. She'd figured when she'd left Phoenix, she'd made a clean break. Obviously not.

But then, she couldn't place the blame solely at Jaye's feet. He had been up-front with her from the beginning. He wasn't the marrying kind. All there would be between them was companionship and sex, sex and more sex. He'd also made it clear when she'd pushed for exclusivity that although they wouldn't date others, it was still just an affair.

He didn't love her and could never love her. She thought that she could be content with their arrangement. Had convinced herself she could settle. But then as time passed, she knew she had deserved more. She'd also known she would never get that *more* from Jaye. The damage his mother had caused to his father's heart was something Jaye didn't just blame his mother for but all women. He would never give his heart to one the way Jack Colfax Sr. had.

Calming her shaking fingers, she reached into the cabinet to retrieve another wineglass and filled it halfway. That's usually all he ever wanted. They would joke about whether the glass was half-full or half-empty all the time.

After topping off hers, she left the kitchen carrying both glasses to find him standing in the middle of her living room, glancing around.

He looked up when she entered the room. "This is a nice place, Vel."

"Thanks," she said, handing him the wineglass. Their hands touched and she felt it and knew he had as well. Okay, so they'd just proved that sexual chemistry was still alive and well between them. Big deal.

She sat and he did as well. He took a sip, and as she watched him, she thought what she always thought, he looked sexy doing it. The way his lips caressed the rim of the glass and how he would take slow, seductive sips…

She cleared her throat. "So why are you here?" she asked for the third time.

Jaye lowered his glass. "It was a rather startling moment seeing you the other night."

She shrugged. "You mean you didn't deliberately buy that bank when you discovered this is where I was living?" she asked coolly.

He took another sip of wine before saying, "Is that what you believe I did?"

She chuckled and shook her head. "No," she said honestly. "It's not in your makeup to care that much for any woman to put out that much effort. I know you being here was just a coincidence neither of us counted on. I'm sure you were hoping never to see me again."

His brows pinched with irritation. "Have you forgotten that you left me and not the other way around? And without letting me know you were leaving and where you were going."

"You sound pissed. Why? I gave you your freedom."

"I don't recall asking for it."

No, he hadn't. He would have been perfectly fine letting things continue as they were. It never dawned on him that perhaps she wanted more. "I did what I felt I had to do, Jaye."

He didn't say anything, didn't even bother to ask her what she meant. She knew that he knew.

He finished another sip of wine and said, "How do you think we should handle things, Vel? To get the bank up and running the way I want, I'll be living in town for about six to eight months. I don't want any awkward moments between us. Any suggestions?"

"Yes, you could stop calling me Vel. Everybody in town calls me Velvet. If they hear you call me that then they'll know we had a past."

"And you'd rather they didn't know that?" he asked.

She nodded. "There's no reason for anyone here to know. What was between us is in the past and it should stay there."

"Alright. Anything else?"

She drew in a deep breath. "Yes. Nobody in town knows who I am."

She saw the bemused look on his face, and then when he realized what she meant, he smiled. "In other words, nobody in Catalina Cove knows you're the Spencer's restaurant heir."

"No, they don't know."

"Even though there's a Spencer's in town? One of the few fast-food places I heard they've allowed to open here?"

Spencer's was a popular restaurant that was known for their hamburgers, french fries and milkshakes. A few years ago, several other items were added to the menu, including pizza. From what Velvet had heard, Reid Lacroix had been against any fast-food chains opening in the cove. However, once his granddaughters made it known that Spencer's was their favorite eating place and the closest one was in New Orleans, he had made sure that one opened up in the cove. The cove had gotten a McDonald's for that same reason.

"Only Reid Lacroix and my friend Sierra Crane know. Both are sworn to secrecy. No one has made the connection and there's no reason they should since I'm not involved in the business side of the corporation. As you know, I have very capable people running things back in Seattle on my behalf."

"Yes, you do," he said. "I hear you're about to expand into Canada and the UK."

"Yes, that's what I'm told."

Her parents had always known she hadn't wanted to be involved in the family business and that being a teacher was her dream. They hadn't been overjoyed but had let her be. Their deaths eight years ago had changed things. While coming home one night from a party, their vehicle had been carjacked and both had been murdered in the process. It had been a senseless killing and had taken away the two people she'd cared about most.

"I like teaching."

"And you're good at it."

"Thanks. Well, that about covers everything."

"Not quite. There's something you need to know."

Velvet lifted a brow. "What?"

"Where I'll be staying."

She tilted her head and looked at him. "Why would it concern me where you'd be staying?"

"Because I'm renting the house right next door. I understand your neighbor Delisa Mills leaves town for extended trips. The Realtor that I hired was able to find me a place with only a six-month lease. Imagine my surprise when I discovered it was next to you. I could try to find another place if it's going to bother you with me being so close."

Velvet tried to keep her features neutral but deep inside she was fuming. For two years she had moved on with her life, trying to get herself free of Jaye, and now, out of the clear blue sky, he not only popped up in Catalina Cove, but *he was moving next door* to her. What on earth did she do to deserve this?

"Vel?"

She glared at him. "No, Jaye, your living next door will mean nothing to me."

He smiled...actually smiled. Did that mean it meant nothing to him, too? He thought it would be okay if he moved in next door and began parading women in and out of his house when she was so close by? There was no doubt in her mind that since their breakup he had gone back to his playboy ways. He'd certainly captured a lot of interest the other night.

"I think we've covered everything, Jaye," she said, taking his wineglass from him—although there was still wine in it—and then turning to head for the door.

"Yes, I guess we have." When they reached the door, he said, "I'll be staying at that bed-and-breakfast in town, Shelby by the Sea, until the first of the year. Then I'll be moving next door."

"Okay. Good night, Jaye."

"Good night, Vel."

"Remember, from now on, I'm Velvet."

"I'll remember."

And then he was gone.

Vaughn stormed inside his home, breathing fire and his body quivering with rage. He could appreciate Sierra's need to not depend on anyone, but didn't she realize that things between them were different?

She'd even ignored the fact he'd said he loved her—or she had been too mad to hear it. All she had to do was trust him enough to listen to what he had to tell her. Then she would have appreciated his involvement. Now she would be going into that meeting with a manipulative ex-husband, who was hell-bent on revenge, and a clueless judge. His woman didn't stand a chance. And whether she accepted it or not, she was his woman. The woman he loved, the one he would marry one day.

And right now, she thought she had every reason to hate his guts. Didn't she understand that when a man loved a woman his natural instinct was to protect her? Granted, she hadn't known he loved her then, but she knew it now and she still hadn't gotten it. She still felt he had stuck his nose where it didn't belong. The hell he had. His nose belonged anywhere that involved her.

Going into the kitchen, he grabbed a beer from the refrigerator and then went to sit outside on the patio. He'd put automatic timers on the Christmas tree inside his home and the one on the dock. The tree on the dock was taller and had a hell of a lot more lights. He believed those kids put over a thousand lights and ornaments on that tree, but he had to admit it was beautiful. Even now he saw how the lights reflected off the water. It looked totally beautiful and, not surprisingly, there'd been a steady string of boaters cruising by to see it. Some were even taking pictures.

He took a sip of beer as his mind shifted back to Sierra. Not that she had ever left it. His anger escalated when he thought of the long hours Deke had worked in such a short time frame to gather all that information on Nathan Flowers.

And damn it, she had thrown it back in his face and said she didn't want to see him again. Hell, the way he was feeling, he didn't want to see her either. Why couldn't she see that she could be the strong, independent woman she was, yet accept there was nothing wrong for someone to want to have your back, protect you from all sides and be ready to kick ass on your behalf if necessary?

Hell, she didn't see that and not doing so was her loss. Maybe one day she would realize he hadn't wanted to hurt her but help her. Too late now. He was done. When she had insisted that he leave and never contact her again, that had been it. He didn't need this kind of BS in his life from anyone.

Jaye entered his room at Shelby by the Sea, noticing that it was a very nice place with all the comforts of home. Jerking off his tie and removing his suit jacket, he tossed both on the bed before heading to the window. He had requested an ocean view, and that's just what he'd gotten. Even at night he could see the lights of several boats, which meant some people were doing night fishing.

He drew in a deep breath as he recounted his conversation with Velvet. He had been prepared to be totally honest with her and tell her the reason he was here—to claim her love.

However, something she'd said had stopped him from being forthright. She had jested about him deliberately buying the bank when he'd discovered this was where she was living. Then she admitted she knew he hadn't done such a thing because it wasn't in his makeup to care that much for any woman. He'd decided at that moment to prove how wrong she was, and that it *was* in his makeup to care that much.

When he felt the time was right, he would let her know how miserable he'd been the last two years and how it had taken her leaving for him to realize how much he cared for her. He loved her. He would eventually tell her he'd hired a private investigator to find her. She would also discover that Larson Barrows hadn't really been ready to retire, it had taken Jaye making an offer that had been so sweet the man couldn't have refused…or he would have been a fool to do so. The same thing with the house next door to hers. He had made it worth Delisa Mills's while, financially, to stay out of the country at least six to eight more months.

Bottom line, Jaye had done what he'd felt was needed to get back the woman he loved. The woman he had lost by his own stupidity. And in the end, she would see that he intended to do what he should have done when he'd first met her, and that was to court her properly.

He loved her and he intended to prove it to her, but on her time, not his. If it took longer than six months, he was fine with that. He'd discovered that Catalina Cove, Louisiana, wasn't so bad. In fact, it was a real nice town.

Jaye was determined that when he left the cove, he would be leaving with Velvet—as his wife.

CHAPTER THIRTY-THREE

Sierra had butterflies flying around in her stomach as she was escorted to the judge's chambers. Even though Marvin had told her that Judge Hargrove was fair, she knew everything that was at stake and she of all people knew how manipulating Nathan could be. It was nothing but a game to him.

She appreciated Velvet for keeping Teryn until she returned. Her sister and parents had given her pep talks and it felt good that she had their support. Dani felt she had blown the issue with Vaughn all out of proportion and thought she'd lost the best thing to ever happen to her. Dani believed any good man would want to come to the aid of the woman he cared about, and she'd seen that Sunday morning at breakfast, clear as day, that he cared about her.

As far as Sierra was concerned, if he cared so much then he would have honored her wishes and let her handle her business. His lack of confidence in her abilities was unacceptable. For the past few days she'd tried not to think about Dani's words or to think of Vaughn, period. That had been hard. What he'd done had hurt. It had shown that he couldn't be trusted to keep his word.

Yet knowing what he'd done had not stopped her from thinking about him whenever she closed her eyes or cried herself to sleep. She should not have fallen in love with him, but she had, and now another man had let her down, had tried stripping away her independence.

When she reached the door, the court assistant opened it for her. The room was empty and the man said, "The judge will be here in a few minutes."

She nodded and entered the room and was about to take a seat at the huge table when the door opened again. Instead of the judge it was Nathan. She immediately saw the coldness in his eyes and knew what Marvin had said was true. He was out for blood.

At that moment another door opened, and the judge dressed in his robe entered. Sierra gave a sigh of relief, glad she would not spend a single minute alone with Nathan.

"Good afternoon, Ms. Crane. Mr. Flowers. I'm Judge Hargrove," he said, shaking each of their hands. "Let's sit at the table here."

When the three of them were seated, Judge Hargrove covered the reason they were there. "As you know, Ms. Crane, although your divorce from Mr. Flowers was pending, and had already been filed with the court, since it did not become effective until after the date of your adoption of Teryn Andrews, legally, Mr. Flowers is also an adoptive parent of the child. Unless you can show just cause why he could not effectively fulfill the role, the law will have to stand."

Sierra saw the smirk on Nathan's face. "But what about the activities he was involved in that led to our divorce?" she asked. "Doesn't that say anything about his character? And what about the fact that he has not once seen Teryn since she was adopted? He's called harassing me, but not once did he ask about her."

"She's lying," Nathan said in a loud voice. "I wanted to see the child, but she wouldn't let me. She even blocked my number, Judge. That's why I feel the little girl should spend the holidays this year with me so she can get to know me, and I can get to know her."

"No," Sierra said, shaking her head. "He only wants her to get back at me for not remarrying him. He is not sincere in any of this. He never wanted children and had a vasectomy so he never would. Now he's trying to make you believe he wants Teryn but all he will do is put her through mental abuse of the worst kind. He has nothing to lose. He doesn't have a job. He is a broken man with only one thing on his mind and that is revenge."

The judge didn't say anything for a long minute, and a part of her felt he was probably seeing her as a raving madwoman. He then said, "I understand you are upset about all of this, Ms. Crane, but Mr. Flowers does have legal rights to the child as well. And since you did have the child with you last Christmas, for him to ask that the child spend this holiday with him is reasonable and only fair."

Fair? Sierra felt defeated and fought back her tears, knowing she had lost. The judge was going to give Nathan what he wanted, and from the look of victory in Nathan's eyes, he knew it as well.

"Therefore," the judge was saying, looking at them both, "to be fair, I have no choice but to—"

Suddenly, there was a knock on the door and an older woman walked in. "Excuse me, Your Honor, this came for you. I believe it's an emergency."

The woman handed the judge a slip of paper. He read it and then looked at them both. "I'm sorry but I need to step out," he said. "This meeting is recessed for an hour."

"An *hour*?" Nathan said, in an angry, impatient voice. "Can't you go ahead and make a ruling so we can get out of here?"

The judge stared at Nathan. "Mr. Flowers, are you trying to tell me how to do my job?"

Sierra heard the curtness in the judge's voice and figured Nathan heard it as well because he quickly said, "No, sir. I'm just anxious to fly to Louisiana and get the child today."

She wondered if the judge noticed Nathan had yet to refer to Teryn by name during the entire meeting. "Mr. Flowers," the judge said, "if I rule in your favor, I will give you the designated dates Teryn Andrews will be with you. Flying anywhere to get her today is a right that has not been granted to you. Ms. Crane will need time to prepare the child for your arrival and for the trip here to Chicago."

The judge looked at his watch. "The two of you need to be back here in an hour. This unexpected emergency should be resolved by then." The judge stood and left the room.

Sierra stood and looked at Nathan. "Please don't do this."

That cold, hard look reappeared in his eyes when he stood, leaned over the table, got right in her face and sneered, "You haven't seen anything yet, bitch."

Sierra refused to let Nathan see her cry and quickly left the room. She kept walking until she came to the nearest restroom and then rushed into the first stall. Closing the door, she leaned against it.

Nathan was so full of hatred. Moving up in his career and becoming wealthy and wealthier was what had driven him, and now he believed Sierra had taken that away, and he would make her pay through Teryn. She could just imagine the mind games he would put her goddaughter through.

Then she thought of Vaughn. She had blamed him for everything when all he'd tried to do was help. Maybe she should have accepted his help, but it was too late now. She had failed and was all alone.

If she had to, she would take Teryn and run away. Leave the country. Change their identities. There was no way she would turn her over to Nathan, no matter what the judge ordered. She still had time. They had no idea how uncaring, cruel and selfish

Nathan could be. Now, fueled by his desire for revenge against Sierra, he would destroy Teryn's life.

Feeling overwhelmed and no longer able to hold back the tears, they came out with the sobs. She had only made a mess of things and it was all her fault. A knock on the stall made her jerk. Clearing her throat, she said, "Yes?"

"Are you alright?" a feminine voice asked, sounding concerned.

No, she wasn't alright. After today, she would never be alright again. But to the stranger who'd been kind enough to inquire, she said, "Yes, I'll be fine."

She wasn't sure how long she remained in that restroom stall, but when she finally checked the time, she saw it had been nearly an hour and it was time to go back. Leaving the stall, she dabbed cold water on her face and tried to redo her makeup. She stared at her reflection and saw that despite her efforts, the evidence that she'd been crying was still there. Her pain could not be hidden.

More than anything at that moment she wished Vaughn was there with her. To hold her like he'd done so many times, and to tell her everything would be okay. She had wanted to be strong but right now she felt so weak. She took out her phone and saw she'd missed calls from her parents and Dani. None from Vaughn.

Honestly, what had she expected? She was the one who had told him she never wanted to see him again and had insisted he not contact her. Not only was she losing Teryn, but she had lost Vaughn as well.

When she returned to the meeting room, Nathan was there and looked up when she walked in. A huge smile stretched his lips and he said, "You look like shit, Sierra. All those tears won't help you now."

Sierra wanted to turn right around and leave, but knew she had to stay and see this out, even though she had an awful feeling about how things would end. Nathan kept talking, saying mean, ugly and vulgar things to her in a low voice, but she tuned him out. She refused to be baited, although she was really tempted to reach out and slap him. She figured that's what he wanted, so then he would claim she was unstable and possibly demand full custody of Teryn. She sat in her chair, refusing to give him any ammunition.

Nathan stopped talking when the judge walked in. He sat at the table and placed a familiar-looking packet in the middle of the table. Sierra stared hard and quickly recalled the dark gray packet looked very similar to the one Vaughn had tried giving to her. She drew in a deep breath knowing it was merely a coincidence—lots of packets looked like that.

"Sorry, I had to leave," the judge was saying. "However, this packet was delivered to me with a request that I review it immediately as it could have some bearing on this case."

Sierra heard what the judge was saying and the more she stared at the packet the more she believed it was the same one. The judge said it had been delivered to him. *By whom?*

She looked at Nathan and saw a confused look in his eyes. "What kind of bearing?" he asked.

"If you recall," the judge said, looking at them both, "earlier I said, specifically to you, Ms. Crane, that unless you could show just cause why Mr. Flowers could not effectively fulfill his role as an adoptive parent, the law would have to stand."

She nodded. "Yes, I recall you saying that."

"Well, it seems, Mr. Flowers, that you were allegedly involved in illegal activities and still are."

"That's a lie!" Nathan stood abruptly, almost knocking over his chair. "I don't know who delivered that crap to you, but it's lies. It's something she's cooked up that's not true. I want to know who gave you that," he demanded, pointing at the packet.

"Sit down, Mr. Flowers, and I will tell you everything you need to know."

Hearing the tone of authority in the judge's voice, Nathan

sat down. The judge pulled the contents out of the packet and said, "This was delivered to me by the FBI."

"The FBI?" Nathan and Sierra said simultaneously.

"Yes." The judge placed what looked like over a hundred sheets of paper on the table. "Mr. Flowers, are you familiar with the club Sherwood Forest that's located on the outskirts of town?"

Sierra saw the confusion in Nathan's eyes immediately replaced with wariness. "Yes, what about it?"

"Then you are aware of what kind of club it is." It was a statement, not a question.

"Yes, I am aware," Nathan said in a cool tone. "It's a private club where members are free to enjoy themselves. It's all perfectly legal and consensual," he ended smugly.

"And do you admit you're one of the owners of the club?"

Sierra frowned. This was news to her. It didn't surprise her that Nathan would go to a club like that, but he was actually one of the owners?

When Nathan didn't answer, the judge asked the question again. Then Nathan said, "Yes, I am one of the three owners, but like I said, everything that goes on in that club is legal. We don't even have a liquor license."

The judge nodded. "That may be so. However, it is alleged that some of your patrons have brought underage girls into your establishment. That *is* illegal, Mr. Flowers."

"That's a lie!" Nathan said, jumping out of his chair again.

"Evidently, the FBI has been investigating. It seems one of your partners," he looked down at one of the papers, "a Wiley Tyndell, was aware of what was going on. Even if you were not aware, as an owner, you may be just as responsible as he is."

"I didn't know any of this," Nathan said, sliding down into his chair. "I just became a partner last year."

"You will have your chance to prove your innocence in a

court of law. Your other two partners were arrested a short while ago, and the authorities are here for you."

No sooner was that said than the door opened, and two guys dressed in dark suits entered along with a police officer.

"As for the custody case," the judge said, "it is closed, pending the outcome of your trial. For the time being, you are not to contact Ms. Crane or Teryn Andrews."

The judge nodded and the men in suits came to stand on either side of Nathan. One of the men flipped his badge and said, "I'm Agent Frigate from the Chicago Bureau of the FBI. Mr. Flowers, you are under arrest."

Sierra watched, speechless, as Nathan stood and was read his Miranda rights. The coldness in his eyes had been replaced with sheer panic. Then the FBI agents and the policeman escorted him from the room.

"What will happen to him?" she asked the judge, not understanding why she even cared.

"He'll have his day in court, and it will be up to a judge and jury to decide his fate. My ruling will probably keep him away from you and the child at least until a verdict is rendered."

The judge stood and, after shuffling the papers and putting them back in the packet, he looked at her and said, "Good day, Ms. Crane, and Merry Christmas."

When the judge headed for the door, Sierra called out to him. "Your Honor?"

He stopped and turned. "Yes?"

"How did you get that packet?"

The judge smiled—the first she'd seen from the man that day. "Like I said, it was delivered to me by the FBI."

He opened the door to his chamber and left.

CHAPTER THIRTY-FOUR

A short while later, Sierra paced her hotel room, convinced that packet Judge Hargrove had received was the same one Vaughn had tried giving her—and she had refused to take it. His very words had been "...*You need to get this to your attorney right away, Sierra... He'll know what to do with it.*"

She hadn't done that. Instead, she had literally told him to take that packet and shove it. Then she told him she didn't want to see him or hear from him ever again. Yet, instead of shoving it, the packet had ended up here in Chicago and handed to the judge in her case. How?

She sat on the edge of her bed and pulled her phone out of her purse. She needed to call Vaughn to apologize and thank him profusely. As she listened to the line ring, a wave of disappointment washed over her when Vaughn didn't answer her call. But then, after all she'd said, she didn't blame him. Chills went through her body when she recalled how mean Nathan had been to her and all the hateful things he'd said before the judge had returned. She could breathe a lot easier knowing Teryn wouldn't be at his mercy. Just worrying about Teryn while she was with him would have driven Sierra crazy...

"Yes?"

She blinked upon realizing Vaughn had answered, right before she was about to disconnect the call. "Vaughn, this is Sierra."

"I know who this is."

She swallowed. His words were brusque, which meant he was still angry, and he had every right to be. Yet, his anger hadn't stopped him from doing what he'd done today. He had saved her. He had saved Teryn. That blatant realization brought tears to her eyes. "I owe you an apology, Vaughn."

"Do you?"

"Yes. I don't know how you did it, but I know you were responsible for the FBI getting that packet. It's the same one you tried giving to me, wasn't it?"

"Yes."

"But how did you do it?"

He paused and then said, "Come to my room and I'll tell you everything."

Her brows rose in question. *His room?* "Are you not in Catalina Cove?"

"No. I'm in Chicago."

Sierra's heart leaped and she drew in a deep breath. He was here in Chicago? Had he come just to bring that packet? After swallowing again, she asked, "What is the name of your hotel?"

"It's the same as yours."

She blinked. Vaughn was here at the same hotel? How had he known which hotel she was staying at? She had a lot of questions for him, so she started with, "What is your room number?"

"I'm in room 3040."

"Thanks, I'll be there in a few minutes."

After she had hung up, Sierra drew in another deep breath. Vaughn was here!

Dani had been right. She'd completely messed things up. Now it was up to her to try to fix it. It was obvious he was still upset with her, but hopefully, she could fix that, too. Looking down at herself, she knew she looked decent. But she wanted to look better than merely decent. She hadn't packed any extra clothing since her plan had been to fly into Chicago and then fly out the next day.

She knew that she needed to make the most of her time. There was a women's boutique in the hotel. Grabbing her purse, she hurried to go shopping.

Vaughn downed the last of his wine. Sierra had said she would be arriving to his room in a few minutes, but that was half an hour ago. Where was she?

He refused to call her to find out. He was still very upset with her, yet he'd known that regardless of what he felt, he would protect her and Teryn from the likes of Nathan Flowers.

Vaughn had flown into Chicago a day ago and met with FBI Agent Frigate, who was a good friend of Deke's. The agent had handled the matter expeditiously. Now it was over. Nathan was behind bars for now, and Sierra could rest easy knowing the man was no longer a threat to her and Teryn.

When Vaughn heard the knock on his hotel room door, he released a deep breath and crossed the room to open it. Had it been four days since he'd last seen her...and she'd told him that she never wanted to see him again? He forced from his mind the harsh words she'd spoken when he'd only meant to protect her.

Opening the door, he tried not to concentrate on how good she looked. His gaze roamed over her and he noticed that her skirt was short. It was shorter than any he'd ever seen her wear before. Had she worn that to her meeting with the judge? Hell, he hoped not. And what about her shoes? She was wearing a pair of black stilettos that had *fuck me* written all over them. Not saying a word, he moved back so she could enter. As usual she smelled good, too.

He could tell she was nervous by the way she was looking around his three-room suite. He studied her in silence. Even her hair was styled differently. Deciding enough time had passed, he said, "So, what did you want to know?" Vaughn knew his voice was a little gruff but he didn't care.

She looked at him. "May I have something to drink?"

"What would you like?"

"Whatever you were drinking," she said, indicating his wine-glass.

He strolled over to the wet bar and grabbed another wine-glass. He filled it with wine and brought it to her. Vaughn tried to ignore the sensations that passed between them and said, "No need for you to keep standing, Sierra. You can sit down."

"Thanks."

Sierra eased down on the sofa and Vaughn sat in the chair across from her. "So, ask your questions."

She swallowed a little wine and then asked, "How did you know about all of that stuff on Nathan?"

He leaned back and crossed his legs. "I didn't. What I did know was that the man was a bully who was making a nuisance of himself. You were worried about him taking Teryn from you. I knew you wanted to handle things your way, but I also knew the risk involved. I didn't want to take the chance of you not being able to stop him. There are times when you have to stop a bully dead in his tracks."

When she shifted to a more comfortable position, he was temporarily distracted by a glimpse of thigh. His gut clenched and he tried to ignore it. He explained, "I have a friend named Deke Hollister who is a former FBI agent. I asked him to get all he could on Flowers as soon as possible. You needed to do things your way, and I needed to do things my way.

"Deke still has close ties with the Bureau and he and I were surprised to discover Flowers was already under an open FBI investigation due to minors—both male and female—frequent-ing the club he co-owned. We found out the FBI was close to making arrests."

She nodded. "And you tried to tell me."

"I wasn't at liberty to tell you everything since it was an on-going FBI investigation. However, I did try to give you the information to pass on to your attorney. I figured he would know what to do with it. But of course, you told me what I could do with that packet."

He saw her flinch and she said, "Yes, and I'm sorry. I owe you an apology, Vaughn. At the time, I saw you as another man thinking I couldn't do anything for myself. I wanted to be strong and independent, but in the end, I almost lost Teryn to Nathan."

Vaughn heard the pain in her voice. "You are strong, Sierra. You are one of the strongest people I know. And you've shown how independent you are. But what you failed to realize is that when two people are in a relationship, it's no longer you or me, it's *us*. We're in it together. We share things, even the problems. What you made me realize is that I had assumed we were in a relationship, but we really weren't."

"We *were* in a relationship, Vaughn."

"Then I wish you had been open to me helping you. I knew I could get enough information to make Flowers go away. Threatening you was crossing the line with me. I didn't give a royal damn that he lost his job. I never shared what was in that packet with his employer. They only got the accurate information about why the two of you got a divorce, which was *his* adultery. He was fired because he'd told his boss a lie, that you were the one who'd committed adultery and not the other way around."

"What!"

"Yes, he was willing to make you look like a tramp and force you to remarry so he could get promoted. I also knew what losing his job meant and I was ready to deal with him there. It was just a matter of time before he was arrested. In the meantime, I wanted your attorney prepared."

"Again, I am sorry, Vaughn. I don't know what else to say."

He leaned forward and met her gaze. "You can say that just

like I know and accept the kind of woman you are, that you know and accept the kind of man I am. There's no way I could let you worry about an issue that I could help you resolve. I'm a man who will protect his woman at all costs, have her back and fight to keep her safe. If that's not the type of man you want and need in your life, Sierra, then say so."

CHAPTER THIRTY-FIVE

Sierra had never heard Vaughn sound so direct before. He was placing his feelings on the table and she could take them or leave them because he'd had enough.

He had pretty much spelled out what being in a relationship meant to him, and now it was up to her to decide if he was the kind of man she wanted. All she had to do was recall what had gone down in that meeting with Nathan and Judge Hargrove. Just how defeated she'd felt when she saw how close she was to losing Teryn.

Then, like a knight in shining armor, Vaughn had come through and saved the day for her and Teryn. What really touched her more than anything was that after all she'd said to him and how she'd acted, he still wanted her, and he was leaving it up to her to give them a chance.

"And if I say you are the type of man that I want in my life then what, Vaughn?" She tried to ignore how good he looked sitting there in his dark slacks and white button-down shirt.

"Then you put up with me, flaws and all, Sierra, and I'll do likewise with you," he said, claiming her full attention. "Then you'll know that although I'll always let you handle your business, I will still have your back and will be there whenever you need me—and even those times when you think that you don't. It also means believing in me like I believe in you. Think you can handle that?"

She nibbled on her bottom lip, nodded and said, "Last week you said you love me."

"Yes, and when I said it, you acted like it meant nothing to you and that you honestly didn't give a damn."

"I was upset and not ready to accept anything you had to say."

"And now?"

And now more than anything she appreciated the generosity of his love. He was so giving, so loving and so protecting. What woman would not want a man like that in her life? A man who would bring her joy in the morning, afternoon and at night. A man who would be there not just for her but for Teryn as well.

"And now I have a reason to be happy because of you. When I think how things could have turned out…"

"They still would have turned out the same way, Sierra. I would have gotten you the best attorney money could buy. An entire team who specializes in family law if I had to. At no time would Flowers have taken you on without getting a piece of me in the process."

With that fierce look in his hazel eyes, she believed him. "And just the thought that you came here, to this city, for me…" Her voice trailed off as she fought back tears.

"I would do just about anything for you, *cherie*," he said softly.

His term of endearment had her easing from her seat on wobbly knees and slowly crossing the room to stand before him. He straightened in his seat and his legs instinctively opened as she stood between them. He looked up at her and she stared down at him. "I apologize for everything I said, Vaughn, and how I acted. I was so afraid of losing Teryn, and the idea of her being forced to spend just one minute in Nathan's presence was killing me. I want another chance with you. I know what and who you are."

★ ★ ★

"What am I and who am I?" Vaughn asked in a low voice.

"You are a treasure and the man I love."

He held her gaze for a long moment and saw the weary lines around her eyes. She looked beautiful but tired. He could imagine how worried she'd been over the thought of losing Teryn. "Do you honestly love me, Sierra?"

"Yes, with all my heart." Then she asked, "Do you still love me?"

He nodded. "If I didn't still love you, I wouldn't be here in Chicago now. Love isn't something you can turn off and on. It's forever, Sierra. It's being there for the person when they need you…even when they think that they don't need you. It's about sharing in their joys and their sorrows. It's about protecting them from all sides."

He reached up and pulled her into his arms, cradling her in his lap. He stared down at her and reached out to caress her cheek. "So, the answer is yes, I still love you."

"Oh, Vaughn," she said, wrapping her arms around his neck. "I love you, too. You make me so happy."

He smiled, brushing a thick lock of hair from her face. "That's today. Tomorrow I might make you mad. That's life."

She chuckled. "That's us."

"Yes, that's us and will always be us. I enjoy having you and Teryn in my life, and yes, I think of Teryn as mine, too. The two of you come as a package deal, one I gladly accept and consider a blessing. She is a special little girl full of love, warmth and vitality."

Vaughn paused a moment and said, "And another thing, *cherie*. I want things I didn't think I'd want again after Camila. I want marriage, babies and a lifetime of love. I have fallen hopelessly in love with you."

Tears began streaming down Sierra's face and Vaughn wiped

them away with the pads of his thumbs. "I didn't say any of that to make you cry, Sierra."

"This has been an emotional day."

Vaughn lowered his head and captured her lips with his. He needed this kiss and he wanted it. He'd gone without tangling his tongue with hers for way too long. The moment their tongues connected every nerve in his body caught fire and it spread through him.

Standing with her in his arms he walked into the bedroom and laid her on the huge bed. He stood back and looked at her.

"I don't ever want to go through another week like this one," he said. "I was miserable. Nothing was the same. I even missed eating your soup."

He saw his words had coaxed a smile from her. "Sorry you missed my soup," she said.

"And you know what else I missed?"

"I can't even begin to imagine," she said, her eyes twinkling with mischief.

"I missed spending time with you, sharing heat with you, making love with you. Especially our lovemaking in your office at night, or any of those other times when I slide inside of you. You've always made me feel whole when we made love."

Walking to the bed, he pulled her against his chest, just wanting to hold her and know she was back with him. Then, he began undressing her and when he had stripped her down to her undies and bra, he shook his head. Her sexy underwear would be the death of him yet. He needed to buy stock in that company.

He couldn't help but stare at how her generous breasts were practically spilling out of her black lace bra with matching panties. "Did you wear that skirt and shoes to meet with the judge?"

She smiled. "Why do you ask?"

"It's way too short."

She threw her head back and laughed. "I thought you once told me that you like seeing my legs."

"The operative word is *I*. That doesn't mean I want every man to see them as well," he said, removing his shirt and tossing it aside to join her skirt and blouse.

"That is not the outfit I had on to see the judge. I wore a business suit. It was important that I portray myself in a positive light at that meeting. I didn't bring any extra clothes since I figured this to be an overnight trip, so I went shopping after you invited me to your room."

"Why?"

"Because I wanted to look sexy for you. I always want to look sexy for you, Vaughn. So that skirt, blouse and my undies are all new. I bought them at the boutique downstairs."

"That's why you were late getting up here. Well, it was worth it. You look sexy."

"Thanks."

"Now are you ready for me, *cherie*?" he asked, lowering his pants and briefs.

He saw the way her gaze roamed all over his body. "Yes, Vaughn, I am ready for you."

The truth of the matter was that Sierra was more than ready. The area between her legs was pulsing and throbbing mercilessly. It always did whenever she saw Vaughn naked. She watched him retrieve a condom pack from his wallet.

That's when she spoke up and said, "Unless you just want to use that, you don't really have to. Since my divorce I've been taking injections, although I hadn't been sexually active before meeting you."

Vaughn tossed the condom aside as a huge grin spread across his face. "I definitely prefer not using it."

"Then don't."

When he moved closer to the bed, she forced her gaze from his engorged penis. She scooted closer to the edge and reached up to stroke his face. "Today you saved me and Teryn. Thank you."

He shook his head. "We save each other, Sierra. You made me believe in love again." He removed her sexy undies but decided to let her keep on her black stilettos.

When he had her completely naked, his gaze raked over her entire body. "You are beautiful and the epitome of perfection."

"I was thinking the same thing about you," she whispered. Feeling bold, she ran her hands over his muscular chest and combed her fingers through the hair there, realizing just how much she missed touching him this week. How much she missed seeing him and being with him.

Reaching up, she tugged on a few strands of his hair. "It's longer."

"You noticed."

"Yes, and I like it. Makes you look like a rogue pirate. I could imagine you being Jean Lafitte himself."

He laughed. "Trust me, the longer hair wasn't intentional. I canceled my regular barber appointment Tuesday."

"Umm, like I said, I like it. In fact," she said as her gaze roamed all over him, "I like everything about you. You are what dreams are made of. Hot. Sexy. Seductive."

"I think the same about you."

When she took his erection in her hand, he moaned. "I need to get inside of you, *cherie*. We will take things slow the next time, but right now your scent is calling out to me."

She could believe it. Her panties had gotten wet the moment he had opened the door, and he'd stood there looking sexier than he'd ever looked before.

"You mean I don't get to lick you from head to toe now?"

"Please hold that thought," he said, easing her back and at the same time using his knee to widen her legs apart.

"I will definitely hold all my thoughts for later, Vaughn."

When he had her flat on her back, she felt not only his heat but the need he was trying to hold in check. He was deeply aroused and so was she. This would be one bone-melting mating and would probably test the limits of both of their endurances, but she was ready.

He began easing inside of her while holding her gaze with searing intensity. He seemed to have gotten bigger and was stretching her insides to the max. He growled and she purred, knowing Vaughn was about to blow her mind.

She was prepared, but when he began moving with long, gliding strokes inside of her, Sierra knew she would never get enough of this. Of him. The total feel of his penis as he moved inside of her, going deeper and deeper, created a sexual enjoyment of the richest kind, the erotic friction of skin sliding against skin, muscles contracting and releasing, over and over again—it was all making her frantic. She lifted her hips and his pace increased, and what they'd missed out on while apart gripped them in the folds of a powerful rhythm.

His thrusts sent sensations rocketing through her that had every part of her quivering and her entire body humming. Being without him for almost a week had done this?

Although her body was aching for release, she wasn't ready to surrender to the magnitude of his vigorous lovemaking. She needed this, the feel of being totally uninhibited with him. She loved the sound of their bodies slapping together, mingling with their moans and groans.

"I'll never get enough of you," he whispered, then lowered his mouth to hers, kissing her with the expertise she was used to.

Then it happened, she felt it all the way to her toes. When his body began shuddering, hers began shuddering as well. He lifted her hips and plunged deeper, and when she screamed out her pleasure, he threw his head back. She slid her hands to his backside, loving the feel of his buttocks contracting. This is what she wanted, what she needed and desired. And she knew it would always be this way.

When the spasms finally eased from their bodies, he slid off her and then positioned their bodies to lie side by side facing each other. Her body was slick with sweat and he leaned in to lick around her breasts then took a nipple in his mouth. Immediately, she felt the area between her legs rejuvenate as she started getting aroused all over again.

"Again?" she whispered.

He smiled and moved to reclaim his position over her. "Yes, again."

CHAPTER THIRTY-SIX

"Merry Christmas, *cherie*," Vaughn said, handing Sierra a small gift-wrapped box.

"What is it, Goddy?" Teryn asked, coming to join them by the huge Christmas tree.

They had decided to spend Christmas Eve at Zara's Haven. Teryn was okay with it after they'd convinced her that Santa would know where to find her when delivering her presents. Teryn had been given one of the guest rooms upstairs and Sierra had been given the one next to that. And later that night, when she was convinced Teryn had drifted off to sleep, she had tiptoed downstairs to join Vaughn in his bed. He had carried her back to her bed just before daybreak. Less than an hour later, Teryn had awakened and rushed into Sierra's room.

Sierra's fingers were nervous as she unwrapped the box. She still had memories of their time together in Chicago. Dani had warned her that there was something wonderful about makeup sex.

They had decided to spend an extra day in Chicago once he told Sierra she didn't need to catch her flight home because he had the Lacroix jet and she would fly back home with him.

After getting assurances from Velvet that staying another day was fine and she'd take care of Teryn, they had continued enjoying their time together…even if it had meant another shopping trip.

After returning from Chicago, there had been a lot of wonderful holiday events, including the boat parade. Teryn had helped Vaughn string lights along the upper deck of his yacht, and she'd been so excited about being a part of it. Sierra had, too. Vaughn had given them all sailor's hats and jackets, which had been a smart idea since the night air had been cool.

To proudly celebrate Teryn's debut as a caroler, they had gone to Spencer's. It was fast becoming one of Teryn's favorite places to eat. She, like everyone else, loved their hamburgers.

According to the newspapers, Nathan and his two partners were out of jail on bond. The whole thing was a big scandal in Chicago. Their troubles piled on when two more teens came forward. Both claimed that although they had gone to the club of their own free will, once they had gotten there and wanted to leave, they had been given the date rape drug. Nathan maintained his innocence and that he hadn't known anything illegal had been going on. So far his other two partners had not corroborated his claim.

"You need help opening that, Goddy?"

She looked at Teryn. "No, sweetheart, I got this."

When they had arrived at Vaughn's house, they had seen three huge gift-wrapped boxes under the tree. This morning, they opened the boxes to discover he had purchased three bicycles for them to go cycling around the cove on nice days.

Now she finally had the box unwrapped and saw the small velvet box. Her heart was rapidly beating when she locked eyes with Vaughn. They were all sitting around the tree and he'd eased closer to her and was now on one knee. She opened the box and saw a beautiful engagement ring. It had to be every bit of four diamonds.

He held her gaze and said, "I love you, Sierra. Will you marry me and allow me to be a good husband to you and a loving and dedicated godfather to Teryn?"

Tears clouded her eyes and she saw the happiness in Teryn's face as both she and Vaughn waited for her answer. She would not keep them waiting. "Yes, Vaughn! I will marry you."

Teryn let out a loud squeal of happiness, and Vaughn pulled her into his arms for a kiss.

"Goddy, did you get your one Christmas wish?" Teryn asked. She was stacking her toys on the other side of the room so she could start enjoying them.

Sierra smiled. "I most certainly did."

"Now can you tell me what you wished for?" Teryn asked.

Vaughn chuckled. He recalled Teryn had tried getting him and Sierra to tell her what they'd written but they'd told her they couldn't tell her their wishes, or they might not come true. "Yes, *cherie*, what did you wish for?"

Sierra released a deep breath and smiled at them. "Happiness. That's what I wished for, and I am extremely happy today that my one Christmas wish did come true."

Before Teryn could turn her attention to him, Vaughn quickly said, "Look, there's a few more gifts under the tree. I believe both are for you, Teryn." He had bought them for her when he and Sierra had gone shopping in Chicago, and she had wrapped them for him.

Teryn clapped her hands in happiness. Sierra reached for the gifts and handed them to Vaughn to pass over to Teryn. He was about to do so when he glanced down and went still, fixated on the way Teryn's name was written on the card attached to the gift-wrapped box. It read, *Teryn Marie*.

He kept staring at it, not for the name itself but at the handwriting. Specifically, the name Marie.

"Vaughn, is something wrong?" Sierra asked when she saw him staring at the box.

"I'm just noticing the name Marie," he murmured.

She tilted her head. "What about it?"

Before he could answer, Teryn said, "My middle name is Marie. I was named after my goddy."

Vaughn swung his gaze to Sierra. "Your middle name is Marie?"

She smiled. "Yes, I'm Sierra Marie Crane. Marie was my grandmother's middle name."

He didn't say anything for a minute as his heart began pounding. "Who wrote Teryn's name on this card?"

"I did. What's wrong with it?" she asked.

"You write your M's different."

She laughed. "Oh, you mean that little squiggly tail I give it. It's an old habit of mine."

He stared down at the handwriting. "I've seen it before."

She shrugged. "You probably have, possibly in my office, although I rarely have a reason to use my full name. I'm sure I've done it at some time or another."

"No." He shook his head numbly. "I've seen the name *Marie* written this same way someplace else."

She lifted a surprised brow. "You have? Where?"

He passed the gifts on to Teryn, who'd been waiting patiently for them, and then said, "Teryn, I need to borrow your godmother for a minute."

Teryn nodded, too excited to answer as she began opening the gifts.

Vaughn stood and reached out to help Sierra to her feet. "What's wrong?" she asked as he took her hand and led her toward his bedroom.

When they entered, he immediately walked over to the dresser and pulled out a packet. He turned to her and asked, "Did you ever at any time communicate with prisoners as a pen pal?"

A look of surprise appeared on her face. "Yes. That was something Rhonda got me involved in. She was always active in social issues or community work."

He nodded as his heart started pounding. "Did you ever sign your name?"

"Yes, but not as Sierra. I used my middle name."

"Why?"

"We were told by the agency not to use our real names just in case one of the prisoners receiving our letters was released and tried to find us. However, we had been assured there was no way they could since we never used our address or provided any identifying information about ourselves. I guess they wanted to take extra precaution.

"The agency asked that we send an occasional uplifting word or two. We sent it to the agency, and they dispersed them." She tilted her head again. "Vaughn? Why are you asking me these questions?"

He covered the distance between them. "Because of this," he said, handing her the packet.

Vaughn watched her slowly pull the letters out and her eyes widened. "These are my letters! How did you get them?"

Reaching out, he placed his hands on her waist. "They came to me. I was your pen pal, Sierra *Marie*. I was the inmate your letters were given to. They kept me motivated and encouraged and I looked forward to getting them. They are the reason I kept a positive attitude and was released three years early on good behavior."

Tears began streaming down her face. "I—I never knew."

"I didn't either," he said, wiping her tears away with his thumbs. "I had no idea until I saw how you'd written the name Marie on Teryn's Christmas card just now. I always thought your signature was unique."

He walked back over to the nightstand and pulled out an envelope. "Now, when Teryn asks me about my one Christmas wish, I can tell her it came true."

Sierra lifted her teary eyes. "What do you mean?"

He handed her the envelope and said, "Please open it."

She did and read what he'd written. *My one Christmas wish is to one day meet my Marie.*

Sierra looked at him as happiness, which had been her one Christmas wish, shone in her eyes. "I can't believe it. It seems everything is full circle. Rhonda is the one who got me involved with being a pen pal, and now, together, we will be raising Rhonda's daughter."

He nodded. "And another thing," he said, grinning. "We laughed at Madam Josey's predictions, but it looks like she was right all along. She said our destinies had been entwined since we first connected six years ago. The timing is about right. We connected not physically but with communication."

Sierra nodded. "Yes, and what she'd told me years earlier came true, too. She predicted that I would live a long and happy life with the man I loved. I believe at the time she knew that man would not be Nathan. It would be you."

Vaughn chuckled. "I believe that as well."

He took the packet of letters from her and put them on the bed. Pulling her close he captured her mouth, elated that both of their wishes had come true.

And they would be celebrating for the rest of their lives.

★ ★ ★ ★ ★